WHERE TIME GOES

With best wishes,

Jules Langton

JULES LANGTON

Copyright © Jules Langton 2023

The moral right of Jules Langton to be identified as the author of this work has been asserted in accordance with the Copyright, Designs and Patents Act 1988.

No part of this publication may be reproduced, stored in a retrieval system, or transmitted in any form or by any means without the prior permission in writing of the publisher. Nor be otherwise circulated in any form of binding or cover other than that in which it is published and without a similar condition including this condition being imposed on the subsequent purchaser.

This book is a work of fiction. All characters and events are fictitious or are used fictitiously. Any resemblance to real persons, living or dead, is entirely coincidental and not intended by the author.

All rights reserved.

Published by Goldcrest Books International Ltd
www.goldcrestbooks.com
publish@goldcrestbooks.com

ISBN: 978-1-913719-49-4

*For Tom Wilson my primary school teacher who
encouraged and inspired me.
You always said I had tenacity.*

*For my friends Jayne, Jilly, Lin, Sally and Sam, who
have all supported me on my own magical journey.*

"My mother is a witch, and that I know to be true. I have seen her spirit in the likeness of a brown dog, which she calls Ball. The dog did ask what she would have him do, and she answered that she would have him help her to kill."

Testimony of Jennet Device
Age 9, Trial 1612

CHAPTER 1

Drifting back to consciousness, it was as if an electrical current - a shock growing in intensity – was spreading from my brain, surging through my body, bringing me back to life. My heart was suddenly frantically beating, trying to catch up for lost time.

In the iciness of the water, a fight for survival kicked in as I tried to struggle free of the clinging riverbed weeds holding me down. Desperate for my first breath, I summoned enough energy to break the surface. Then I was hanging on to the riverbank for dear life – indeed, for my life – gasping for air, naked as the day I was born.

At the very moment the strong current loosened my desperate fingers from the soil of the bank, I felt hands on me as Sandy and Alice, combining their strength, hauled me out. I was in deep shock, my body shaking and spasming in an attempt to kick-start a healthy blood flow. Then the aggressive retching began; it felt like the whole river was being expelled, water spewing uncontrollably from my mouth and nose. As the painful flow slowed to a trickle, the two women swiftly laid me down on prepared blankets, roughly rubbing me up and down with towels until they were satisfied I was dry, whereupon they swaddled me tightly until I was as cocooned as a newborn and equally helpless.

Thank God I was alive. I'd survived the last test. I'd drowned. I'd proved the power of the protection spell. I tentatively wiggled my fingers, then my toes, as much as possible within the warmth of my wrappings. Everything seemed to be working. My mind was clear too, I felt normal – better than normal – and while I'd never taken life for granted, I was aware of an invincibility, a stronger force electrifying my being. Any lingering doubts about how protected I was had been summarily dismissed, and there could be no further doubts; it was a strange sensation. As I looked up at Sandy and Alice, I had a momentary intense flash of déjà vu as if all this had happened before. How bizarre. I shook my head fractionally and the impression dispersed. The sun was dazzling, promising a beautiful day. My two guardian angels were haloed, and an Emily Brontë quote came to mind, *No coward soul is mine*. So true, a revelation, a turning of the page onto the next chapter of my life. I was brave, that I knew for sure. I vowed to put on the silver necklace I'd found in the spell book and never take it off, in honour of Hettie and her lost soul. I wished she'd used the spell and understood the impact. Or maybe she'd tried, like me, but it hadn't worked, an ancient typo in our version? But I had to live in the present, in my time. I couldn't change the past.

Sandy and Alice were one hundred per cent on my side. I'd trusted them with my life to prove the power of the spell. And now I was liberated, free of the shackles of fear which had bound me for so long. I must confess, it had crossed my paranoid mind more than once that maybe one or both of these women had crossed to the other side and become witch hunters, just biding their time, waiting to pounce. I'd wondered whether they were concealing their own secrets; after all, I knew all too well that not everyone was who you thought they were. Now I felt remorseful, I should have trusted them from the start; they were the good guys. They'd tried everything, hadn't they? Burning, garrotting, and now drowning, I'd gone through the murder mill and survived. Onwards and upwards, I was alive, a kick-ass witch. No one could touch me now, but that wouldn't stop me from appreciating and living each day as if it was my last, with an appreciation of everything life had to offer.

Alice was the first to speak. Difficult to know what to say when you've just witnessed your best friend drown. She couldn't disguise the look of utter relief on her face now that she knew I would be OK.

"You see, Ellie, you should have trusted us. We have your back, always have, always will."

I managed a weak smile. "Thank you."

Sandy's smug, told-you-so expression spoke volumes. "Congratulations, Ellie, this is it. Nothing and no one can harm you now." She smiled. "Come on, sweetie, let's get some clothes on you and get you inside before you freeze to death."

Mindful of my modesty and making sure we weren't being watched, I quickly scrambled into my clothing. I felt energised, my body tingling and exhilarated. The spell had certainly powered right through my body, and I jumped up as if nothing had happened in the river. The only clue was my wet hair which I hurriedly bundled into a towel and, grinning, muttered, "Drowning is not for the faint-hearted, is it? Should come with a public health warning." They both laughed.

We headed back, amiably arm-in-arm, to the house. We'd managed all of this without any of the farm workers noticing what we were doing. Quite an achievement when they seemed to be everywhere at the moment, like worker ants. There was always so much to do both on the land and in renovating the various buildings. Sandy, Mike, and Alice had done everything to keep things normal, but it only took one person to blab, and that would be the end of the game. We were all protected, but Sandy and Alice were much needed by the witch community so we couldn't afford for anything to go wrong. Because they didn't need any distractions from the locals, they kept themselves to themselves, not joining in with activities in the nearest village, and maintaining a low profile. I wasn't sure what was involved in their plans but was certain I'd be enlightened before too long. I hoped so, anyway.

Mike had come into his own as our security guard. Up with the lark, making sure any other early risers were distracted, occupying them with the day's tasks, so there was no excuse to be anywhere near the fields or the river. He was much in demand, brewing up builder's tea the colour of mud, and toast with lashings of butter – they were slaves to their stomachs, and any chance of a free breakfast and a cuppa ensured they stuck around. If there had been prying eyes, what would they have made of what they saw, midsummer murders perhaps? Mercifully, as we made our way back, the only reaction we had were waves from the builders, grinning at us nutters taking a freezing morning river dip. My teeth were still chattering as Sandy and Alice hurried me into the living room where there was already a welcome roaring fire to which I huddled as close as possible.

After the testing of the spell, things got back to normal surprisingly quickly. I had mixed feelings, everything felt just a little anticlimactic, and living at the farmhouse, I was starting to feel I needed my own space. I was an adult in my own right, but through force of circumstance we'd gone straight back into the mother/child relationship, habits of a lifetime being hard to break. On a positive note, we'd made it up big time, and our relationship was so much better now that I understood and respected Sandy's motivations, especially with what was happening in the wider world. We'd both shared our secrets – or at least some of them in my case – I'd told her all about the drowning dreams, the past life experiences with Hettie and the strange happenings on the London ghost tour. Sandy had been unsurprised, and said she'd had her suspicions about my dreams, she'd always thought there was a possibility I was astral travelling, that my soul was leaving my body.

"You see now," she'd said, "why I tried to protect you,

suppress those tendencies. How on earth would you have handled all of this as a young child? I'm so glad you didn't have full-on time-travelling experiences then. Mind you," she added, "it wasn't an easy task I set myself."

"Well, even as an adult, it freaked me out," I'd admitted. I recalled Mike was with me when I experienced the time slip in London at my leaving party. Looking at him, I'd asked, "Did you know what was happening when I collapsed?"

He'd shaken his head. "No, not then, but I told Sandy, and she nearly had a fit, especially when I reported that you'd said 'I am Hettie' in front of everyone! I knew then that I had to get you away quickly before the men in white coats arrived to take you away."

Sandy had said, "I think you really only started to recognise your abilities once you were in Yorkshire, although I was horrified at the time. But now you have fully understood and unleashed that power, it will only get stronger, and you can use it for the greater good." She ignored my raised eyebrow and continued, "Going back into the past will help you see things from a different angle, some great life lessons to learn."

"But I still don't know how to make it happen," I'd protested. "It seems to be completely random."

"Ellie," she'd said firmly, "you always over-analyse things! Just accept it as an amazing gift, one I wish I had. The fact you can do it is enough for right now and maybe it's only being in a certain place at a certain time that triggers some magnetic pull, especially when there is an important message to be relayed."

I'd nodded slowly. "Makes more sense when you put

it like that, but how do you explain why I met the funeral director, going back in time just ten years? That was bizarre!"

"Maybe you were meant to meet a particular ghost, not the funeral director himself?" she'd suggested. I thought of the beautiful ghost of Mournful Maddie, maybe Sandy was right, and I was only meant to meet her spirit, not Maddie when she was alive. But I still couldn't work out whether there was any message. I couldn't help wondering if I'd missed something. Sandy saw the look on my face. "Darling, stop overthinking. Your power is growing daily, you'll understand in time. You may meet someone in the future who can help you hone your skills."

"Hope so," I'd said, although I wasn't sure how that would happen as, for our own safety's sake, we were obliged to keep our heads well below the parapet.

I knew for the sake of our ongoing relationship that it was probably better if I moved out of the farmhouse. Otherwise, the lectures were going to be endless, Sandy couldn't help herself. However, there was no doubt we shared a newfound mutual respect, and I didn't want to spoil that. I was careful nowadays to count to ten rather than snapping back with an instant answer when I thought she was wrong. I could see how Mike handled their interactions, often taking the easy option rather than heading into a row and I took my cue from him. I knew she'd only ever had my best interests at heart and her mission to protect me throughout my childhood hadn't ended now I was an adult, and I understood. All she ever wanted was my safety, and she was petrified I'd put myself in a dangerous situation without fully understanding my heritage. She certainly had a point, as my recent history proved. Nevertheless, I knew I needed to move out sooner rather than later, so I could start adulting again!

CHAPTER 2

It was a further six weeks before the barn was ready for me to move into, with the building and decorating completed and only a few nagging issues and decorating touch-ups still to be dealt with. This just left the garden to be landscaped, but that could be achieved from the outside without anyone intruding into my new home. Admittedly the area around my abode still looked like a building site, but I was assured I'd soon have the promised courtyard garden, natural hedging, and reclaimed railway sleepers as raised beds. Never one for waste, Sandy was making use of everything left behind by the previous residents. A low-maintenance area was the plan, with an abundance of shrubs and herbs, no lawn in sight so no need for a lawnmower.

I knew that this wasn't necessarily going to be my forever home, so I'd been happy to let Sandy have a free hand with the decor – she might have other uses for it in the future. It would make a perfect holiday cottage rental. But right now, and for the foreseeable future, it suited me perfectly, and Sandy had said I could stay as long as I wanted. In addition, she wasn't planning on charging rent. I didn't feel bad about that as I'd recently discovered the extent of her wealth, which had increased dramatically since my father's death, with a generous life policy and pension. I sincerely hoped that as a wealthy widow, she'd taken care to protect her assets, but she was a lawyer after all, so she almost certainly didn't need my input – like teaching grandmother to suck eggs, as they say. Of course, Mike might be incredibly wealthy in his own right too, you should never judge a book by its cover. Had his work as a company chauffeur just been a cover for his clandestine lifestyle? I was sure there was still an awful lot about him I didn't know.

I was calling for Alice on my way to the barn, ready to give her the grand tour. It wouldn't take too long; it wasn't a huge place. We'd been banned from the site until it was fully decorated and furnished, so it would surprise us both. Sandy's rules, of course, and we obeyed them! She'd promised it would all be fully kitted out, ready for me to move straight into, and was proud of using as much as possible from our old family home, recycled stuff she found around here, and pre-loved items from the local antique shops. I was somewhat dubious about this, remembering the elaborate and glitzy decor, but as I wasn't keen to take on even soft furnishing choices, I'd just gone with the flow. I knew Sandy had raided the enormous on-site storage container, and I expected to see a few familiar items, but at least she wasn't throwing things away and adding to the landfill problem.

I'd asked if there was a name for the barn yet. Sandy laughed and said, "It housed pigs when it was a working farm, but I didn't think you'd want to live at *The Piggery!*" I giggled; she wasn't wrong. It would be nice, though, for it to have its own identity, maybe a witchy name, nothing too magical, though, or the locals would talk. Imagine the postman delivering mail to *Hex Cottage,* which had been my initial thought. Maybe I could change it to *Heck Cottage, subtle change, but I'd know what it meant!* Sandy left the choice to me, and I'd gone through a long list. Now I was being silly: *The Old Haunt* or the *Witches Lair* were candidates, but probably far too risky. I'd also considered *Hallowed Woods Barn* but eventually decided just *Wood Barn* would be more sensible. Innocuous enough for the postman and local gossips.

Alice was especially thrilled with my imminent move as it meant I'd be putting down some roots, at least for the time being. In our retreat there was safety in numbers, and she desperately wanted me to like it here, feel settled and stay put in Wood Barn forever. It didn't look like she was planning on going anywhere else any time soon. I wasn't keen to think about the future because that always seemed to get me into trouble. Right now, I had every intention of settling down and going for an easy life, at least for now. Daydreaming now, I could get another cat, remembering Mia, the beautiful Ragdoll house cat I had in Hampstead, but did I really want to take care of a pet? Not sure I did. A house cat in a farm environment didn't seem too practical either. Perhaps a common or garden black cat that would be more independent, wandering around the grounds of the farm, would be more suitable, but then again, possibly too obvious – the witch link again. There was, of course, a distinct advantage to acquiring a feline; it would keep the vermin at bay. I wasn't happy to have seen the odd rat out and about and knew mice were rife in the barns.

CHAPTER 3

We headed over to Wood Barn, both of us impatient and excited to finally see what Sandy had done to the place. I unlocked the double locks on the front door – there were some horrendous stories of rural burglary and crimes of violence were going up all the time and Sandy wasn't taking any chances. She'd also fitted a high-tech alarm system; I held the instructions in my hand. I felt I was taking part in one of those TV programmes, think Kirsty and Phil on *Location, Location, Location*, where they show a wild card home to a prospective buyer.

Still working automatically to Sandy's rules, we discarded our muddy shoes onto a carefully placed mat at the front door and entered the spacious hallway. There were antique stripped pine doors off the hallway to the other rooms, and the original oak beams had been retained and restored. The living accommodation in this barn conversion was all on one level, with no stairs to climb. There was a beautiful Victorian-style Minton tile pattern on the floor, in white, black, and terracotta, and the walls were a soft neutral grey. I recognised the colour, maybe Farrow and Ball?

We opened the door into a lounge, and the welcome sight of the open fire Sandy had already lit. The wood crackling behind an ornate wrought iron fire guard gave off a lovely glow, and the scent was divine. Alice and I glanced at each other and smiled. It was starting to feel like home already. They say home is where the heart is, and my bestie was with me. The room was wonderfully spacious, I imagined all the original partitioning had been knocked down. The same Minton flooring and subdued grey wall colour had been carried through from the hall, and I could see a few familiar pieces of furniture – the sideboard that would be perfect for my music system still at Lavender Cottage, along with matching side and coffee tables. I thought wistfully, I did miss my vinyl, streaming music was just not the same without the crackle!

Alice chuckled. "The theme's a bit Victorian mahogany. But it works, what with the beams and all." I plopped myself down on the super-plush, rich aubergine-coloured velvet sofa. Sandy had scattered different shades of velvet cushions to add splashes of orange, mustard, and teal to great effect, and it faced its twin against the opposite wall. Alice, meanwhile, had perched herself elegantly on a buttoned, teal velvet chaise longue. "Everything looks awesome, I know they came from your old home, but they look so different here – as if they were made for this place."

I nodded. "I agree. I'm surprisingly happy with this look, and everything is in pristine condition, I reckon Sandy might have used a little magic, don't you?"

"Too right, although I don't think this chaise longue was built for comfort."

"Not for your bony arse," I said.

Alice mock-frowned. "How rude!" Then continued, "Walls look a bit bare though, maybe a few black and white or sepia pictures?" I visualised some of the Victorian pictures on the wall, the so-called death pictures, maybe a bit too much on the spooky side. I grimaced, thinking of those I'd found at Lavender Cottage, now safely installed in the Whitby Museum, ready for ghoulish Victoriana enthusiasts to savour.

"I'll have to explore some antique and art shops in the area. I'm sure I'll find some perfect gems. I'm just pleased Sandy hasn't filled the walls with those botanical prints she's so fond of. Don't you think it's funny how she's changed her decorating style – maybe Mike's influence?"

"Perhaps she just fancied a change – new place, clean slate. After all, she'd lived at her previous home for a long time." I nodded but wondered whether she'd wanted to erase her history with my father and not replicate it here. Alice continued, "Anyway, you have a blank canvas on the walls, ready for the Ellie touch. I suppose you could use your magic if you wanted?"

I laughed. "Not sure I can materialise pictures, that's a step too far. I could do an illusion spell, but it wouldn't last, I guess I'm just going to have to go out and buy! I can also visualise a luxury deep-pile sheepskin rug here, and maybe one of those pedestal pot plants that the Victorians used to have, with a cheeky aspidistra. That would do the trick."

Alice grinned. "I can see it won't take long for you to put your stamp on the place." She glanced over at the glitzy, ornate gold mirror above the mantelpiece. "You know that mirror's totally over the top but somehow just right in here, or maybe I'm just growing more mellow and old-fashioned in my old age."

"You and me both." I grinned and, looking around, added, "I don't remember some of these things, but our old house was massive, and there were rooms we never used. I'm relieved she's used white shutters rather than those chintzy flowery curtains she used to favour!"

"You are planning to stay around, aren't you?" Alice said anxiously. "Not absconding anywhere?"

"Don't worry, darling, I'm here to stay, and I think I'll be very happy here."

She looked relieved. "I've lost you once, I don't want to do it again!"

The next stop was the bedrooms. The first one we came to had a generous-sized en suite, so I'd bag that as mine and leave the other bedroom as a guest/dressing room. There was a feature wall papered with tiny, Victorian-style, dark pink rose buds on a white background, not to my taste, that would have to go. The other walls were in Sandy's signature soft grey. The carpet was a slightly darker shade with, I noted approvingly, a luxurious deep pile. The furniture was all mahogany: a generous double wardrobe, a matching chest of drawers, a dressing table, and bedside tables. The pièce de résistance was the magnificent four-poster bed, which would have looked at home in a stately pile but seemed to work here, too. As I went over to the impressive dressing table with its matching stool, I smiled, the perfect place to put on a full face, but as I looked into the mirror, a shiver ran down my spine. I felt a little lightheaded and had a strong feeling like I'd looked into this mirror many times before. For a chilling, riveting second it wasn't my reflection looking back at me, it was a Victorian woman, her face obscured by a mourning veil. I jumped back and screamed.

Alice, shocked, jumped in turn. "Ellie? What the hell?" I cautiously turned back again but, thank God, only my reflection now showed in the glass.

"Holy fuck," I said shakily. "That was beyond weird, I swear someone else was looking back at me! Remember those horror movies we watched at uni, hiding behind our popcorn?"

Alice moved to my side, cautiously taking a look. Seeing the acute apprehension reflected on both our faces she laughed, "Don't be daft, you've got too vivid an imagination, that's your problem! You gave me a proper scare though, you idiot!"

I smiled weakly; what was that? A past life looking in? A ghost? An encounter waiting for me in my future?

"The first thing I'm going to do is change this room around, the dressing table has got to go, and as for the rosebud paper, a bit too authentically Victorian for my liking!" Alice grinned. She knew I'd be like a dog with a bone, and this room would be changed pretty damn quick.

We moved swiftly into the other bedroom, decorated in the same vein but with a less impressive bed. I wasn't expecting visitors any time soon, so it'd make a great dressing room. I'd ditch the Victoriana in here too. The Victorian feel in the bedrooms had unsettled me. I wasn't even sure I wanted to stay the night until I'd changed the look. I didn't say anything to Alice, but maybe someday, when times were safer and we finally got in touch again, Sarah and Lizzie could stay over. This would be the perfect place for them, with a few tweaks here and there. Perhaps I could invite the Hampstead crew one day, too, including Lily? But maybe not Lily. I wasn't sure about bringing Matt back into the frame. He was such a nice guy, but it was a complicated situation, he was firmly in the past. I shook my head; this wasn't a day for maudlin thoughts. I mustn't lose sight of my new mantra, "look forwards not backwards, and lose the guilt!"

Opening the door into the generous family bathroom, we saw a huge white enamel claw-footed bath with bronze legs, quite the in style. Sandy had certainly gone full-on Victoriana with the old-fashioned toilet with its overhead cistern, chain pull, and heavy wooden toilet seat. Alice, looking around appreciatively, said, "I can imagine you making the most of this, candles, a bubble bath, a glass of vino, and a good book."

I nodded. "Just what I was thinking." Although, as soon as the words were out of my mouth, I realised that while I loved the idea of a luxurious bubble bath, I'd probably stick to my modern en suite. This was a little too gothic for me – something was troubling me. There was something a little gross about the reclaimed Victorian lavatory, had it come from our old house or elsewhere – eew!

The last room was the best surprise of all. It was immense, a delightful mix of antique and contemporary, giving it an almost industrial feel. Thankfully, there wasn't a splinter of mahogany to be seen. I loved it – much more my sort of thing. It served as a kitchen, dining, and living area, with bi-fold doors opening onto what would be the patio in just a few weeks. I could imagine entertaining in this room; it'd be perfect when the garden was finished. There was the same Minton flooring, a black wood burner Sandy had lit, and an enormous Aga. It was super-warm and cosy, and I could see myself spending most of my time here, away from spooky mirrors and Victoriana! Maybe treat myself to an Aga cookbook, encourage me to be a little more domesticated and do some baking and cooking. OK, let's not get too carried away! Domestic goddess was not one of my strengths.

Alice started opening drawers and cupboards with approving murmurs, and I spotted some of Sandy's Le Creuset and Denby pottery on show. The kitchen units looked bespoke, and I recognised the colour as Cashmere, bang on trend at the moment. A stone-coloured granite counter complemented the units.

"Wow," said Alice. "Pretty well-equipped kitchen, some real top-quality, useful stuff. With this Aga, you'll have to make some serious recipes, become the new Nigella."

I laughed. "Now, that is where I'd need my magic, but I promise I'll make you supper one evening. It's a fabulous space. I'm sure I'll spend most of my time in here."

"It's perfect for you."

"I just need to cosy it up a little more with some rugs, throws, and, of course, pictures for the walls – I can feel a shopping trip coming on or maybe I'll have a rummage through the storage container, see if there's anything else I can repurpose." ... and some new furniture that isn't mahogany! Sandy had put two huge, brown, squashy leather sofas in there, both with an assortment of scatter cushions, and there was an oversized farmhouse dining table which looked somewhat familiar.

Alice seated herself at the table, as further investigation showed me Sandy had kindly filled the fridge with some basics – milk, butter and, eggs – and there were coffee pods and a coffee machine on the counter. A freshly baked loaf, croissants, and locally made preserve were left in a basket. She'd thought of everything, what a sweetheart.

"Coffee?" I said.

"Thought you'd never ask."

I waltzed over to the coffee machine, detouring to put one of my spooky playlists on the Bluetooth speaker. We always used to have uplifting background music on when the girls were over, but that was then and this was now, and I was currently obsessed with darker music; one of my newest discoveries was the UK band Broadcast, who'd acquired a cult following in the 90s. I opted for "The Book Lovers", one of my favourites.

"Wow, Ells," Alice exclaimed. "Bit spooky and psychedelic, not our usual!"

I laughed, fully recovered now. I should be used to strange and spooky experiences and perhaps embrace the mysterious woman in the mirror, whoever she was. Maybe I'd imagined her? But I was still going to change the furniture and decor as living in a totally Victorian ambience might be a step too far, although I won't deny there was a temptation to go and look in the mirror again. "The World Backwards" came on, and as I made the coffee – mine particularly strong, Alice's with more milk – I sang along to the deep and dark words. "OK, not my usual genre, but I do love it." Alice said, "And you, what a gorgeous voice," as sarcastic as always about my musical attempts.

I refused to take offence and laughed. "Sometimes it's good to try something different. I relish a haunting playlist, after all, I am a witch and proud of it."

A grim expression briefly crossed her face. "Maybe keep quiet about that." Then, as Radiohead's "Karma Police" started, "No, Ellie, this is too much! Maybe this is why you are getting more weird experiences; you are attracting the macabre. I'm putting my foot down, not Radiohead. I have my limits. What's wrong with you? It makes me want to slit my wrists."

I laughed. "OK, I've got the message, what's your choice then?"

"Something from the old days, uplifting and lively, and where's that coffee?" As I stirred our drinks, I thought about my new music choices, which tied in with my emotional roller coaster. There was no doubt this genre of music had got into my soul. For now, I found an old-school 90s dance classic, "Dreamer" by Livin' Joy. It brought back good memories as I moved to open the bi-fold doors to their full capacity, getting some fresh country air into our lungs, although it made me gasp.

"Oooh, Eau de Vache, the smell of cow dung."

"Don't worry, after a while you don't smell it any more. You get used to it."

I suddenly screamed. "What the fuck, something has just brushed between my legs. A giant rat?"

Alice smiled. "Ahh, it's Kasper, he lives in the village with Mack and Jan who run the local pub. He gets under their feet, so he likes to make himself at home around here where he gets more fuss and catches a mouse or two. Although we haven't seen him for a while around the farm, we did wonder if something had happened to him. Maybe he knows there's a new girl in town, ready to pamper him!" I laughed as I realised Kasper was a black cat, with one thing missing – his tail! I wondered how he'd lost it. But it didn't seem to bother him, as he sauntered into the room as if he owned the place. Maybe this answered the question of pets – this cat had found me. I wouldn't have to feed him or worry when I wasn't at home, but he was welcome to call in whenever he wanted to, and of course keep the area free of vermin – win-win! Alice asked, "Where are your bowls?" I pointed to one of the cupboards. She took a small bowl out, filled it with water, and Kasper gratefully started drinking. I must admit he was cute, he could come again, and a cat with no tail was the perfect companion for a witch; I was sure he had a few stories to tell himself. Although I thought it must be cupboard love on his part as he sauntered back out again, now refreshed.

As we sat at the table, coffees in hand, "Stop Crying Your Heart Out" by Oasis came on. We smiled, this was another of our old-school classics, no need for words. I wiped away a tear, it always made me emotional. Distracting myself, I looked around this room, making plans – a bookcase in here, or maybe in the lounge if there was room, and a change of bedroom decor, of course! With more time on my hands, I'd been catching up on my reading. As a child, I'd been an avid reader, my nose always in a book while I was at boarding school, but work and socialising later got in the way, and I was more likely to leaf through a magazine than bury myself in a book. But now I was breezing through the back catalogue of the Brontës and had just finished Wilkie Collins's The Woman in White – vivid stories woven by Victorian authors. I was gaining a strong feel for what life might have been like, at least for the middle to upper classes. It was an era with which I was particularly, perhaps morbidly, fascinated. Maybe this era was getting too much into my psyche. Perhaps, as Alice suggested, I was encouraging the macabre. As we sat in companionable silence sipping coffee, life was good, and I just hoped Sandy and Mike didn't have any plans to repurpose the space any time soon. I felt I could stay here forever. I was fed up with running. Apart from the furniture, the general vibe of the property was good. It had been expertly restored to maintain a historic feel, and there was an enticing aroma of beeswax, varnish, and fresh paint. For an old building, it all felt nice and draught-free. Sandy, keen to share lots of detail, had told me she'd had triple glazing fitted, but as it was in a protected area, no plastic or aluminium frames were allowed, so the frames were wooden. My heart skipped a beat as I was sadly reminded of renovating Lavender Cottage a lifetime ago.

Finishing her coffee and croissant, Alice came over and giving me the biggest bear hug, said, "I need to get back. I've got some work to finish, and I want to hit the shops."

"OK, wait for me to lock up, and we can head back to the house."

As we walked arm-in-arm I looked up. "Hey, look, it's a mackerel sky." Alice looked puzzled. "Weather folklore," I clarified. "Haven't you heard that before?" She shook her head. I didn't say it had been part of Seb's lectures, my favourite subject. "There's an adage," I told her, "Mackerel sky, mackerel sky, never long wet, never long dry. Means weather's on the turn, it's an old country saying. You know the sky paints us a different picture every day." I became aware of Alice looking at me oddly. This was very far removed from my usual ramblings.

"I've heard of Red sky at night shepherds delight, red sky in the morning shepherds warning, I think everyone knows that one, but that's about it," she said. "Anyway, I really must go, babes. I know you'll be super-happy here. I can see it already in your sweet little face, you're looking more relaxed. Enjoy your last few days as a lady of leisure, just another week to go, and you'll be joining us!"

As we hugged, I won't deny I was excited at the thought of joining the family firm. I wasn't quite sure what to expect, but I was more than ready for a new chapter and a new challenge. My recent experiences taught me never to take anything for granted and to find inspiration in the small things. Goodness, I was developing mantras by the minute! I'd decided to stay at the farmhouse tonight and was tempted to go back in and take another look at the creepy mirror. I was split between totally freaked and fascinated.

CHAPTER 4

My week of leisure passed quickly, and I was to report for duty at the office at the back of the farmhouse the following day at 8.30 prompt. OK, they hadn't actually said that, but they might as well have. I wasn't clear exactly what they'd want me to do and was unsure how well my skills would transfer. They'd gone very cloak and dagger, so I was still in the dark as to how I could help the cause. I'd been wracking my brains but hadn't yet found an answer. I'd sort of discounted the roll out of the protection spell, the mission to save the Witches. I know we'd talked about it, but how on earth could this practically be done on a massive scale. Yes, I wanted to help humanity, but if I was totally honest, I didn't believe we could pull something like this off. I'm sure when I found out exactly what they had planned for me it would be an anti-climax.

I wasn't sure why I felt so fidgety, and there was also

a slight feeling of dread that had crept in. Rubbish, I told myself, just a bit of new-girl nerves, but did they really want me on board or were they only going to employ me to keep me busy? Braving the gothic bathroom, I decided relaxing in the warmth of a bubble bath, with candles and a playlist, and an early night were in order to get me fighting fit. Liberally applying a rich moisturising hair and face mask, I kicked back into the exquisite-smelling bubbles. It was bliss. I had a glass of bubbly and some artisan chocolates I'd picked up locally, so it was a fair old while and wrinkly-fingers-time before I dragged myself out, but I did feel ready for anything. Wrapping my hair in a fluffy white towel, I yawned. Once I'd sorted my unruly locks out, I'd settle down with a good book. It was stupid to worry about the next day – it was Sandy and Alice, for God's sake, I shouldn't feel nervous or intimidated.

I have to admit that I'd felt a little spooked for the first few nights sleeping at Wood Barn. There was a chill in my bedroom, which I couldn't seem to dispel, however high the heating was hiked up. Plus, as in any unfamiliar new room, night-time shadows created some insanely spooky shapes, and I still wasn't used to the night noises made by any structure, old or new. There was a lot of creaking and moaning, although that was probably just the wind through the trees. I don't think I was yet used to the absence of traffic, countryside sounds being very different from those in the city, and even the silence had a weight of its own. I'd turned away from my Victorian authors and gone for something a little more frivolous, some chick lit, light-hearted romance. As I settled into the comfort of the four-poster bed with its comfortable mattress, I felt as if I was the princess without the discomfort of the pea and, amusing though my book was, I don't think it was long before it fell from my hands, and I slept.

Someone was squeezing me tightly from behind, I couldn't see who it was, but it didn't feel threatening. Then a whisper in the air, as light as a feather, so soft that I nearly missed it. "Let me take you on a journey." And in the next breath, it felt as if we were flying at breakneck speed, scenery passing in an indistinguishable blue. Then we stopped, the grip on me loosened, my head was spinning. I had no idea where I was and didn't recognise anything around me. It was flat for as far as I could see, sandy, arid – a desert, the heat rasping in my throat as I took a breath. My lungs ached as the dusty acrid air hit them. My eyes stung from the sunlight reflecting orange from the sand. Then, I was grasped tightly again. I tried to look round but couldn't turn my head, and we were on the move again. When my dizziness passed, it was freezing, snow-capped mountains were in the distance, and my breath clouded before me as I shivered in biting wind-driven snow.

It was deathly quiet. There was only the unseen presence, now holding me gently. I felt no fear, they meant me no harm, and we flew again, spinning through sunrises and sunsets, days to nights, following the turning of the earth until we were in the dark of a forest, in a clearing, silent except for the creaking of trees and a lone wolf howling to a moon in an ink-black sky, no light pollution here. Where was I? Why was this happening? Even in my dream state,

I felt confused. I tried to call out but couldn't. My guide had relinquished their hold on me once again, although I knew they were still there and in no time at all we were in a boat on the open sea, the sun high in the sky. I was reminded of the Maldives, although I could see no people on the beach, just palm trees moving in a soft breeze. OK, I thought, this is good, I'd be happy to stay here with the clear water lapping around the boat, but I was jolted alert by the wail of a woman:

"Please help Ellie." Then another desperate voice: "Come, find us, we need your help."

Finding my own voice, I called back, "Who are you? Where are you?"

"You know who we are." Voices now in unison, and with a shiver of shock, I did know. It was Lizzie and Sarah, without a shadow of a doubt, but as I drew breath to respond, I was gripped tightly again and abruptly yanked away from the voices of my friends, whirling around and around again until the hold on me relaxed, and I fell to earth with a thump, the presence behind me disappearing as quickly as it had arrived and I wasn't on the ground, I was in my bed.

My head was throbbing, and not just from the dream, I must have been thrashing around a lot because I'd hurt myself on one of the decorative bed-posts, and was that just a dream or more of a nightmare? The desperation in the voices of Lizzie and Sarah had been dreadful, even if only a figment of my overactive dream world and my mixed-up mind.

I didn't understand, from what Alice had said, they'd

left the country, and I knew Lizzie was somewhere in the US, but was she safe? I couldn't be certain of that. And why would Alice not be more specific about where they were? Did Sarah and Lizzie even know that Sandy was a witch? I had a feeling in my bones that Alice was in touch with them, yet that made no sense. Did they even know I was alive, and if so, surely they would want to hear from me? I was aching to speak to them, even if it was just a quick phone call. Then again, could it be that she was protecting me from them – or was it the other way round? Could I put them in danger? I'd ask her again, but today was not the day. I knew I missed them with all my heart and prayed they were safe and well. Did the spell protect them too? Then a dark thought – maybe they were on the wrong side, witch hunters, which was why she was keeping me well away from them. Had Lizzie been enticed by the dark side, the Salem witches. Or had they been brainwashed against the witches; it did happen after all. But surely not, they were my best friends.

Shaking off the anxious feeling from the dream, I concentrated on getting up and ready for my first day at work. I wasn't sure what to wear but planned to take my cue from Alice: classic, understated, and smart. Although, in the past, I knew she was far more formal when she was in court – sharp black suit, white blouse, high heels aiming to intimidate the other side – she was more casual in the office. Kitten heels or smart patent loafers, with simple but classic-cut trousers and a silk blouse. Alice had never done grunge, even at uni. I'd put together what I thought was a suitable wardrobe. Not jogging bottoms and a slouchy top, but not city wear either. I wanted to feel I was going out to work, even if it was only a few paces to get to the office. I smiled as I recalled having to call Mike to take me to work. How weird that he was now firmly ensconced in the farmhouse with my mother, life certainly had its surprises. I'd already picked up some new threads at one of the many boutiques dotted around; black was always safe, wasn't it, and my Mulberry bag was big enough for my iPad and phone, so I could either take notes or record them.

Turning on the shower, my mind wandered back to the dream, was it more than just a night terror? Was it my subconscious searching for my friends? Had I actually travelled and heard them? I'd read somewhere it was good to name that unwelcome negative voice in your head. I called her Doris. "Shut the fuck up, Doris, I don't need to hear from you today of all days," I muttered. I'd ask Alice again when the time was right. For now, I had to put it to the back of my mind. I shuddered as I stepped into the cold shower, but it did the trick, washing away the uneasy feeling of dread. I trusted Alice with my life, she must have her reasons.

As I got myself ready, making sure my hair covered the bruise which had come up like an egg, I realised I was starving. I took a few moments for a few bites of croissant, and a glug of ice-cold milk, did a few yoga stretches, and a quick 10-minute meditation – calm, deep calm, and breathe – that felt better. I finished the rest of the croissant before clearing away.

CHAPTER 5

Right, head in gear, I was ready, a little early, but knowing Sandy and Alice, the consummate professionals, they'd probably been at their desks for hours. I'd like to know what I'd be doing. Would I get stuck in straightaway? I put on some kitten-heeled, black ankle boots – smart but comfy – it was too rubble-strewn around here for high heels, I'd break my neck walking through the building site that was my garden. I teamed the outfit with smart black tapered trousers, a frilly black chiffon blouse and my leather biker jacket. Picking up my bag, what else did I need? Phone, iPad, lippie, and other girlie stuff. I headed out of the door, buzzing with excitement but at the same time with a churning nervousness at the pit of my stomach.

Not far to go to work, just a short walk to the office suite at the back of the farmhouse, away from prying eyes. Of course, to the outside world it appeared normal, just another law firm, most of the time run from the farm, with staff manning the other office in the nearby town, where client-facing appointments ostensibly took place. In fact, with the work becoming increasingly sensitive, Sandy and Alice often met clients at their own homes – far more private and discreet.

As expected, they were already seated at their desks, hard at work, but both looked up when I made my entrance.

"Morning, Ellie," Alice said, getting to her feet. "Coffee?"

"D'you have to ask?" I said. "Caffeine hit always welcome."

"Your desk." She nodded at an identical third desk, this one uncluttered by papers. "You can leave your bag there, but don't get too comfortable, we're going straight into the boardroom." That sounded formal.

Sandy caught my dubious expression and laughed. "Don't worry, just us today. The rest of the team is working at the main office. I banished them. You'll meet them in the next few days."

I carried my coffee cup and saucer into the boardroom in one hand, my iPad in the other. Once seated, I gratefully sipped – a nice strong blend which hit the spot.

Sandy followed me in. "You won't need to take notes today, it'll be more of an introduction, showing you the ropes, getting you up to speed with exactly what's been going on." I nodded. "Actually," she added, "Probably best not to write anything down – nothing that could be used against us." Now that did sound ominous. What exactly, I thought, were they going to ask me to do?

Sandy continued, in serious mode now. I'd never worked with her before, but knew that she was exceptionally focused on whatever she was dealing with; those she worked against always called her a hard-faced bitch, so I knew she was good. "As you know, we're doing what we can to help the witches, representing them from a legal point of view, but we feel we can do much more."

Alice interjected. "The Purge is gaining momentum, and we think there will be another push soon. That means increased action and aggression. The vibe seems to be changing, and from what we hear, I'm afraid it's becoming more threatening. Most concerning is that the perpetrators seem to be less and less concerned about being found out. It's a political game changer for the prime minister, this plan to eradicate the witches within legal parameters, but despite that, there's a lot going on where the same end is being achieved by whatever means necessary." She let that hang ominously before going on. "We've already launched a major humanitarian mission, but we need your help." I took another sip of coffee and waited. I still couldn't see what possible constructive contribution I could make.

Alice continued, "As you know, I don't have a magical bone in my body, I'm just the legal side of the operation, but Sandy has made sure the spell fully protects me, otherwise I'd be in deadly danger. And that's where you come in, if you're serious about helping."

Sandy interjected, "It was important you had all the trust issue sorted before you came on board. To put it bluntly, we knew you had to drown again for you to believe you were protected." She wasn't wrong, they knew me better than I did myself.

I nodded. "Yes. OK. Now I can be one hundred and ten per cent committed."

Sandy looked sideways at Alice; a look between people who were comfortable together. They were like a double act, completely in tune. No wonder they worked well, they were single-minded as well as tough – you wouldn't want to cross either of them! I'd always teased Alice about never letting go of anything, like a Rottweiler. What, then, did that make Sandy? Perhaps a Bull Terrier, one of those vicious dogs trained to fight? I hoped I was making the right decision to join them.

"We are planning on taking our surgery on the road – eventually across the UK – a series of roadshows," said Alice. "Particularly to vulnerable areas, where we're needed the most." Whitby sprang instantly to my mind. I guiltily brushed it aside as she went on. "We're testing an experimental concept on some of our clients alongside our regular legal representation. The uptake has been gratifying, if a little overwhelming, and truthfully, it's been putting the law practice on the back burner, which is concerning, we can't afford for that to happen."

"This," said Sandy "is where you come in. Thankfully, the witch hunters have been giving us an extremely wide berth, we think our involvement and knowledge of the legal process gives us a certain level of immunity."

"Any research we do," put in Alice, "seems to go unquestioned. You can find whatever information you want on the internet, and it won't be sanctioned."

Sandy continued, "The law of the land must be obeyed, they are not allowed to intimidate lawyers. We're not in the dark ages – yet!" I didn't say anything but disagreed with her last comment. With the increase in suicides and mysterious disappearances, I was convinced the law was being taken into individual hands and was also sure there was a news embargo. There were no more headlines screaming war against the witches, but from everything I knew and from what Sandy and Alice were hearing, it hadn't gone away. If anything, the momentum had increased, flourishing under the radar. Neighbour crossing neighbour, friends and family turning on each other.

Alice saw my worried look and understood without me saying a word, she knew me better than I knew myself. "Dangerous times, Ellie, and of course, there will be risks."

Sandy broke in, she couldn't help herself, and I saw the dynamics in their close bond, they were more like mother and daughter than Sandy and I were. "The long-term aim is to disarm the witch hunters. If they can no longer harm or incarcerate the witches, then what's the point of the Purge?" She was right, but I wished they'd stop being so long-winded.

Sandy said, "To sit back and do nothing is dangerous, putting all of us in jeopardy. As a legal firm, it's important that we are seen as neutral. But as you learn more about our supporters, the underground resistance, you may be surprised when you find out who works for us."

"Anyone I know?" I said. She smiled but didn't answer, so I said, "Look, maybe I'm being thick, but I still don't know how I can help with all this. I don't have any legal training."

"Don't worry, you'll do an amazing job once we're travelling around the country with our other services – that's when you'll come into your own. Your official role will be marketing and hospitality organiser; you'll have a role in the firm and a salary."

I took a breath, it all sounded so formal. Was this me? I was used to doing things my way.

Sandy could read me like a book. "You'll love it, you can put your stamp on it, the organisational side is just a small part. You'll be responsible for booking venues and hotels, advertising the roadshows, and deciding where we go first. You were always excellent at finding luxury hotels." Well, that sounded easy enough. "The lawyers in our firm, including myself and Alice, will take appointments at these roadshows." She held up a hand to forestall me. "We have a secretary to deal with all our meetings." I promptly opened my mouth to ask why they also needed me if they had a secretary, but Alice again read my mind.

"You need a proper title, but it doesn't cover everything because when we meet up with potential clients, they'll also have the opportunity to have a private consultation with you."

"What the fuck for?"

Sandy hated swearing. I'd forgotten how often I'd been reprimanded in the past. "Language, Ellie, please. We're on a mission and can't just sit back and ignore the crisis. We need to be proactive. If this pays off, we will be helping humanity." Wow, she was thinking big. "If this works, and we're convinced it will, it's a game changer, the witches will be empowered and can fight back."

"Fight back? We're not getting violent, are we?" I caught another look exchanged between my mother and my best friend, and they laughed.

"Hardly fisticuffs, darling, no hands-on stuff." Sandy stood. "I need to stretch my legs – and I need the bathroom. Alice, be an angel, get us another round of coffee, please."

"I'll do it," I said, and then, once we were all settled again, "Come on then, spit it out!"

"Think of it as a Witch Protection Scheme," said Alice.

For a moment, I was silent as it sank in, it was insane. "You mean I'll be using the spell?"

"You've finally clicked," said Sandy. "About time. As we see it, the witches have two major problems. They go through the legal process, and whether we win or lose the case for them, it's tough, and their reputation can be pretty much ruined – you know, people will always think no smoke without fire. And, of course, if they lose, they get a hefty sentence, and who knows what goes on behind closed doors?" She didn't need to say more. We all knew the barbaric practices to which officialdom turned a blind eye and which most often seemed to lead to coerced suicide, or in other words, murder. "If we can make good our plans, the witches and sympathisers will be protected. You will teach them the protection spell and the fly on the wall spell. With invisibility at their fingertips, they can disappear the hell out of awkward situations."

Despite the seriousness of the conversation, I couldn't help but laugh. "Sorry? You mean right in the middle of being arrested they vanish into thin air?" – I paused – "Ohhh, you mean when they're imprisoned?"

With more than a little sarcasm, Sandy said, "You've got it. Think of it like a vaccine programme, they will be double jabbed – two spells for the price of one."

"Buy one get one free," added Alice. "It'll give them additional protection. They will be able to disappear from a prison cell."

"Right," I said. Then, as another thought occurred, "Can sympathisers also be protected? Is it possible to teach a non-witch a spell?" Alice smiled, and one moment she was there, the next, she disappeared, before reappearing. She chuckled. "That answer your question? Sympathisers can be protected too, don't worry."

"Sooo," I said slowly, "if all witches and sympathisers are protected and can disappear, witch-hunting will become pointless!"

Sandy said, "Think of it like a game of cat and mouse, Tom and Jerry. If the cat's never able to catch the mouse, there's no point in trying."

I sat back in my chair. Could it be that simple? Could this actually work? Could we really save the witches? Did it seem too good to be true? But I could already see the biggest fly in the ointment. "How on earth can I physically administer the spell to so many?"

Sandy snorted. "Silly goose, we've already thought of that!" Silly goose, I hadn't been called that since childhood, I decided to see it as a compliment and bit my tongue. "You will be *training* them on the spells, not getting involved in the physical implementation, that would be impossible! Think of it as a high-level training role."

"Ah, well, that certainly makes it far more practical," I admitted.

Sandy continued, "We've already been doing some of the work locally with our existing clients, and so far, it seems to be working well. There are more witches around here than you would ever imagine, they blend in, never stand out, you don't see them."

"Using the fly on the wall spell?" I queried.

"Right," she said, in the tone of one congratulating a child. "They avoid a sticky situation by not being seen."

"We are not sure how barbaric things are countrywide," said Alice, "but you'll be our eyes and ears – listening to the witches, seeing what's going on under the radar."

"There will be some heart-rending stories," I said. "Some horrific accounts, I'm sure."

"Indeed," Sandy agreed soberly. "And there's no time like the present to start. You will have total discretion about where you choose to go, although known problem areas are probably the best places to start. Your first job will be to compile a priority list, and then we will work from there. You'll have a great deal on your shoulders, but you'll be doing worthwhile work."

CHAPTER 6

Things were moving fast. I'd met the employees based at the office in town, an awesome group, lawyers and support staff alike, and a hundred per cent committed to our mission. They obviously had to be of a sensitive persuasion to work with us, and the business naturally attracted a majority of female lawyers. But there were also some guys on the team. Alice's role was to vet them before they were properly interviewed for the job. They didn't have to be witches, but they were all confirmed sympathisers. There was great care taken with due diligence, and as well as scouring social media there were other more unlikely sources of information. The firm did its research and knew exactly who they were dealing with before that person even entered the room. Additionally, of course, the legal team also had to have the right legal credentials behind them. Those who made the grade were cream-of-the-crop lawyers, top of their game, and the best in the country.

All staff had to sign a non-disclosure agreement ensuring they didn't discuss anything that went on behind closed doors. Alice, firm-lipped, said the motto was *What goes on in the office, stays in the office.* Discretion was the name of the game. She explained that every employee had been given the magic treatment for their own safety, witch and non-witch alike, and I found it hard to tell one from the other, they were so discreet. They were able to use the fly on the wall spell, too, so if they found themselves in a menacing situation where there was no alternative, they could simply disappear. It was emphasised they had always to remain objective and support their client following the laws of the land. They'd been told about my official and unofficial roles, and at some stage, every one of them would join us for the surgeries.

Our awe-inspiring reputation had gone before us. The list of those who wanted to join our firm was a mile long, as was the one for those who needed our services. And the big surprise was I'd been made a partner. I had the feeling they'd planned this all along, but I wasn't grumbling – the increase in salary and benefits was a welcome bonus. I suspected that this was what Sandy had always wanted for me, and although I hadn't followed her legal path, I still had an important part to play and was now in the family fold. She was beyond delighted, and maybe just a little smug – but I wasn't going to hold that against her.

I'd been asked to organise a couple of social events for the firm, bonding exercises before we started our tour of the country. It would give me a chance to get to know the lawyers more informally as well as an opportunity to acknowledge appreciation of the hard work done so far. I was in my element, and what better activity than an evening of fine dining at the fabulous Wild Rabbit at Kingham, just outside Chipping Norton, one of my favourite haunts. To look at us, you'd think we were just a group of polished professional types getting together for dinner. Not a word was spoken about our work, we stuck to small talk. Because of our backgrounds and the fact that Alice had vetted everyone, we were all on the same wavelength. I was sure I'd make a good friend or two along the way. It would be good to start growing my currently non-existent social circle.

I also organised a well-deserved weekend break for those who could join us. An overnight spa stay at the delightful Bamford Wellness Spa in the grounds of the Daylesford Farm, the site of my favourite local deli. I'd booked us some heavenly treatments, and we came out looking dishevelled but feeling amazing. We'd gossiped in the steam room, sauna, and Jacuzzi as I told them about the other treatments I'd had here – reiki and reflexology, so relaxing and restorative. We continued lively conversations over lunch and dinner, finishing the evening with pornstar and espresso martinis after copious champagne. I'd gelled with a couple of the lawyers – both around my age – Jasmine, or Jazz, as she was called, and Asha, both witches. They had the same spark as me and worked and played hard. I was ready to socialise and made sure we'd get together again. I had to admit, Alice had become a bit of a party pooper of late; she had her head down most evenings, bogged down with work and burning the midnight oil, although I appreciated it was more of a vocation for her.

I loved living in the Cotswolds, it was easy to see why it was so popular with the rich and famous and why so many of them lived around and about. I'd certainly be happy to settle here for the rest of my days and was pretty sure that was Alice and Sandy's plan. The only flaw in the new order was the two people I yearned for the most, like missing pieces of the puzzle – Sarah and Lizzie. I wished I could share all of it with them. But I didn't have time to dwell on these melancholic thoughts, there was important work to be done.

Could we pull this off? We were ready to start our first surgery, and speed was of the essence – the unprotected were in more danger than ever, especially in the case of revenge killings. Our goal was a utopian time with no threat. We'd all live in peace, but until then, we'd have to live in hope. Practising our magic without retribution, we meant no harm, and it goes without saying we all abided by the Witches' Charter.

The hardest part had been deciding where to go first. Whitby might have been the logical choice with its Mystical Ladies, the Whitby lockdown, the Purge, and the fact that things seemed to have kicked off there first. I did feel conscious-stricken that I'd abandoned them in their time of need – survivor's guilt? But I'd had no choice. Would it be a waste of time to go back? Surely it was too late for them anyway, that horse had already bolted. Anyway, there were too many personal issues involved in returning, namely Seb. It was probably selfish but, in the meantime, I'd just have to reassure myself that the witches of Whitby were OK. Maybe I'd underestimated them, perhaps they were already fighting back hard? I thought often about the mixed bunch of women to whom I'd become so close. And the truth was I'd never seen or experienced the wrath of the Whitby witches, all I'd seen were harmless, frivolous spells. But who knew what power had been hiding behind those, power that now might have been unleashed.

I did know, though, that I'd have to deal with it all in the not-too-distant future. I had to sort out the Lavender Cottage situation; leaving it unoccupied wasn't ideal. It would fall into disrepair, and that would be so sad after my loving and meticulous restoration. Of course, it wasn't sensible to leave it unoccupied, it could be ransacked, or there was even a possibility squatters could move in and then where would I be? No, it would be far better to sell it, let someone else love it as I had, put its heart back in place. For now, I had bigger fish to fry and more urgent issues. But where to start? It was all a little overwhelming.

Another area I'd considered putting at the top of my action list was Hampstead, I had lots of links, and there was no doubt the place was heaving with witches. The downside was the thought of bumping into Seb again, that terrified me, even fully protected as I was. The main problem with both Whitby and Hampstead was the heightened personal risk, I'd have to be brave and tackle that at some stage. In the meantime, I felt bad I was potentially deciding the fate of others, but I was sure there were lots of areas that were just as desperate, and Alice and Sandy had left the decisions to me.

I took a couple of welcome sips of the steaming cup of coffee left for me. I'd be caffeined-out at this rate. My head was buzzing, but today that was welcome, keeping me focused. A couple of mini pastries had magically appeared, sitting temptingly on my desk. I'd been so nervous that I hadn't felt hungry, but now I was ravenous. I was trying to be good – not eating too much crap – but there were so many tasty goodies around here, most sourced from local farms, just what the doctor ordered to satisfy my hunger. I loved the pain au chocolat which I scoffed down, it was oozing with chocolate. Thinking about the number of carbs I'd just eaten, I smiled when I thought of a saying I'd seen in one of the local gift shops – *I save my carbs for wine, it's called having priorities.* Well, now I'd blown my allocation on pastries, so no more wine for me tonight. Or maybe just one glass in celebration of a good day at the office.

Pondering over my computer, I looked at the geography of the UK. Where to start? Maybe see where the news was worse. That'd be OK, to check for research purposes. Sandy and Alice had said a firm no to keeping notes on my computer. They said it could be infiltrated and provide evidence to be used against us. But I was OK to use recognised research on Google and other search engines, as this could be considered part of our legal research – I was part of the team and the study was legitimate. I'd started to feel like a spy in a movie – didn't they eat the evidence, tearing it up into little pieces and swallowing it with a glass of water? There was so much material about witchcraft, both past and present. It was a dreadful truth that there weren't too many differences between what was happening then and now. Witches were totally misunderstood and feared, and nothing had changed through the centuries.

I'd initially focus on past places of persecution. I knew something about the Pendle witch trials of 1612 – who didn't? Funny enough, nothing about this historical persecution was taught at school. It seemed witchcraft wasn't welcomed as a subject for study. I wasn't sure what was happening today in Lancashire, but it seemed as good a place as any to start. Call me snobbish, but prior to living in the Whitby area, I hadn't tended to go up north very often unless we were visiting lovely Lizzie in Manchester. Even then we didn't venture far from where the footballers' wives lived and socialised in nearby Cheshire. Maybe we could visit this area again and do some retail therapy. I pulled myself back down to earth with a well-deserved thump. This wasn't a jolly. We'd be working hard, although I was determined to bring a bit of pleasure into the mix – we still had to eat and drink, might as well make that as pleasant as possible. Sandy's brief for the surgery was that our chosen venue had to be as private as possible, remote, with plenty of parking and vast grounds, so we'd be undisturbed and not overlooked. I immediately thought of the boutique hotels of which I was so fond. It also helped that money was no object when it came to food and accommodation. I didn't foresee that finding the best location off the beaten track would be a problem.

The more I read about the current and past witch situation, the more I felt I was disappearing down a rabbit hole of facts and information, and it was all blending into one. It was interesting to note that Sandy appeared unbothered if we crisscrossed the country and Whitby didn't come up as a subject. I hadn't completely bared my soul to the two women who meant the most in the world to me. For whatever reason, I simply couldn't explain the enigma that was Seb. I also kept to myself the danger I'd foreseen if I'd stayed in Yorkshire, and even Hampstead, after my two sightings of that dangerous man. And even if I had told them anything about him, I certainly wouldn't have shared that he was working for the government as a witch hunter. But, as you know, that was only part of the story. I still felt a sense of shame at how easily I had been taken in. I didn't want to admit my weaknesses to them.

CHAPTER 7

With a month's worth of work behind me, I was no longer getting the dreaded Monday morning feeling. Certainly nothing like past work experiences when I'd have to haul myself out of bed after a particularly enthusiastic weekend of partying. I felt on top of everything, workwise, especially now I'd sorted our first surgery location. I'd had to work quickly to secure the venue and ensure the team was ready and waiting to launch some carefully worded publicity. I was beyond excited!

My fears that working in the office with Sandy and Alice would be problematic proved unfounded. Most of the time, when they weren't at the farmhouse, they were out and about, seeing clients, or at the office in town. It took me a while to get used to not working in a crowded office, but I now found it to be a refreshing change, allowing me the freedom to do my own thing, and anyway, the other two often dropped in at the end of the day which gave us a chance to catch up. Other than that, they left me to my own devices, and most of the time, I worked with my earpods in, the outside world zoned out while I focused on whatever it was I was doing.

Truthfully, I felt I had the best end of the deal, and they were working far harder than I was, toiling away and hardly coming up for air. That morning I started a dream pop compilation, *"Space Song"* by Beach House, one of my favourites. This was followed by a classic chill-out playlist, with *"At the River"* by Groove Armada, which always reminded me of exotic holidays. Today I needed light and breezy rather than dark gothic vibes, I'm not always in that melancholic frame of mind! This was the perfect working environment, and I appreciated that there was no formal start or finish time. The other two women trusted me not to take advantage, and I didn't. I'd sometimes eat at my desk and work through, at other times nip out for lunch at the local deli, then trawl through some of the many delightful bookshops. Here in the Cotswolds, several traditional independent bookshops did a roaring trade. Books, like vinyl, had made a massive comeback, and there was a huge rise in people preferring to read from page rather than screen. I tended to get a migraine if I read too much online, so physical books were my preference. Plus, I was a secret book sniffer, you couldn't beat the smell of ink on paper.

I relished my time in the local bookshops, particularly as an inordinate amount of shelf space seemed to be bizarrely devoted to witch history. As a boarding school child, I'd dwelt in the different worlds I found in books; yes, I had friends, but books kept me sane. I loved Roald Dahl and, like Matilda, I wanted to find my very own Miss Honey, who would whisk me away to a cottage in the countryside and smother me with kindness. As for Charlie and the Chocolate Factory, well, who wouldn't want a tour? But in this new phase of my life, I'd learnt to avoid the local shops when hordes of weekenders descended. Early on I'd gone shopping on a Saturday, been accused of parking space pinching and received a mouthful of abuse – there were certainly some anger issues and car park rage that needed resolving there. I was, of course, fully capable of giving as good as I got, but it wasn't worth it, and I drove off. I now made sure weekends were spent at home relaxing. Call me middle-aged, but it turned out that I loved a little light gardening, potting up flowering bulbs that flourished alongside my favourite herbs.

Our first surgery was going to be – drum roll please – in the north west, specifically Lancashire, also known as Witch Country, it'd be rude not to start in one of the most important landmarks! I wanted to pick up a relevant book or two before setting off at the end of the week. Not that I'd get much time for reading once we got the show on the road. I made a point of dropping into my favourite bookstore The Book Den, it was one of those places that had a bit of an identity crisis, it could have been a music shop, as I entered the shop, I could hear a familiar tune as I walked through the door, "Echo Beach" by Martha and the Muffins. Although they only had the one hit over here, their music was pretty cool. Unusually for a bookshop, there was sometimes music playing, depending on who was working there on that day. I was glad to see there was no one else in the shop, Mondays were always slow around here. I smiled – my favourite, Liam, a young Prince Harry lookalike, was behind the counter. He worked different shifts on a part-time basis while studying for his degree in English Literature; he was also a history nerd. His face lit up as he saw me, he always kept me up to date with the bestsellers, and I suspect he had the hots for me.

"Hey, Ellie, how are you? You won't believe it, such good timing you've come in today! Two incredibly awesome books have come in, literally hot off the press. We've been waiting for them to come back into print. But if you're interested, now's the time to say, most were pre-ordered, I only have one of each left." He was always enthusiastic, a real read-freak; he hadn't even told me what genre these prized books were.

He chuckled, reading my mind. "Sorry, got carried away, they may not even be for you, might not be something a glamorous sophisticate such as yourself would go for."

I grinned back at him. "Flattery will get you everywhere." But as it happened, he wasn't my type, too puppyish, too keen, and too young, plus I'd never fancied Prince Harry. But it didn't hurt to have some banter, show that I still had it!

"Witches!" he announced dramatically. Well, that certainly caught my attention! The fact that we were on our own made him braver, and he waved two books literally under my nose. I laughed. "Hey Liam, calm down, let me have a look." I noticed one was called Daemonologie, well, with that title it certainly wasn't for the faint-hearted.

"You won't believe it, but these bestsellers were both written over four hundred years ago. Daemonologie was written by the King of England, James I, himself, in 1597."

"Why on earth would the King of England write a book?" I asked. I knew a little about King James I from my own research, but I didn't want to give too much away, and Liam was flexing his knowledge, like a badge of honour. Obviously, he thought his knowledge of history and the witches was a way to a girl's heart. "Who'd have guessed that these publications, which went like hot cakes in the sixteenth and seventeenth centuries, would be so popular now? We've even got them on repeat order, and people can't seem to get enough. Crazy, isn't it?"

"So what is the other book about?"

"This one is called *The Wonderfull Discoverie of Witches in the Countie of Lancaster,* by Thomas Potts." He smiled. "Yes, it's also written in Olde English, like the other one, and it covers the 1612 Pendle witch trials if you are interested in that sort of thing." He paused for breath, giving me a chance to comment, although I kept it casual.

"As it happens, Liam, I am interested – by pure coincidence I happen to be off to the Pendle area next week. Maybe I should get in a bit of historical research before I go." I maintained my best poker face, which wasn't easy as I'd spent the last week or so mugging up on Pendle witch material I'd found online. He was delighted at my response, grinning from ear to ear, and I didn't have the heart to mention the bit of spinach between his front teeth. I knew he'd blush like a beetroot.

"Ooh, you going on a witch hunt, Ellie? You must

brush up on your knowledge before you go, these two books will be perfect for you!"

I smiled. "No, just some business in the area, but it'd be interesting to read about what went on around there, won't do any harm."

"Right," he said. "I'll put a copy of each behind the counter, just in case anyone else comes in while you're browsing. Don't be put off by the Olde English language, once you've got your head around that, and read a few pages you'll find it easy to follow."

I teased him: "I did a history degree myself, I'll have you know, but if I can't understand it, I will drop back in and you can interpret it for me." He blushed even more, but he was on a roll now, and was droning on. I feigned interest, but he could bore off. I could do my own research.

"Of course, it was all just fiery sixteenth-century propaganda, whipping up witch-hate frenzy, playing on pre-existing fears, folklore and suspicions of the time."

"Nothing has changed then?" I replied. Why did I say that, I was meant to be staying objective. He gave me a quizzical look for a moment, and as I didn't take the bait he kept on with his commentary. "Did you know the King had already had a brush with witchcraft when he was James VI of Scotland?" I gave my best surprised look and said, "No I didn't know." He carried on.

"He believed that there had been an attempted assassination against him, in the form of a violent storm when he was on his way back to England from Denmark. It was said the storm had been witch-raised and this led to the North Berwick witch hunt, and accusations against a woman called Agnes Sampson amongst others, she was a local healer and midwife." I knew that those with herbal knowledge were always amongst the first to be accused and, as for midwives, they seemed fair game. "That sounds absolutely ridiculous doesn't it. Being blamed for a force of nature?" He nodded, and was getting redder and redder by the minute, as he got more excited with a captive audience. "Blame was placed firmly at the door of witches. They even had their own social media, with a propaganda pamphlet distributed covering the trial of Agnes Sampson and the other witches as a warning to others. Once James became the King of England, he became even more obsessive, and it was his mission to wipe out ungodly practices and practitioners. You have to put it in the context of the time, there were famines, plagues, and battle losses and what better way to redirect blame than to blame all misfortunes on witches, they were the enemy of the state." He whispered under his breath, "The enemy of all." He was enjoying this, but just then, thank God, the tinkle of the bell as the shop door opened and another customer entered the shop. He swiftly put the books in a brown paper bag with the shop's logo on it, and I said, "Great, thanks for the info, now point me towards romantic fiction. I'm going to also need some easy poolside reads, light and breezy."

I could tell from his grimace I'd gone right down in his estimation, maybe he felt he'd wasted his time on this history lesson. "Well, if it's chick lit you're after—" he pointed over his shoulder towards the back of the shop. "You'll find a whole load back there." I laughed at his expression; he certainly wasn't going to help me with this selection. Being a literature student had made him a literary snob, but you can't beat a trashy novel, as well as witch lit, and as a currently single woman, a bit of romantic fantasy never did me any harm. I swiftly chose the four most gaudily coloured, tacky-looking books, exactly what I was looking for and paid for them together with the two books Liam had carefully put aside for me. I didn't recognise the other person in the shop, they were waiting patiently for help from Liam. I wonder if they would be ordering these two books, and would get the history lesson?

I had an odd thought as I left the shop. It was illegal to practise witchcraft, as evidenced by the Purge, and, in fact as recently as 1735 it was still a crime to accuse another of using magical powers or practising witchcraft. And, in truth, witch-hunting had never stopped. Hettie had been murdered, and law or no law, how many more unexplained deaths over the years were due to people taking the law into their own hands? And yet there remained the indisputable fact that people were still so fascinated; they couldn't get enough of witchcraft, as proved by the popularity of the books Liam had recommended. I was dying to dip into these books before I started working, but had little time to eat on my way back to the office. I dropped into Wood Barn, picked up some leftover chicken salad from last night, threw the chick lit books down next to my nearly fully packed case, and settled at my desk back at the office.

As predicted by Liam, Olde English wasn't a smooth read, and rather than start at the beginning, I chose random pages, but after a while, I adjusted and was angered beyond words by the gruesome methods used to obtain confessions. One account described using thumbscrews to rip out fingernails, and the sheer brutality chilled me to the bone. Even children were not immune. Even so, the book was a fantastic insight into the sentiments of the time – but what had changed? Maybe we didn't ask children to testify these days, and I'm sure we didn't use instruments of torture, but people were dying for our craft nevertheless. How crazy that propaganda from centuries past could still whip up fear and paranoia today, tapping into people's anxieties and building a picture where witches ran amok, casting spells and curses left, right and centre.

Certainly, in Daemonologie there was plenty to influence opinion against witches and tie into the stereotype of evil old hags causing havoc and harm. It seemed witches were perceived today much as they had been in the past; superstition was still rife. Unbelievable, I know, but it was being used to justify the treatment of witches and our sympathisers alike. It seemed that where there was even the sniff of something out of the ordinary going on, or an intelligent woman with a mind of her own who spoke up, she was immediately labelled. By perpetuating the myths, contemporary witches were still seen as non-human, which made harming them appear a little less evil. Thinking of the so-called current suicide contagion within our supposedly sophisticated twenty-first century, it seemed nothing had changed. History was repeating itself.

I picked a random page. There was an incredible argument between Philomathes and Epistemon – the latter being pretty much unhinged when it came to the supernatural – discussing the disproportion of men to women involved in the craft. There were roughly twenty women accused and tried against one man. The view seemed to be that not only were women frailer in body but also a lot weaker in the head! Of course, it was this which made it so much simpler for them to be bemused, taken in, and seduced by the devil. This toxic idea hadn't changed down the years, borne out by the fact it was still mainly women being persecuted. With an awful and growing recognition, I understood I was reading a book written centuries earlier that could just as easily have been written today.

Witch fear was endemic, and over the bridge of time, the past was pacing back to bite us. Nothing had changed, not in isolated communities where suspicion and finger-pointing ran riot, and not in supposedly sophisticated areas such as the nation's capital. Bigots, zealots, paranoia, and the willingness of people to so swiftly buy into the worst still prevailed, and because of that, history played and replayed. I slammed the book shut abruptly, letting it fall onto the table. I couldn't read any more, and I only had five minutes before a scheduled Zoom call. I needed to calm down and compose myself a little. I certainly felt, though, that I'd got a clear insight into the thinking of His Majesty King James, the whatever!

I didn't get around to looking at the second book until my working day was finished, and I was back in the barn, which was probably better for my blood pressure. What I was going to read about might hit a little less hard if I was in homelier surroundings. Liam's second recommended bestseller had been written in 1613, just a year after the Pendle witch trials and maybe I should've gone for this one first because it was relevant to where we were going. I was more than a little witched-out after the previous shocking book which had sent shivers down my spine, but I had to read more, I was fascinated.

The Wonderfull Discoverie of Witches in the Countie of Lancaster was by one Thomas Potts, Clerk to the Lancaster Assizes, who'd been ordered by the trial judges to document proceedings, making these accounts some of the most authentic on the Lancashire witch trials which took place on 18 and 19 August 1612. Amongst the accused were the Pendle witches. Eleven were found guilty and hanged, and one defendant was sentenced to the pillory for speaking seditious words. The pillory was a devilish wooden construction with holes for head and hands. This meant the unfortunate victim was forced into a horrendously bent position while being publicly abused. Some poor souls even had their ears nailed to the pillory, or cut off altogether. The others on trial were acquitted, but I wondered about their fate as they'd already been tarred with the witch brush. Were they able to blend back into society, or were they ostracised on the basis that there's no smoke without fire?

I was only too aware that I'd soon be stepping on the same ground as these poor unfortunates when we headed to Lancashire in just a few days. I was tired but hooked and couldn't put the book down, there was so much I could learn from this research. The Pendle witch trials were important and well known, but what else had been going on that was undocumented? I wondered if we'd find descendants living in the area, still practising skills passed from generation to generation, but maybe with enough risk aversion to stay below the radar. Would I meet them? I really hoped I would, it wasn't a coincidence I had chosen this as our first stop, and now I was raring to go.

CHAPTER 8

I desperately wanted to get to the bottom of why the Pendle witches had been singled out for special treatment in the past and was determined to finish the book before I set off for Lancashire on Friday. A dark thought about Seb had occurred to me – as a history professor, had he read these two books? I assumed so much of his research must have been based on these same events and I wondered how much that had influenced his thinking as he pursued today's witches.

Surprisingly, my reading had shown me that although we tended to think of our forebears as far less sophisticated and past times as simpler – other than technology, which obviously had come on in leaps and bounds – not that much had changed in 400 years. I'd already felt the undercurrent of that in Salem; how we treated each other, and how we interacted within society, had changed little. Bizarrely, even the names of those accused were familiar, sounding ordinary, there were any number of Sarahs, Alices, and Elizabeths. The main difference between then and now was that then, whatever happened in a village stayed in the village, whereas nowadays news spread far and wide with incredible speed, even if the bigotry, paranoia, and oppression were unchanged.

But now we were fighting back on behalf of the persecuted, and maybe we'd even be able to clear the names of the unjustly accused from the past. Ellie was back, the go-getting, hard-arsed bitch, on a humanitarian mission to save and empower fellow witches and all our sympathisers. We could do it! Together with Sandy and Alice, and all the others working with us, we could change the world.

It was a long week before I was able to lock up Wood Barn and head for the hills – Pendle Hill, to be more precise! What with traffic along the way, it was a longer drive than I'd expected, and I was knackered by the time I got there. I arrived before Sandy and Alice; they'd far too much work to finish at the office to leave early, but they planned to join me for dinner at 8 pm. I'd booked the restaurant at the hotel after checking the reviews; they were mainly excellent. Sandy said money was no object, and I'd taken her at her word and found a delightfully luxurious country hotel not too far from Pendle Hill in the Ribble Valley. A beautiful, remote, windswept location, away from prying eyes. It ticked all our boxes, being secluded in its own grounds, with plenty of car parking, private meeting rooms, and the perfect spa facilities – you know me, never averse to mixing a bit of pleasure with business! The spa looked sublime. I could do with a full body massage right now and was sure it would be exactly what Sandy and Alice needed after their hectic work schedule. It was my responsibility to make sure everything was ready to roll for our launch on Monday morning, and I was excited and nervous at the same time. Everything had gone smoothly so far with no hiccups, and once I'd gone over all the details, I'd have the rest of the afternoon free. I could go to the spa or the pool but, quite frankly, couldn't be arsed to get changed or wet. I'd take a rain check and relax in my room until dinner.

Since I started work, I'd been in a booking frenzy and had several venues around the country reserved for future events. I was keeping the marketing team manically busy, and they, in turn, were working with the media experts advertising the events. Sandy suggested I slow down a little as, although this was a mercy mission, we couldn't see everyone or be everywhere all the time; we had to look after ourselves too. She insisted I put some short breaks in the diary so we could recuperate back at the farm, plus a two-week sabbatical where the diary was firmly closed. In the past, we might have jetted off somewhere exotic, but we agreed we'd be better off at home recharging the batteries, making sure we didn't burn out. Maybe when we had done as much as we could for the cause we could truly relax and unwind somewhere hot.

Right now, I wished I could find an energy spell; it was what we needed. I'd ask Sandy, I was sure she had more than a few more tricks up her sleeve. I chuckled to myself as I remembered that advert for energy drinks. I needed those wings! Because it was such short notice, I was concerned we wouldn't have anyone attending our first event, but I needn't have worried. The team were excellent; they'd pulled out all the stops to get the message out there, working their very own magic. I was worried about history repeating itself in Lancashire and could only imagine the fear and panic over the Purge. Were descendants of the original Pendle witches still here, or had they fled as fast and as far as possible after the original trials? It seemed, though, that the word on the street had spread, and we were inundated with enquiries. To my delight and surprise, we were now fully booked for Lancashire and already filling up for our next location when we were heading across the country to Northumberland, from the north west to the north east.

We'd be based just outside the historic town of Alnwick, after we left Pendle. My research on what was happening in each area was obviously focused on witchy, ghostly, or inexplicable occurrences. Alnwick, in particular, struck me as a magical place, with so many ancient castles and a rich history Alnwick Castle was where Harry Potter was filmed. I know he wasn't real, but the area and atmosphere might attract a certain type. I suppose my only frustration was that at each of our stops, I wasn't going to have as much time to explore as I'd have liked, because this was no holiday, but rather a whirlwind of practical activity and assistance.

Alnwick appealed as there was a second-hand bookstore based at the old railway station building, and that was definitely on my list to visit, if there was time. I'd seen photographs and loved its open fires and model trains, and I was sure I'd find an interesting first edition witch book or two. Then maybe tea and cake at the delightfully twee Grannie's Tea Room set in a flagstoned basement. I'd take a book with me but, in fact, would be listening in on as many surrounding conversations as possible, getting a whiff of what was going on. Reviews on the place called it "small but perfectly formed, with cake to die for", but I was far more interested when they said ". . . convinced the place is haunted! We were served by a waitress, who kept bobbing a curtsey, she took our order then disappeared. When we asked, we were told it was Eliza, the resident Victorian ghost – we never knew whether that was genuine or just a tourist trap!" I desperately wanted to meet Eliza too; Grannie's Tea Room sounded just my sort of place, with spooky happenings and cake. What more could you want? But first let's concentrate on witch country. Pendle here we come!

I know, I know, I'm getting ahead of myself and starting to sound like a tour guide, and we still had to survive Pendle. But it was all about savouring the atmosphere as we travelled around the country – for me anyway – I'd spent enough time being a lady of leisure; I was happy to immerse myself in the thick of things again and find out under the radar what the hell had been going on. There were still elephants in the room: Hampstead, and my beloved Whitby and the North Yorkshire Moors. But I'd finally bitten the bullet, and now they were on our list of bookings. Hampstead last but one, and Whitby and the North Yorkshire Moors last but not least. I hoped that by the time we were ready to visit, the dire situation would have eased, as would the personal threat to me. When the impact of what we were doing around the country finally hit home, along with a growing realisation that the witches couldn't simply be eradicated, perhaps the tide would turn. One day maybe the witches would be revered and appreciated, lauded, rather than feared and hunted. The current dark truth was that we were a long way away from that utopia.

I'd promised myself that when things calmed down, I'd do another road trip to all the beautiful locations but this time with all my girls – Alice, Sarah, and Lizzie. For the present, I'd have to be satisfied with these whistle-stop tours and a trip to the spa in between. This weekend would be the most relaxed time for the next few weeks. We'd be heading off again on Friday evening, ready for the Monday to Friday surgeries the following week in Northumberland.

CHAPTER 9

I'd already suggested to Sandy that we might go on a real-life witch hunt to research further about the Pendle witches of 1612. Take in their haunts, soak in the atmosphere, walk in their footsteps, but I was fighting a losing battle; they weren't up for it. I'd persevered, but they both firmly stamped their spoilt little manicured feet, banning anything more strenuous than the spa.

"Darling, you can't be serious; we'll have had our fill of witches at the end of the roadshow. My aim is to enjoy whatever is on offer," Sandy had said. I didn't hide my disappointment, and Alice had piped up, "Sorry, hon, you may still have energy to spare, I certainly don't. I'm with Sandy, just want to chill. I've already booked back-to-back treatments!"

"Anyway, you can go on your own," Sandy said. "Don't be afraid, nobody's going to get you, just dress up as a regular anorak, you'll fit right in." I nodded, thinking of my country-casual look. I'd certainly need to tone down the glam look. "How about we do Sunday lunch together, though? Choose somewhere a bit spooky for us if you'd like?" I nodded. I was sure there'd be plenty of places around here, cashing in on the witches' plight past and present.

Reluctant as I was to go on my own this was an opportunity too good to miss. I'd finished the Thomas Potts book about the Lancashire witch trials, read it from cover to cover. I know, a bit obsessed – I'd felt pulled right back in time to the warring families involved in the sorry saga. One thing that kept popping up in my googling was the popularity of witch tours; so many to choose from, some more serious than others. I wanted one that was as authentic and authoritative as possible, something that would dig down to the real stories, and then I might get a clue as to how things stood today. Of course, I was happy to hear the myths and superstitions, they were part of the fabric of life, but I'd discounted the tours where you were supposed to turn up as a ghost or ghoul, although I guess that sort of thing was fine for a hen do or a birthday party, where you wanted a spooky laugh.

Our image on the sites wasn't great, the stereotypical image – hairy, warty, black pointed hat, black clothing, and, of course, a broomstick – the same image that had been around since the twelfth century. Certainly didn't fit with the witches I knew. Most looked ordinary and wanted to live peaceful, meaningful lives. Incidents like Hettie cursing her lover and the hexes and curses of others were only after provocation, life-threatening situations.

Wouldn't anyone use what resources they had? And above all, we had the witch's code of conduct to follow, and most of us did.

My head was spinning. Trying to find the right tour was more stressful than I could have imagined. I'd already discarded those that did a walk up Pendle Hill, as I was never one for hiking. Others weren't so exhausting but looked crass, just trying to cash in, and their reviews were pretty dire, but it seemed the more the witches were persecuted, the more they were fair game for commercialised, gruesome voyeurism. The baying public couldn't get enough; it felt as though they wanted to bring the gallows back, and how about the pillory? I'm sure some would like to throw a rotten tomato or two.

Just near the point of giving up I finally found exactly what I was looking for. A full day, which included a walk through a mystical wood, a sculpture trail, a visit to the Heritage Centre, and then on to Lancaster Jail, and back to the village of Barley for dinner. To get me in the right mood, I'd put some melancholy music in the background while I searched. This always motivated me, the more melancholic the music, the happier I felt and the more productive I became. Yes, I did need a check from the neck up, but I wasn't the only one. Some of these retro tracks were making a real comeback. People wanted misery. Today I listened to The *Virgin Suicides* by Air. It always hit the spot, *"Bathroom Girl"* and *"Cemetery Party"* particularly.

I liked the profile of the tour guide on the trip I decided to go for. A retired history professor, Jennifer Davis, who had made the Pendle witches her life's work – Project Witch, she called it. She was born and bred in the area, so she wasn't just an outsider trying to cash in on what was happening. Maybe she was even related to one of the original witches. Her tour came with a warning. This was an objective historic tour, and she wouldn't be drawn into discussions or gossip about the present-day situation. Her site painted a wild and wonderful picture of Pendle Hill, isolated from Bowland Fells and the Pennines. There was a map of the forty-five-mile trail taken by the accused from their homes through the lonely roads of the Ribble Valley to Lancaster Castle, where they were incarcerated before they stood trial. Reviewers raved about this tour, the general theme being "We went to dark places that spooked us out, not for the faint-hearted!" and "Fantastic historic information, we felt sorry for the Pendle witches!" Unsurprisingly, this one was anonymous. Maybe they could bring this attitude forward to the present day. Another good one said "Prof. Davis knew her stuff; she was born in the area. These were bleak times. A truly historic tour, highly recommended. We were chilled to the bone visiting Lancaster Jail, especially." And this last one sold it for me! "If you're scared of the dark, or hate macabre stories, then this tour isn't for you."

When I called to book, Jennifer Davis herself answered and said yes, she could fit me in.

"Usually pretty fully booked, but you're lucky. For how many?"

"Just me, please. My friends have opted for a spa day instead!"

She laughed. "Certainly a more relaxing choice. OK, you'll need comfortable clothes, walking shoes, and waterproofs – just in case – and bring a bottle of water. It's a pretty gruelling day!"

"Sounds like the Girl Guide trips I used to go on, but I've read your reviews, and everybody raves. I'm looking forward to it."

My mission as I set out on the roadshows was to feel the atmosphere of this infamous place for myself and gauge public feeling: were they on the side of the witches, or did they despise and fear them? Good, bad, or indifferent? Had we really learnt from the past, as nothing much had changed really, had it? The Purge and draconian laws were evidence of this. I couldn't understand, though, why the persecuted hadn't used magic to save themselves in the past. Did they know about it, were they searching as I had been, or had they found it and it had gone wrong as it had for me?

Of course, it would have been harder to get the message out in those days, what happened in the village stayed in the village, and they wouldn't know what was happening in other areas of the country. That way, the witch hunters could contain their actions. Today, things were different. I'm coming for you, sisters – and brothers – to help you in your time of need. So far, I'd identified the places I felt we were the most needed and, if I was perfectly honest, had the most interesting histories, but I knew that this was just the tip of the iceberg.

All I knew was witch mania was endemic in society, a morbid interest in the plight of the witches, and no more so than around here because of the gruesome history. Ghoulish tourists gone mad for the place, wanting to see the links between what was happening today and the early seventeenth-century witches. What could I learn from the witches of the late sixteenth and early seventeenth century? I hadn't learnt that much from my trip to Salem, so would Pendle and other mystical areas around the country be any different? It struck me again, maybe there were still descendants living in the area of the original witches – would I meet them? Maybe they'd come along to the roadshows? I knew from my own experience that the witches had never gone away, but did they stay close to their ancestors, keeping themselves to themselves, especially in these dark times? How many generations were there from 1612 to today? There were over 400 years of dark history, so whoever they were, they carried a heavy legacy.

CHAPTER 10

I was determined to do this tour come rain or shine but was hoping not to get a soaking, so my spirits were lifted when I opened the blinds in the morning. I thought crossly that it would have done Sandy and Alice a world of good to get some old-fashioned fresh air into their lungs, but I wasn't going to waste any further breath in persuasion.

The group was to meet up at the car park in Barley at 7.45 am, and it was noted that public facilities were available, making it pretty obvious there wouldn't be loo stops along the way. I thought back to our student days, sharing toilets in clubs or wild peeing behind a bush when caught short. I'm never keen on public toilets, I'd far rather cross my legs and wait. Luckily, I'm blessed with a strong bladder. I guess that's why I wasn't fond of the Victorian toilet back at Wood Barn, it reminded me too much of the ones at school, with the scratchy toilet paper endured by generations of students.

Before heading towards Barley, and checking that there was no one around, I'd done a simple spell, tweaking my look so I'd blend in with the type of people I thought would tend to opt for this more serious tour with its emphasis on history rather than hysteria. I didn't want to appear too glam, so I went for mousy brown hair and little makeup. I put on a khaki parka, baseball hat, and walking shoes, and Alice had lent me a rucksack just big enough for a bottle of water and the essentials, my phone and a couple of energy bars. I'd have to make sure I changed my face back before guests at the hotel spotted me. I didn't want to cause confusion.

The car park was quiet for a Saturday, but it was still early, plus there wasn't much else to do around here. I found a space and parked up – free parking, that was a pleasant change. There was a bright purple, super-modern minibus that looked the height of comfort and luxury, and I made my way over. "You must be Ellie?" smiled a middle-aged, capable-looking lady. "I'm Jenny. If you want, you can leave stuff in the minibus to save carrying – we'll be doing our walk first." She was immaculately turned out with a short, neat blonde bob, not at all how I'd pictured an eccentric history professor, and I'm sure her ultra-trim figure resulted from all the walking she did. She reminded me of Sandy, that generation of simultaneously intelligent, manicured women, glamorous and smart at the same time.

I nodded thanks, dropping my waterproof jacket on one of the available seats; it didn't look as if it would be needed. The driver, an elderly but fit-looking gentleman, silver fox-type, smiled at me, so Professor Jenny wasn't doing this all on her own. I wondered if they were together or just colleagues, they looked well-suited. "I'm Malc," he told me. "I'll be staying on the bus most of the time while you do the tour, and if I do leave it, trust me, it will be securely locked, so anything you leave will be well looked after."

Turning round, I saw a small crowd had gathered, nine people in all. It was 7.45 am on the dot, so everybody was surprisingly prompt. I joined the others, hovering at the back, and some turned to look at me as if I was late. Goodness only knows what they'd have made of Sarah and her timekeeping. Jenny did a swift head count and nodded, satisfied everyone was present and correct. Just ten of us, a sensible number, and fine by me.

I put on my most sullen bitch-face, I wanted to keep myself to myself and make sure nobody would try and make friendly small talk. After a quick scan, I'd already clocked that I was the youngest by several decades, not that I was ageist but they certainly weren't spring chickens. I looked at them with some concern. Surely they were more suited to moochinng around a garden centre or National Trust property? I hoped we weren't going to be constantly waiting for them to catch up on the walk, patience, as you know, not being a virtue of mine.

Jenny, beaming, addressed the group. She had a sunny disposition, a glass-half-full rather than glass-half-empty personality. "Splendid, all here and all on time, and for once, the weather's kind. Let's seize the day." She was right, it was a spectacular morning, clear blue skies with just the odd fluffy white cloud, promising a lush day. Jenny fell easily into tour guide mode. "Ladies and gentlemen, if you look to your left, you will see Pendle Hill where from the summit on a day like today, you can see as far afield as Wales and Blackpool and, if you look extra carefully, a glimpse of the sea!" Now I was seeing it in real life I was even more grateful I hadn't committed to climbing it, to me it looked more like a mountain than a hill.

Blackpool didn't hold much interest for me, it wasn't on the agenda, but we'd be going to Wales at some stage, which I knew had a bit of a mystical reputation. So far, I had only English destinations booked, but as well as Wales, we would also be taking in Scotland and Northern Ireland, the whole of the United Kingdom. I tuned back into Jenny.

"... if you want to do a walk another time, there's a great Halloween tour. They climb at night, so all you see is a line of spooky moving lights. Now, before we set off, does anyone need to nip to the lavatory?" She pointed to the toilet block. Holy crap, I thought, who says lavatory these days? I noticed one of the more elderly couples hurrying off. Why couldn't they have gone before, I thought with impatience. I wanted to get going and seize the day, as Jenny had said.

Having made a summary judgement of my tour companions, I couldn't help but be impressed that they all seemed to have some very professional rambling gear. Slimline rucksacks for water and other necessities, and then, as if from nowhere they'd all produced spiked walking sticks, obviously I'd missed that memo. These were serious ramblers. I might have looked like an "anorak" with my gear on, but these guys seemed to be the real deal.

We headed to Aitken Wood, Pendle Hill looking even steeper close-up. As if she'd read my mind, Jenny said, "It is a pretty steep incline, isn't it? Depending on your fitness levels, climbing to the top will take thirty-five to forty minutes." Even the professional ramblers looked relieved we weren't going to be attempting that, and Jenny chuckled at our expressions. "As you take in the beautiful scenery, spare a thought for the twelve unfortunate souls, all locals from the surrounding villages. They were used to seeing this hill every morning from their windows but probably never dreamt under what circumstances they'd be forced to walk the dreadful journey over several days, some forty-five miles or so from their villages all the way to Lancaster Castle to face trial for witchcraft. Today we'll be following in their footsteps."

There was certainly a palpable atmosphere to the place, and we appeared to be the only tourists at the moment; everything was unnaturally quiet. I had little time to reflect because I had to concentrate on keeping up with the group and was forced to ditch my early concerns about them slowing us up. In fact, they were putting me to shame, having picked up their pace, using their spiked sticks to full advantage. While they were making it look like a walk in the park, I was trailing behind, puffing and panting. I couldn't believe how unfit I sounded.

Much to my relief, Jenny stopped at certain points to indicate things of interest. "If you look over there, you'll spot the Ogden Reservoirs. As you can see, it's a windswept, desolate countryside with hills as far as the eye can see and, as you can imagine, it would have been even more isolated in the seventeenth century." I thought it looked pretty isolated today too, but was grateful for a pit stop. I got my water out, I wasn't going to let a group of old codgers beat me. Gaining a renewed bout of energy, I'd show them.

There was no doubt the bleak scenery was spectacular and seeing Pendle Hill from a different angle, it looked stunningly beautiful with endless snaking pathways. I had to admit I was falling in love with the Great British Isles, which was a surprise. I thought with sadness back to Lavender Cottage and the beauty of Whitby and the North Yorkshire Moors. The Cotswolds were pretty stunning too, but I'd hardly had time to explore since I'd moved there. In the past, I'd closed my eyes to the beauty around me, searching for it elsewhere in locations far and wide and not finding it, but it was here all along. Right now, I was here for work but maybe when the nightmare times had passed, I'd come back and explore the special places, and I already knew this was one of them. I felt so close to the persecuted Pendle witches, and it seemed, as I filled my lungs with fresh country air, that I also breathed in some of the area's magic.

We reached Aitken Wood, ready to follow the sculpture trail. It wasn't too long a walk, but I hadn't exercised that much recently and regretted not using a rejuvenating spell. But this was neither the time nor the place to start doing anything suspicious, and certainly, the sculpture trail wasn't as challenging as Pendle Hill would have been. I was still at the back of the group with the fitties marching ahead, off in their own world. I had to take my hat off to them, they were super-fit, total respect!

We followed Jenny's neat figure into the woods. Malcolm was accompanying us for this part and as I observed the banter between him and Jenny, there was no mistaking the chemistry between them. Maybe he was a retired academic; he reminded me of the suave actor Bill Nighy.

As we made our way into the forest, Jenny started speaking again. Her accent was posh, not a trace of the north, even though I knew she'd grown up here. "They only installed the sculptures here in 2012," she told us. "They've proved so popular the plan is to extend the trail in the forest, as more and more art installations are added."

One of the group murmured, "Magic through art," and we all nodded.

"The safest kind," agreed Jenny and for a second, her glance caught mine, then moved to focus on the rest of the group. "You will spot magical and mythical creatures within the trees. This is ancient woodland, so what better place." We all nodded again; honestly, it was the quietest group I'd ever been a part of. Then Jenny added in a softer tone, almost under her breath. "Can you feel the magical vibe? It is said the unquiet spirits of witches wander these woods." I was nearest to her at that point so may have been the only one to hear that comment.

When she spoke again, it was at a normal level, and,

as we made our way deeper into the forest, the sunlight struggled to break through the magnificent trees. "These ancient woods are known to have a life of their own, and don't be surprised if you think you see the sculptures move; it's the shadowy environment. You may see things that look alarming, but they're only the effect of the light." She paused, then added, "Most of the time." She saw alarm on several faces and laughed. "Only kidding." Well, I thought, all these professional ramblers aren't looking so brave now.

Jenny continued more seriously, "Some of the sculptures do look a bit sinister the deeper we get into the forest, but," – she put her hand to her chest – "hand on heart, I've never seen any paranormal goings on around here myself." She looked at me and winked, this time I was sure I hadn't imagined it, she was singling me out! It was strange. In this beautiful woodland setting, I felt an atmosphere. "In the early seventeenth century," Jenny continued, "this would have been an area for foraging, firewood, and magical meetings." Ah, I see. I silently added, I bet there are still meetings today.

As we weaved our way in and out of the trees, Jenny pointed out some of her favourite sculptures. "The Quaker Tree – although Pendle Hill is notorious for the witch trials, it was also the inspiration for George Fox, who founded the Quakers. In 1652, he climbed Pendle Hill and had a revelation, an epiphany which inspired him to form the religious group. This is what he said," she closed her eyes briefly and quoted from memory. "'As we travelled, we came near a very great hill called Pendle Hill, and I was moved of the Lord to go up ... When I was come to the top, I saw the sea bordering upon Lancashire. From the top of this hill the Lord let me see in what places he had a great people to be gathered.'" She finished with a sigh, opening her eyes. "Like the witches just a few decades earlier, Quakers were persecuted for their beliefs." The group was riveted, this was a woman who certainly knew how to work an audience.

"Right," she broke the silence briskly. "On we go." And she led us further along the trail to a ferocious-looking sculpture. "A demonic black dog, you'll find them a lot in English folklore. As you can tell, they represent evil." I was in my element, although I could see several others weren't enjoying these darker elements of the tour as much as I was. Jenny must have also sensed their discomfort, and we moved swiftly away from the dark dog to a more conventional figure, a sombre gentleman in formal seventeenth-century dress, although, as it turned out, he wasn't so nice either. "This," said Jenny, as we all gathered around her again, "is the Witchfinder, based on Roger Nowell, the magistrate who investigated and prosecuted the Pendle witches. As you can tell, the persecution of the witches and their historic importance has inspired and been interpreted by today's artists."

Next, Jenny moved us on to the Magic Chair, a genuinely weird and wonderful creation. "Look carefully," she instructed, and unnervingly, the more I looked, the more I saw, and from the murmurs around me, I wasn't the only one. The chair had arms and legs, the odd eyeball, and ears. It was very cleverly done and equally unsettling.

I thought this was my favourite piece so far and knew at some stage I'd come back on my own, when I'd be able to spend more time. Jenny had already walked us to a sculpture called The Pendle Witches. "A particularly soulful piece," she said, "portraying the witches chained and making their way across the landscape. We don't have time today, but if you visit again, you can look for the ten ceramic plaques, one for each woman hanged." I know I wasn't the only one with a tear in my eye for those poor souls, and there was a distinct lightening of the atmosphere when we followed Jenny out of the woods and back to the minibus.

As we piled back on board, I looked forward to the rest of the day. Our guide was an amazing storyteller, an accomplished tour guide, and had all the facts at her fingertips. I was sure she had a lot more information on witches and was also sure there was a lot more to find out about Prof. Jenny herself.

CHAPTER 11

We made a stop at the churchyard at St Mary's, in Newholm, where Alice Nutter, the wealthiest of the Pendle witches, was said to be buried. I said a silent prayer at her family's grave; it felt like the right thing to do, pay my respects. I couldn't see her name engraved, but that wasn't surprising. Witches weren't allowed to be buried in hallowed ground. It was alleged she got caught up in the whole sorry tale of the Pendle witches because she passed by Malkin Tower on Good Friday on her way to a Catholic gathering. She couldn't admit to this when accosted because it was illegal to attend such a meeting. Jenny promised us more information about Alice later in the tour. "Nobody knows for sure whether she was there at Malkin Tower, or whether she was genuinely an innocent passer-by." I was appalled at how easily a woman with money and a privileged life could be brought down. Was there a similarity to my own life? Could I end up on the gallows? We learnt more about Alice Nutter when we later got to Roughlee, her home village, where a statue had been commissioned after a local campaign. It seemed that even after 400 years it was felt hers was a wrongful death. She'd lived at Roughlee Hall, a grand manor now surrounded by 1970s housing – really bizarre – the neighbours now mowing the lawns of their neat front gardens. The statue itself was beautiful, and fresh flowers had been left in her folded, chained hands.

Our next stop was to see the tiny Witches Galore shop, which Jenny told us had its own supernatural reputation. "A young woman who lost her lover in the war has been sighted several times, wandering through the building. We'll stop for a few minutes, give you a chance to pick up a souvenir," she said. I wasn't sure I wanted anything other than to savour the atmosphere. As I took my turn to enter the shop, a massive dog slobbered up to me, appearing from nowhere. I smiled; perhaps this was the owner's familiar, nice change from a black cat. Having patted the dog's head, I felt it would be rude not to buy something, and I picked up a book that looked interesting.

When we pulled up to the Pendle Heritage Centre Museum, Jenny explained she would take a break and leave us to wander on our own around the exhibition. "It's not huge," she said, "so I'd suggest you finish off by dropping into the tearoom. We'll reassemble in an hour. I recommend their Victoria sponge. Let them know you're on one of my tours, and you'll get a generous portion, big enough to share." Not likely, I thought, there'd be no sharing as far as I was concerned. A large calorie-laden piece of cake would do nicely after all that exercise; I was ravenous. I whizzed through the exhibition, it didn't take long, and with nothing new to learn here, my mind turned to cake. Others in the group had decided they'd use their free time walking around the eighteenth-century walled garden. More walking – I couldn't believe it. Not surprisingly, I counted myself out. They probably already had me sussed out, as an antisocial loner. OK, yes, I know one day I will be old and watching my pension, but I'd like to think I'd be more refined, like Sandy or Jenny, for example, and still enjoy a cup of tea and cake in a tearoom!

I'd visualised something rather twee – flowery china cups, paper doilies, and knitted tea cosies – but the reality was far more modern, and a friendly young waitress breezed over to where I'd elected to sit in the beautiful walled garden. "Good choice," she said, when I ordered the Victoria sponge.

"Jenny, our tour guide, recommended it."

She smiled. "Jenny's lovely. Are you enjoying her tour?"

"Very much. The witch history is incredible, isn't it?"

She lowered her voice. "I agree, and I don't tell many people, especially with what's going on nowadays, but my grandma is related to Alice Nutter."

"Really!" I exclaimed in a tell-me-more way. I smiled to myself, if her grandma was related, surely she was too?

"The Nutters still live around here you know, but naturally changed their name ages ago, they had to, after what happened." She bustled off to get my order, returning with tea and the biggest slice of cake. I savoured every mouthful. I was delighted and intrigued by her comment confirming Nutter descendants were still in the area.

Back on the bus, it would have been easy to nod off after all the fresh air and exercise, but I was captivated by Jenny and didn't want to miss a thing. I was sitting on my own – Billy no mates – but it meant I didn't have to make small talk with anyone. I know, I sound like a total frightmare, don't I? I'm sure they had me down for a miserable, stuck-up cow, but that was fine. As Malc drove us around the spectacular countryside and through beautiful villages. Jenny announced, "We're now on the forty-five-mile Pendle Way, the last journey for the Pendle witches. Legend has it their spirits still roam to this day." She gave us a moment to reflect on that, then continued, "I've lived here all my life, so you probably think I'm biased, but in my opinion, nowhere can beat Lancashire when it comes to stunning scenery combined with fascinating if problematic history."

I couldn't argue with that. I still favoured my memories of the Yorkshire Moors, but maybe this came in a close second. There were so many similarities between the two areas. Jenny broke into my reverie.

"We're just about to pull up for our lunch stop at the *Gossiping Monk*, which serves delicious traditional pub grub." I wasn't sure I had much room for lunch, maybe I'd overdone it with the cake, so I chose the lightest and healthiest thing I could see on the menu, salmon with asparagus and a glass of sparkling water. The meal was a surprisingly quiet affair as everyone else had been saving themselves by skipping the tearoom. I watched a little enviously as they all dived into various pudding choices but I just opted for coffee.

Malc joined us for lunch, and body language – the light brush of hands, and the arm leading Jenny to the table, where they sat next to each other – confirmed they were indeed a couple. As everyone sat back, Jenny told us more about the pub. "There have always been ghostly sightings here, indeed in a lot of the pubs around this area." She made a joke about spirits being attracted to spirits, and we all chuckled dutifully. "Many inns, alehouses, or taverns, as they were known then, have been around for centuries. Ale was brewed to make the water safer to drink, with the added benefit that it makes you feel good – in moderation, of course." She waited for another laugh. I assumed she worked from a well-memorised script and knew exactly when and how to lighten the atmosphere between dark tales.

"You'll also have heard about the murderous highwaymen, ready to hijack travellers, violent robbers on horseback. Some say in the dark hours you might hear the sound of hoofbeats and feel a rush of air as the ghost of a long-dead highwayman in dark clothing passes. There are even those who maintain they've seen him, in a black cloak and with just a skull for a head." She paused. "But I'm sure he won't be out and about at midday." She truly was skilled at working her audience, and the group were full of questions. I was more of a passive observer; a little smile of acknowledgement here and there from me seemed to be all that was required. I knew the conversation would turn back to witches, and sure enough, one of the men said, "Jenny, I've heard there are still witches around these parts; we've all heard about the trouble they're causing."

There were murmurs of agreement from the others. Jenny gave a swift look towards me and held my gaze for just for a second. I knew then that she knew who I was. She turned to the questioner, and I could see from his expression he was surprised by the change in hers.

"I'm sorry, Brian, I thought I'd made it clear to each of you when you booked. I'm a history professor, therefore I specialise in the past, not the present, and that's where this tour firmly stays." Well, that shut him down. He looked sheepish and muttered something. I wondered how he'd feel if he knew he was, in fact, lunching with a bona fide witch, and maybe more than one!

CHAPTER 12

Lunch finished, we continued our journey. Jenny was in her element. For whatever reason, in the pub, she'd kept the subject to ghostly goings on, maybe walls have ears? Though now she was unleashed, and it was all about the Pendle witches. You could tell she was passionate about her subject, after all, wasn't it what everyone had come along on this trip to hear? All about those poor desperate souls from the past, whose ghosts were rumoured to roam. I thought how different it would be for present-day kick-ass witches like me, now we could finally protect ourselves against the perpetrators, we could finally fight back. As Malc expertly tackled the twists and turns of the winding country roads, Jenny equally expertly wove a web of stories. She had an amazingly calming voice, and we all listened, enthralled. I wondered who she really was, behind the professional tour guide façade.

"If you've grown up in this area," she'd started,

"witch folklore is ingrained in your psyche. Their memory lives amongst us, their lives and their tragic end never forgotten." She paused before adding, "Or forgiven." Bloody hell, she was certainly pulling on the heartstrings now, but was I the only one who shivered a little at her last phrase?

"After my history degree," she continued, "there was no question but that I'd do my PhD thesis on the Pendle witch trials. There is a wealth of material around if you want to find out more, including my own published thesis." She smiled. "Just a quick plug! Let me take you back in time to before the witch trials of 1612. Witches always lived around here, they were generally accepted, and certainly weren't always associated with evil, they were seen as wise women or healers, and they helped the community using the 'old ways': lotions, potions, and spells." As she spoke, I was thinking about the Mystical Ladies, all we ever wanted to do was help others. Nothing bad or evil was ever done. Yes, we'd help true love on its way and change our appearance, amongst other spells, but never to anyone's detriment. I zoned back into Jenny's commentary as she carried on speaking.

"Let me put this in the context of the time. King James I was a fearful man who was appalled and frightened by witchcraft. He'd had a brush with witches while he was King of Scotland, and he was particularly concerned when Lancashire was brought to his attention. He became convinced the area was contaminated, that the people involved meant him harm. He subsequently passed an act that imposed the death penalty for the following reasons: 'Making a covenant with an evil spirit, using a corpse for magic, hurting life or limb, procuring love, or injuring cattle by means of charms.'" I shuddered and saw a few of the others in the group exchange alarmed glances. "He made sure witchcraft was a treasonous crime, both against the crown and God." She paused for breath and took a sip of water from a bottle, then carried on. "Although today we see a stunningly beautiful backdrop, with lovingly restored cottages and stunning rugged scenery, back then life around Pendle Hill was far bleaker, the area was remote, it was a hard life. Few outsiders visited, so it was an insular community of scattered tiny hamlets, the population very much left to its own devices. In such isolated circumstances, it was all too easy to fall out, and two particular families were constantly arguing and accusing each other of various crimes. Each family was headed by an elderly matriarch. Anne Whittle, known as Old Chattox, lived with her daughters Elizabeth Whittle and Anne Redferne. Old Demdike, real name Elizabeth Southerns, headed the other family. She lived with her daughter Elizabeth Device, known as Squinting Lizzie, and her grandchildren, Alizon, James, and Jennet." I couldn't help myself, I snorted inappropriately at the Squinting Lizzie label. It broke the tension; a giggle is always contagious. I'd have to put this in the memory bank for when I next saw my very own Squinting Lizzie! Jenny smiled patiently while we composed ourselves, it hadn't put her off her stride.

"In different times the story might have ended there, but superstition was rife. The war between the families escalated and it wasn't long before accusations of witchcraft were flying around." She raised an eyebrow and smiled to acknowledge the broomsticks, which immediately popped into our heads. "Things worsened on 21 March 1612 when Alizon Device had an altercation with a certain John Law. He was a peddler who travelled from village to village selling his wares. Alizon wanted some pins, but he was suspicious because they were rumoured to be used by witches for nefarious purposes, and he refused to sell them to her. She allegedly cursed him, and he was struck down. We now know he most probably had a stroke, but at the time even Alizon herself was convinced her curse had worked, and with that, the die was cast for the family's demise. There were already rumours that they had put curses, hexes, and spells on those they disliked. Inevitably, Alizon came to the attention of Roger Nowell, the Justice of the Peace for Lancashire, and it just so happened he was looking to score brownie points with the King. He knew a successful set of witch trials would do his career no harm at all. He started putting together a case."

She continued, "Later that spring, on Good Friday 1612, there was the alleged meeting of the witches at Old Demdike's home Malkin Tower – sounds imposing, doesn't it – but it was only the humble cottage of a family who lived hand-to-mouth. But it seems it was this meeting which sealed their fate."

One of the group raised a hand to interrupt. "Did they think even young Jennet was one – a witch, I mean?"

Jenny shrugged. "There's no evidence of that, she was very young after all, but she did testify against her whole family at the trial." She paused. "Of course, nobody knows how they got this testimony from her!"

Someone else called from the back of the bus, "What sort of accusations were made against the women?"

"Good question," said Jenny. "I was coming to that. Everything from sickness within a family, cattle falling sick or dying, they were even blamed for yeast not fermenting when local bread and beer were made. One of the more absurd charges levelled against them was the overflowing of the river Ribble, which breached its banks. This was held to be directly due to the Malkin Tower meeting. In truth, anything and everything that went wrong was laid at the feet of the witches."

I frowned, I couldn't begin to imagine a spell for flooding a river, but I had no doubt that there was much witch lore I had no knowledge of and maybe when the chips are down and everything and everyone is against you, you have nothing left to lose. Perhaps they were wreaking revenge in the only way they knew. Or maybe it was just Mother Nature, after all, rivers still flood to this day, why would I think they had cast a spell? Surely we were a different breed today, and I certainly would never do a spell that could harm. Of course, it could have simply been hearsay and rumours, a way of damaging those who were generally disliked, it wouldn't take much for people to turn on them and make baseless accusations. I thought of my heart-shaped mole, the same one as my birth mother, Anna. That alone might have been enough to convict us, in those troubled times we wouldn't have stood a chance. But these were troubled times too, history was repeating itself, the past had come back to haunt us. Jenny was expertly linking the past to the present, it was subtle but I saw it, even if the others didn't get the connection. She was a witch sympathiser at worst, a witch at best and shortly, with the commencement of our roadshow sessions, I'd be finding out the local lie of the land for myself.

I wondered what the rest of the group were thinking. Did they think the witches were innocent or that they deserved everything they got? Then someone asked, "Have they confirmed exactly where Malkin Tower was located?"

Jenny shrugged again. "Nobody is really certain. There have been a couple of important excavations in the last few years, indeed they found what they think may have been the house of a witch. It was in an amazing condition, preserved because it was buried under a grassy mound. It was a seventeenth-century property, but there was evidence of nineteenth-century inhabitants. They found a cat buried in the wall. I'm afraid it was a common, if barbaric, practice to wall up a living animal in a building, it was thought to protect the inhabitants of the house from curses and spells. Whether that was proof of a witch living there is open to debate, but more likely it was someone who feared them." I thought back to Lavender Cottage; even though Hettie was a witch, the family still used the withered hand of glory to ward off evil spirits, after all, witches weren't evil. Then I recalled the mummified cat in the boot of Steph's car, the tour guide who met us at Robin Hood's Bay. She'd said she was using it as an artist's prop. Was that the truth?

"But coming back to Malkin Tower," Jenny continued, "it's thought that it was most likely demolished shortly after the trials. The superstitious locals wouldn't have wanted to be reminded of the evil amongst them. The only firm evidence for its location came from the official court records and placed it somewhere in the Forest of Pendle." She lowered her tone. "Maybe we even walked over its foundations earlier." There were a couple of nervous chuckles which Jenny acknowledged with a smile, turning to a bag on the floor of the bus. "If you find yourself fascinated by all you're hearing, I have a few copies of my book available to purchase." I put my hand up, I'd certainly buy a copy to add to my reading pile; several of the others did too.

Jenny had just finished handing out the books and accepting payment as we arrived at Lancaster Castle, and handed us over to Peter who was to take us round the Castle. "He's the expert," she told us. "He's worked here for so many years he's part of the fixtures and fittings." She wouldn't join us on the one-hour tour, she planned to give her voice a rest but said but we'd all meet up again in the courtyard, and Malc would then drive us back to the Barley Mow pub.

CHAPTER 13

We met Peter outside the dark and imposing castle entrance. He looked more like the lead singer from the band Sparks than a guide – a throwback from the 70s. I liked the fact he had a dark sense of humour. "Keep with the group at all times," he said, adding ominously, "You really wouldn't want to be left behind." They had ghost tours and paranormal group visits here, so we knew what he meant, and we all laughed nervously.

He started with some background. "There has been a prison on this site since the twelfth century, and we saw our last inmates here in 2011, three hundred and ninety-nine years after our most infamous occupants, the Pendle witches. As you will know from Jenny, the witch-finding frenzy had reached Lancashire, and the most infamous witch trials in history were held here. I'm afraid Lancaster has a long and dark history. It's known as the Hanging Town, second only to London in the number of people hanged."

He was full of further grim facts as we moved slowly from room to room. I'd never heard about the debtor's prison before, but Peter explained, "There were up to four hundred people housed here, they were those who could not pay their debts and had to work in return for food. They had more freedom than the other inmates, and their families could visit them, some were even allowed to do additional work to pay off their debt more swiftly. The lucky ones eventually left the prison. Others didn't. Perhaps you know that Charles Dickens's father was held in a debtor's prison."

"Can we go into one of the cells?" asked a man from the back of our group.

"Certainly, just remember when you're in there that there would have been up to twenty prisoners crammed in at any one time." Three brave souls chose to venture in, and Peter shut the door and turned the lock. In response to gasps from both those inside and out, he chuckled, and kept them there for a minute or two before unlocking it and letting out the three men, noticeably paler than a moment ago.

There was a darkness about the castle, and it wasn't just due to the lack of light and the damp chill, there was a brooding atmosphere of despair. Our guide skilfully wove a series of fascinating stories of witchcraft, persecution, crime, and punishment, but when we followed him into one of two courtrooms, what he said chilled me to the bone. "You're lucky to be able to see all the rooms today, they still use Lancaster Castle as a Crown Court." Oh my God, were people still tried here for witchcraft? I didn't dare ask for details, but then he went on to quote, in sonorous tones, "'For making a covenant with an evil spirit, using a corpse for magic, hurting life or limb, procuring love, or injuring cattle by means of charms: the death penalty.' The Pendle and other Lancashire witches were all tried here." And, I added silently, witch persecution is still going on today.

In a circular room with two large black wooden chairs, Peter invited anyone who wanted to try them out. "Comfortable? You're sitting in what they called the Lunatic Chairs which were used to hold the more troublesome prisoners. Those leather restraints tightened the more the prisoner struggled." He relished in sharing these ghastly stories. Moving on, he led us to the tiny dungeon below Well Tower. "Better known as Witch Tower. It's where they were kept when awaiting trial. The assizes trial judges only met twice a year, so there was sometimes a very long wait. In fact, the oldest of the accused, Old Demdike, died in these miserable conditions before she ever got to trial." I could see I wasn't the only one of our group who was glad to get out of the damp and dark. It was all too easy to put myself in the shoes of the women held there. I could only hope there weren't plans to revert to these punishments in the current purge. Peter continued, "At that time, they were utilising a pretty gruesome hanging method – the short drop, which meant a drawn-out death by strangulation." I gulped and shivered, how barbaric. I was beginning to find the whole thing more and more unbearable and while the rest of the group was taking in Hanging Corner and the unmarked, quicklimed graves of the victims, I faked a headache and moved to where Jenny was waiting.

There was no one else around, but I couldn't quite bring myself to ask her the question I wanted to. Instead, we made small talk. I asked about her accent, which certainly didn't sound local.

She laughed. "I spent time at university in London and at that time, a northern accent didn't go down well, so I had elocution lessons. I must admit it's something I came to regret. The Lancashire accent is beautiful and part of my identity, but I can't get it back. At the time, I wasn't planning on returning, but I couldn't resist the pull of home."

I nodded. "I know what you mean. I lived in the North Yorkshire Moors, similar in some ways to around here. I loved it there but had to move back to London. I'd love to get back there again one day. Some people find it lonely, but I loved the moors." I didn't go into details as to why I'd left, but she said, "I imagine you'd be more sensitive than others to atmosphere." Before I could ask why she felt that, she'd neatly changed the subject. "Where in London did you live?"

"Most recently Hampstead, before that Richmond, but I was brought up around the Surrey Hills until I went to boarding school." Somehow, we got onto the subject of which pubs we went to, and she mentioned that a favourite watering hole of hers was the Prospect of Whitby, which stopped me in my tracks. What a coincidence, I told her about my leaving party at the pub, obviously omitting the time slip. While we were talking, I wondered about her name. Davis was very close to Device, could she be a descendant of Jennet Device, the young girl at the centre of the witch trials? She smiled at me knowingly, even though I hadn't voiced my thought, and turned away swiftly to speak to the others who were wandering back.

The journey back was quiet, we'd covered the tour programme, and I could see Jenny and Malc had switched off and were deep in their own private conversation. Jenny and I hadn't spoken again, but I was sure she knew a damn sight more than she'd recounted on tour. Unfortunately, I only had a week here and my time would be taken up with the roadshow so I probably wouldn't have the chance to find out more about her. Shame, she was an interesting character, like the yummy mummies in Hampstead, hiding in plain sight behind a stereotype. My witch radar was getting stronger, but I'm not sure someone else would be any the wiser.

I settled myself into a chair at the edge of the group as we reassembled in the lounge area of the pub. The conversation had turned to growing roses and other gardening issues, not an area of expertise for me. Apart from a little light gardening, I'd left all that sort of thing to the gardener at Lavender Cottage, I thought wistfully about how I missed my beautiful cottage garden. Wood Barn just wasn't the same. Being in this part of the country reminded me so much of the moors. I'd feel brave enough to return to my beautiful eighteenth-century cottage someday. For now, I concentrated on the menu. I fancied something a bit stodgy for a change; I needed some energy after all the walking and settled on a seafood linguine. I always tried to have fish or seafood when I was out; I was not too fond of the smell of fish cooking in the barn.

The Barley Mow pub had a history. There'd been a drinking house on the site since at least the sixteenth century, well before the infamous witch trials. I asked one of the staff where else they'd recommend locally for our dinner the following day with Sandy and Alice, and the lovely waitress even offered to call them and book for me, very kind, nothing was too much trouble here. The place had recently been taken over and modernised, with trendy wooden panelling, lots of leather and wooden chairs, squashy sofas with brightly coloured cushions, and rugged wooden tables. The walls were full of pictures and mirrors, and there was a welcoming open fire.

By now, though, listening to these oldies drone on, I was a little bored and tired, annoyed I hadn't opted to return to the hotel at the end of the tour. I could be sitting in the spa or sipping a chilled glass of champagne with Sandy and Alice rather than listening to these old codgers. The subject had now changed to the cost of living. I appreciated that not everyone was financially in the same boat as me, but enough was enough. With regret, I passed on the pudding. They had my favourite, sticky toffee pudding, but I wanted to make a quick getaway after I'd finished my main course. Jenny was now off duty and making small talk with the group, listening to them whinging; she didn't seem to mind, her workday nearly finished. She worked part-time and was semi-retired, so she could relax tomorrow. She and Malc seemed amiable, happy to chat with everyone, even though I'm sure they'd heard it all before. As far as I was concerned, they could bore off. I feigned tiredness with a yawn, thanked Jenny, promised a rave review and said my goodbyes to the rest of the group, who didn't look as if they'd miss me overmuch, and nipped to the ladies on my way out.

Renovations hadn't yet reached this area by the look of things. I passed through a corridor leading to what might even have been part of the original Jacobean building. The ceiling was claustrophobically low with dark wooden beams, and felt particularly cold, the chill was all the more noticeable after the warm and cheerful lounge area. I could see the ladies sign at the end of the corridor, but a middle-aged man was blocking the way.

"Excuse me," I said. He was dressed in black trousers and a T-shirt printed with the pub logo; perhaps he was the landlord. If so, he wasn't the picture of hospitality, and he'd been quietly cursing at the wall where there was a pile of rubble and a gaping hole, you could see through to the wattle and daub, the original construction. He hadn't heard me, so I coughed to catch his attention, and he jumped as I repeated what I'd said and added, with a nod at the wall, "What's happened here then?"

"Don't ask!" he said, grimly.

"Is this your pub?" I said. "It's amazing."

"I'm Chris, and yes, I'm the landlord, for my sins."

"Alice," I said, goodness knows why. I didn't need to give a name, let alone a false one.

"Not related to Alice Nutter, are you?" he said. That was strange, or was it just a local in-thing they said to anyone of that name?

I smiled. "No, not from around these parts. This is my first visit, it's a beautiful place."

His smile faded. "Sinister, more like, strange goings on at the moment." He pointed to the wall. "I'm not the only one finding holes like this, it's as if someone's searching for something in these old buildings." I was unsure why he was sharing this with me, a total stranger and a southerner at that. I must have had a trustworthy face – this transformed face, anyway.

I smiled. "Maybe one of your ghosts, isn't this supposed to be the most haunted pub of all?"

He grimaced. "Not sure it's a ghostly presence, maybe someone closer to home and very much alive. Nobody's been caught in the act, it's a mystery."

"Why's it just started now?" I asked.

He scratched his head. "Don't want to say too much, tempting fate and all that, but it's no coincidence they recently started work on the Manor House just outside Barley. The old owner died, been in the family since Elizabethan times, but he was the last of the line. It's changed hands now. Place is a wreck by all accounts, he only ever lived in a couple of rooms; the rest has gone to rack and ruin. He was a hoarder, house is filled to the rafters with rubbish, vermin too, naturally. Whoever bought it got it for next to nothing because they had to clear it. No one locally had the inclination or the money. An outsider with deep pockets, southerner, we think."

"Sounds gruesome."

He nodded. It seemed now he had an audience he didn't want to let go. "Weirdest thing, on the boundary they found an old lady living in a tiny, almost derelict stone cottage built into the hill. Hermit-like, she was, totally self-sufficient, no one in the village knew she was there, never even knew about the cottage. She was not all there, if you know what I mean. Social services got involved and couldn't leave her there. They've lodged her with one of the locals. They don't give her long to live, though."

"What's the new owner going to do with the house?" I asked, intrigued.

"They've already split the land," he replied, grim-faced. "Reinstated the original ancient boundary, donated both the cottage and its garden to the National Trust. I was there when they went in – I'm a member of the local history group – but nobody bargained on what we found." He paused for effect. "A hidden door, leading to a secret room, like a small cave built into the hill. They expected to find contraband, instead, there was the mummified body of a woman!"

"No!" I gasped.

"They think she'd been there for centuries, but because of the conditions – cold as a fridge it was in there – she was preserved. I'll not forget that fixed toothy grin in a long time, and that's not all; there was evidence of witchcraft. They questioned the old lady about the room but couldn't get any sense out of her."

With an effort, I maintained my poker face. "How fascinating; I'd love to see the cottage."

He shook his head. "Not in the public domain yet, but you can probably take a sneaky peek. The locals all know where it is, but you wouldn't be able to go inside;

there's scaffolding up and all that, apart from which it's said there may be a curse on the place, there's all sorts of gossip. Some say it may be a spell to protect whoever lives there."

I was thinking how strange he'd told me all this, a stranger with a fake name. Could he be one of us? I wanted to ask more, but he was already putting up a health and safety sign near the hole. He inclined his head and hastened off. I hoped they'd find the woman in the hidden room had simply died a natural death and hadn't been murdered for her beliefs.

I continued to the loo, then splashed cold water on my face, even though it was so cold I was getting hot sweats; I smiled at the reflection in the mirror, seeing the funny side, who the hell was staring back at me, with a fake face? I made my way out of the back of the pub. The car park where I'd left the car that morning was just a short walk away. I didn't want to bump into Jenny or the rest of the group. I wondered if she knew about the tiny cottage, she hadn't mentioned anything. Maybe what happened in the village, stayed in the village, protected by the locals, kept secret from ghoulish trophy hunters and the tourists seeking the macabre.

CHAPTER 14

The old Manor House was set in its grounds between Barley and Roughlee. It had been built in Elizabethan times to flaunt power and wealth. Once resplendent, it now looked sadly neglected, badly in need of repair and renovation. It looked just the sort of old pile that TV ghost hunters would love. My renovation of Lavender Cottage was nothing to what was needed here, and first and foremost was loads of money. It had the potential to be brought back to its former glory but at what cost? Whoever owned it now seemed to have made a start. There were several full skips awaiting collection. Of course, money wasn't the only issue; I was certain such a historic property was listed, so the new owner would have to jump through hoops before full-on work could start.

I drove a bit further around the perimeter of the land, having spotted the scaffolding Chris had mentioned, which I guessed marked the location of the newly found cottage. I could see it would originally have been within the ancient wall surrounding the main house, but what with the deterioration of the wall in many parts, as well as the overgrown trees and bushes, it wasn't surprising nobody had known the cottage was there. It looked like they were currently reusing the fallen stones to rebuild a wall to establish a new boundary and separate the cottage from the main house. It could be an appealing tourist attraction before long, especially with its intriguing back story.

Chris had mentioned the scaffolding but not the protective fencing and tarpaulin. Police tape still wound around what had become a potential crime scene with the discovery of the body, and I assumed it would stay until they'd established cause and date of death. From the outside, there was little to see, and dusk was approaching; the sun was slowly setting, and it was starting to get dark and spooky, the witching hour. I'd come here on impulse and health and safety certainly wasn't going to stop me. I reckoned it couldn't be that unstable if someone had lived there until recently. I checked no one was around, then squeezed into a gap in the protective fencing, making my way towards the front of the building, parting the tarpaulin and locating the tiniest wooden door. It was open. I had just a moment of hesitation. Was I opening a Pandora's box? Had something dark been unleashed after the disturbance of a long-dead body in a secret hiding place?

I had to stoop to get through the doorway, and the first thing to hit me was the smell. I expected an aroma of dampness and decay, but instead the strong scent of lavender hit me, and a woody, smoky smell; centuries of open fires had seeped into the stone structure of this tiny dwelling. The old lady lived alone here, but even one person in this small space would have been a crowd. It was a multipurpose living room and kitchen combined, but with no electricity or running water. I could see evidence of candle wax in nooks and crannies around the room, but there was no sign of a secret hiding place, just a table fashioned from a fallen tree trunk. Two roughly made wooden chairs had seen better days and were set near the fire; neither looked comfy or inviting. Surely more up-to-date furniture had already been removed? There was a push towards natural living, but this took it too far. I thought it was too risky to look for the hidden door, I didn't want to delve too deeply, I might find more than I bargained for. A set of steep curved stairs led upwards. I knew I had to look but, to be honest, I was already more than ready to scoot back to the comfort of my luxury room at the hotel.

I trod carefully; the wood of the stairs was visibly rotting and I shuddered, as much from cold as from fear of a gruesome death, tumbling down the stairs, alone in the cold, with nobody having the faintest idea I was here. I reached a tiny landing with a room on either side. Stooping to enter, they were similar, with low ceilings and dark, exposed beams, more the size of large cupboards than bedrooms. Nothing to see other than grime and cobwebs. Hard to even figure out how a bed would have fitted; maybe the old lady had simply slept on the floor on a mattress of straw and hessian sacking, like in the olden days.

There was no sign of a bathroom or even a toilet. It must be outside like the one at Lavender Cottage. The old lady would have had to go out whatever the weather, or perhaps she kept a chamber pot where she slept. No wonder she looked the worse for wear when they found her. I couldn't date the property, but it looked older than Hettie's; hard to believe there were no signs of modern living. What a hermit existence, but perhaps she'd not been unhappy – just self-sufficient, undisturbed. I wondered how well she'd settle into the twenty-first century in her new lodgings. There was a rustling in the corner of the room, and I knew what that meant. I made a hasty retreat down the stairs and out through the tiny door.

I wondered why the new owners had gifted this cottage to the National Trust and not restored it for their own use. Maybe the spiralling costs of the main house made this a project too far, or perhaps it was the ghoulish discovery and link to witchcraft that frightened them off and made them happy to wash their hands of the place. People were as superstitious and as scared as they'd always been when it came to curses, and properties protected by spells. It was weird, I thought I might have felt something here, a sense of the past, was I a little disappointed I hadn't felt even the remotest malevolent vibe? I wondered what they'd find when they examined the body they'd found. Had she died of natural causes, and how long ago? Was she one of the poor unfortunates murdered in her own home? It was possible she was hiding in the secret room and became trapped. I'd have to leave with a lot of unanswered questions.

I closed the door behind me and, parting the tarpaulin, felt a chill. While I'd been inside it had become colder and darker outside and I was more afraid of the living than the dead right now. I didn't want to be caught snooping around. One thing was certain, this evening I wasn't going to catch up with Alice and Sandy; I'd already messaged them saying, Eat without me. I've had supper. On my way back. I wanted to be alone; I was shattered and needed to process all I'd seen and heard today. I'd had a glimpse of the past in these parts, and I couldn't help but compare it with what was currently going on.

Using my phone as a torch, conscious I couldn't afford to trip and fall in this godforsaken place, I made my way back through the tangled, overgrown weeds, and trees, a couple of times catching my hair in low-hanging branches. Relieved to be back at the edge of the land, I found the gap in the fencing, grateful that I hadn't sustained any injuries or seen anything gruesome on my unauthorised jaunt. Time to make my escape. But before I could squeeze myself back through the fence ...

CHAPTER 15

I felt strangely lightheaded, and then that familiar electrical current running down my body, the magnetic pull so strong I could hear the crackling noise getting louder and louder, ringing in my ears. The sky turned sepia. A frizzle of exhilaration added to the surging electricity within me, and the air quality changed, became fresher, cleaner. My body violently jolted as I landed hard on the ground. Dusting myself off – I'd worry about bruises later – I was more euphoric than scared. What would I see, who would I meet, and what era had I travelled to? Would there be another past life to meet? A message? Or was my time with Hettie the exception rather than the rule? Maybe another random experience, like meeting John Hackett in Hampstead Cemetery? Had I somehow willed for this to happen, or was the tiny dwelling drawing me in to tell me its secrets and that of its residents? I had no idea how long I'd remain there, but I'd savour every moment, seeing it as the incredible gift it was.

There was, of course, no trace of builders' rubbish, tarpaulin, or scaffolding around the cottage. The stone wall was now intact around the original border of the big house and included the tiny dwelling on its land. The garden still looked overgrown with greenery growing up and between the stones of the cottage walls and a once-beautiful wisteria hanging on for dear life against encroaching ivy. But on closer inspection, it was a productive area. The low-hanging branches burst with apples, plums, and other fruit. I couldn't resist. I picked up a juicy, dark purple plum and took a sweet and delicious bite. There was an enviable vegetable patch full to the brim with fresh produce and an abundance of herbs. I brushed a hand over lavender, rosemary, and thyme – echoes of my own cottage garden. I started at a noise, then realised it was just chickens clucking and scratching around their rickety-looking wooden henhouse, while industrious bees buzzed between the wildflowers and a beehive at the end of the garden. It looked as if anyone living here would be completely self-sufficient; how envious my lovely Alice would be of this way of living, although it'd be a little tidier under her care, she'd soon get it ship-shape. For a moment, I thought perhaps I should get bees and chickens for Wood Barn, but what was I thinking – that really wasn't me at all.

There was a wispy plume of smoke from the chimney; someone was home. I walked to the tiny, now familiar front door and knocked gently, not wanting to startle anyone. After a moment, I rapped again, a little louder. This time the door opened a crack, and I looked down into a pair of unblinking brown eyes framed by long dark eyelashes. She opened the door a little wider, a tiny slip of a girl with a snub nose, maybe twelve years old. On her head she wore a bonnet that had once been white, and her dark brown hair was held in a rough side plait. She had a pale, natural beauty, but her fashion sense left much to be desired. She was in a shapeless, roughly made dress of linen, which reached her feet, although it was so heavily stained and patched to cover tears it was hard to tell what colour it had originally been.

Untidy and unkempt as she was, beneath the grime was a lovely young girl – but she smelt rank, personal hygiene not a priority. I'd never smelt anything like it before, stale body odour mixed with something else putrid, an aroma impossible to describe. I wanted to hold my nose, but that would have been rude. I'd have to get used to it. On a positive note, she didn't look emaciated. I suppose she ate the produce grown in the garden, and her skin was glowing, not a blemish to be seen.

She smiled straight at me, so I knew she could see me, and there was no sign of fear on her face. Her mother had obviously not warned her of the stranger danger Sandy had drummed into me as a child. The girl's teeth were surprisingly straight but almost green with obvious signs of tooth decay. She reminded me of the raggedy children I'd seen back in time in Whitby, but unlike them, she had a happy aura around her. "Won't you come in?" she said, a voice so soft I almost missed it.

I assumed I was at least as far back as Hettie's time, from what I could see. The tiny room didn't look much different from just a few moments ago. It was dark and gloomy, but this time there was smoke from the fire; the chimney could certainly do with a sweep. The windows were covered by makeshift curtains made from rough sacking material, similar to that used for the potatoes Sandy had delivered to the farm. I imagined the sacking also provided some insulation, although I shivered as the wind picked up outside and a draught came through, it must be freezing in the winter. As my eyes adjusted to the dark interior, the only light sources were flickering candles and the fire. Every house had its own smell, and even though the young girl didn't smell great, the room itself was scented by bunches of lavender and rosemary tied and dotted around the room. Something was cooking in a big pot suspended and steaming over the fire, and it, too, smelt quite pleasant, although I could have done without the sight of a brace of pheasants and a partially skinned rabbit hanging from hooks in the ceiling. Still, it seemed whoever lived here was eating well. Not sure where the food was prepared, I could see only the rough table and chairs I'd seen in my day, although in better condition, how amazing that they had been so sturdily crafted they'd lasted all this time. There was no sink I could see; there must be a nearby stream they used. Where did the inhabitants go to the bathroom? I wasn't going to ask.

A couple of small milking stools stood by the fire, together with a rocking chair and what looked like bales of hay with animal skins laid over them. The girl gestured I should sit. I chose one of the chairs and tried out my voice.

"What a lovely warming fire, and what a delicious smell. I'm Ellie, what's your name?"

"It's pottage for dinner, and I'm Isabel."

"What year is this, Isabel?"

She showed no surprise as she answered, "It is 1615, the year of our Lord." With shock I realised I'd travelled back to just three years after the witch trials.

"Where are your mother and father?"

"My father is long gone. He died some years ago. My mother is up at the big house."

"How old are you, Isabel?"

She shook her head. "I am not certain of the exact date of my birth but believe I am around thirteen years."

"A teenager," I murmured, more to myself, and she gave me a look of incomprehension. "Shouldn't you be in school?" I asked.

She laughed softly. "School is not for the likes of us, but the children at the house have a tutor, and sometimes they help me. So," she said with some pride, "I have started to learn to read, and I can scribe a few odd words."

"What does your mother do at the house?"

"She helps." She smiled at me as if I should know what she was talking about. "In her special way, you know." She giggled. "I am surprised you ask. You are magical yourself, are you not? That's how you're here with your strange way of speaking and odd attire." I was intrigued, how did she know? But she didn't offer more, so I said, "But after all that went on, why would you stay here? Aren't you in danger?"

"Where would we go? Anyway, we are protected."

"Protected?"

"By the Manor House, they keep us safe, won't tell anyone. They charge us no rent in return for services. I sometimes help too." She was so matter of fact, and I was baffled.

"Are there witches living at the Manor House?" I asked.

She laughed aloud at that. "No, of course not, but they value my mother for her lotions, potions, and spells." At my expression, she hastened to add, "All are well hidden. There is no fear they will be found. We have a secret room. It is a safe hiding place for us, too; it was needed when witch hunters came banging on our door. But now we feel we are safe again, at least for the time being. My mother has also cast a protective spell around the cottage and the big house and it seems to have worked so far."

"And are other witches brave enough to stay in the area?"

She shrugged. "We don't mix with the village, but I expect so, some are better than others in keeping themselves to themselves, especially if they have protection as we do. Jennet was the only person from the village who ever visited us anyway."

I tried to keep my expression neutral. "You don't mean Jennet Device?" She was the young girl who had testified against her family and others in the village including Alice Nutter.

Isabel inclined her head. "Yes, she was my best friend."

"And where is she now?"

"When all the troubles happened, she was taken away

to stay with a church family who wanted to redeem her soul and release her of the devil. She'd been reprieved for her honesty, so she was allowed to go." Isabel's face reflected her sadness.

Of course, I knew all this from my own research and from Jenny. Nevertheless, it was a shock to hear it spoken of so casually.

"When I am older," she said, "I will travel the country to find Jennet."

"Jennet knew your mother was a witch? And you too?"

"Naturally, but Jennet was powerful. Quicker-witted than all the rest of her foolish family put together."

"But if she saved her own skin by betraying her family, there's no honour in that. And if she knew about you and your mother, how were you not betrayed too?"

Isabel shook her head. "Jennet had a traumatic time at Malkin Tower, she was neglected and abused by her family, there was no surprise she betrayed them. They treated her shamefully. My mother only showed her kindness. She cared for Jennet as much as she did for me. She had many meals here while her family was too busy arguing. Her mother, Squinting Lizzie, was a nightmare, and her grandmother was even worse." What Isabel was saying confirmed what I'd already gathered from my research, but why Alice Nutter, what had she done to harm Jennet?

"She was very ill," Isabel continued. "At one stage, she nearly died. She came here for refuge, and her family didn't even realise she was missing. My mother nursed her back to health, and one thing we've always had is an abundance of food. Without my mother's kindness and nurturing, she wouldn't have fared well, and Jennet repaid that kindness by keeping her mouth firmly shut. She never breathed a word about our activities, even in the midst of the witch hunts. She was loyal to the end."

She read my expression of amazement. "I know it always feels strange when you folks visit, especially as you know what you've read from the history books, but often those don't tell the accurate story."

I asked, "But why Alice Nutter, she wasn't a witch, was she?"

She shook her head. "No, she wasn't, but I'm sure they made her say it, she was going to tell the truth. They didn't like Alice, saw her as a troublemaker and tarred her with the same brush as the witches, she was a Catholic you see." That made sense, and Jennet was only nine years old, I bet the poor soul was scared to death.

"Did the family at the house know Jennet too?" I asked.

"Yes, she was the only one from the village allowed in the big house. She knew about our secret room and that we would have hidden her, if need be, but she was still taken away from us. I miss her, but it was probably better for her than staying. Many still feared her, didn't believe she had no involvement with her family's crime, so she had to speak out if only to save her own skin."

"But she was only a child."

Isabel smiled wryly. "Childhood is no protection, we must work as soon as possible. I have been helping at the big house since the age of five."

"Were the family there drawn into all the troubles? Were they suspected of anything?"

She shook her head. "They are rich, well-respected, and they put a great deal of money back into the village, it buys silence. No one was going to search their house or land."

"Can you show me the Manor House?"

She hesitated. "I suppose, but you can't speak to me while we're there. No one else will see or hear you, but they will wonder at my reaction."

The Manor House in its heyday was magnificent. The owners were prosperous and happy to flaunt their power and wealth. Isabel led me to the servants' quarters, she wasn't allowed to go uninvited to other areas of the house, but the kitchen itself was immense and full of busy people rushing around. While many of them acknowledged Isabel, nobody saw me, and during the time we wandered around the vast room, there was no sign of her mother. As we returned slowly to the cottage, I was lost in my thoughts until I realised, I desperately wanted to see the secret room before being pulled back to my own time. When I asked her, she was cautious, like she was backtracking, regretting opening her mouth earlier.

"Isabel, I know about it from my time." I said nothing about the body that was found. "You mentioned it before and I'm intrigued."

"Well, I suppose I can," she said, as we re-entered the cottage. "But you must swear not to speak of it to anyone. My mother would kill me if she knew I had shown it, even to someone from beyond." The door to the room was hidden in plain sight – it was tiny, blending almost imperceptibly with the surrounding stone wall and obscured by the rough table and chairs.

I was amazed at what was beyond the tiny door as Isabel led the way with a candle and I squeezed through behind her. The space opened into a cave-like room, much bigger than I'd imagined. It cut deeply into the hill the house backed onto and had been kitted out so a family could sleep and live here for a time, with bedding made of hessian sacks and straw. It was a space used for storage as much as anything else, and food had been stockpiled, so they could hide for some time without being discovered. I was immediately struck by how cold it was in contrast to the rest of the cottage, and there appeared to be a small stream of fresh water running along the side of the room. All around were obvious signs of witchcraft.

"We keep our craft secrets here and we were ready to hide if need be, when they were rounding up the witches. No one would have ever known we were in there." I shivered. She misunderstood. "Don't worry, Ellie, we have plenty of animal skins, the big house gives us the skins from the farm animals when they die. I know it doesn't look the most comfortable of places to be, but better than being hanged as a witch."

The room was starting to feel like a fridge, and I suddenly felt claustrophobic, and I was glad to move back out again. She carefully closed the door and pushed back the furniture, and I asked if I could see the rooms upstairs. Very little had changed since I'd last seen it, just a few minutes ago, although there was a makeshift mattress in each room. The lack of storage space explained why her outfit was so dirty. She may have only had one dress, how crazy was that idea. I had now gone totally nose-blind and couldn't smell her any more. I thought of my life in my time. How would I manage without all the technology and other comforts I took for granted, although, of course, Isabel knew no different. I'd love to take her back to my time and show her a different life. The first thing I'd do would be to get her teeth sorted.

It was what she said next that freaked me out more than anything. "I have seen others like you before from beyond." I whispered, "Others like me?"

She nodded. "I've been expecting you, Ellie. One of the others told me you would be coming someday soon."

"Who are these others?" I wanted to know more. She ignored my question, but she'd shocked me to the core. Was I just one of many time travellers?

She laughed at my bafflement. "My mama always thinks I've gone mad because she can't see any of you. 'Talking to your imaginary friends again, are you, Izzy?' she says, but she's warned me many a time not to boast about my gift."

"Wise words," I said. "You must do as she says." Isabel seemed to have decided, as I was one of them, that it would be safe to confide in me. "They come from different times, not just yours. Men, women, and bairns. I love it when they are my age. But I know in your time witches are again being persecuted, the hate has never gone away, has it?" The fact she had this information was proof of what she was saying.

"Let me get this right. You've seen people from other times and someone from the twenty-first century, my time? Who was it?"

She nodded eagerly. "Someone who knows you well; they thought you might visit sometime soon." I shook my head. I didn't know anyone who had the same skills as me. Certainly, Sandy didn't know how to time travel, and it wasn't something I'd discussed with anyone else.

"Isabel." I took her gently by the shoulders, looking directly into her eyes. "Please tell me, who did you meet?" She understood, then, I think how important it was to me and started to tell me, but while I could see her mouth moving, I could hear no words. "Noooo," I tried to shout but was now soundless too. She looked distraught; she was trying to shout but knew it was too late, she'd seen it all before. And then everything went black.

CHAPTER 16

My head was banging as I came to. The first thought in my mind – who was the person Isabel was talking about, someone who knew me? That was super-weird in a world full of weirdness.

I was looking up into two pairs of concerned eyes. Sandy and Alice had come looking for me, although I had no idea how they'd known where I might be. As they helped me up and brushed me down, Sandy was unusually flustered.

"We were so worried. Are you OK?"

"Fine." I produced a weak smile, but I don't think anyone was convinced, least of all me.

Alice said reproachfully, "We've been calling and calling, and messaging you with no response. Eventually, we called the pub, but they said your group left a while back ... and you left before the rest."

"I did, but I bumped into the pub landlord he told me

about this old cottage they'd found recently, and I just had to have a nose around. Then, before I knew it, I found myself back in 1615, and I'm sorry, guys, but no phone signal!"

"1615 – what the hell! We thought you'd been kidnapped," Sandy said, in no mood to be amused. "It was getting dark, and we were panicking." I thought that was a little over the top, but I didn't feel able to go into any more detail at this point. My head was spinning, I felt completely disorientated and wanted some space. "Listen, I just need to process all this. I'm so sorry you were worried. I didn't mean for that to happen, but I found out so much more than you'll ever read in the history books. Can we please just get back to the hotel? I'll get some sleep and then tell you more about it."

I could see from a glance at my phone there were numerous missed calls and messages. It was so odd. I hadn't felt I'd been out of touch for that long. The time spent with Isabel had seemed to fly by, but then my relationship with time was obviously not the most reliable. I was also guiltily aware that there were things that had happened back in Yorkshire that I'd kept from Sandy and Alice. I wasn't even sure how I'd tell them that someone else who knows me is also able to time travel. Who could it be? I knew for sure it wasn't Sandy, she would have told me by now, wouldn't she?

By the time Monday morning dawned, I still hadn't managed to tell them the whole Isabel story. I was still reeling from the experience. I'd gone straight to bed as soon as I arrived back at the hotel, had a splitting headache all day Sunday and cried off from our planned dinner, and now it was Monday and down to business. Our mission was to help the witches; my misadventures had to be put on the back burner. The week flashed by. Sandy and Alice were inundated with enquiries from women, and surprisingly more men than we thought, wanting legal help for themselves or beloved family members. Much of what was handed out was advice, but many were ready to be represented. Reasons for an arrest were often bizarre, sometimes serious, and all carrying penalties. You would think we were still in the times of Isabel or Hettie, from centuries before.

Blame was laid at the door of supposed witches for what seemed ridiculous things, but they were treated with seriousness in the eye of the law. Urban witches, for example, were blamed for any malicious behaviour, everything from internet trolling to Wi-Fi dropping, and for a spate of car crimes – tyres slashed, paintwork scratched, as well as all kinds of thefts and break-ins. The most laughable was a spate of divorces in a particular area – some sort of anti-love potion in the water was blamed. In the more rural areas, nothing much had changed, droughts and floods, spoilt crops, small businesses failing, and even the bigger picture of global warming were all said to be due to witchcraft, and these were the more civilised accusations. The increase of protective graffiti, the pentangle and other symbols carved into buildings, farmers using corn dollies, and the rise in wearing precious stones such as tiger's eye in jewellery was taking hold. We also heard about unexplained deaths. Hearsay is a powerful thing, and vigilantes taking the law into their own hands organised an unofficial council of witch haters; it was barbaric, and very scary. With all these horrific accounts in just one week, you could say that we were the dream team here to save witches from a gruesome fate.

We'd worked out between us an incredibly simple way of interpreting and passing on the spell to share with others. This involved briefly putting someone into a hypnotic state and implanting the knowledge in their subconscious, making it easily recoverable with a post-hypnotic keyword so they, in turn, could pass it along. It was a huge game changer. Sharing the spell this way was not only swift but ensured it could be handed on accurately, the vital information spreading like ripples in a stream. We'd decided there was no question of charging for it, even though Carol, or Cassie, or whatever she was called, had taken money to extract me from my predicament. We viewed it as a humanitarian mission and hoped that once taught, the spell would be well-used and would travel the country like a Mexican wave. We were exhausted by the time we finished each night, and although we had dinner in the restaurant together, it was too public a place to risk being overheard, so we kept our conversation on everyday matters. There was no chance to detail my time trip, and then, when we'd finished our meal, all we wanted was our beds.

By the time Friday arrived, our thoughts were already on our next location and also on the opportunity for a few days' rest before everything restarted on Monday. My sightseeing plans had gone out the window. It had been a very busy day and, as our time here was drawing to a close, I thought I had time to have a breather; maybe everyone who needed to see us had done so, but then, with surprise, I saw a familiar face. I didn't think for a minute Jenny, the professor-cum-tour guide, would recognise me, because I'd done a different transformation spell for the tour. But she had seen straight through it. I'd been fairly certain she was a witch, but now it was confirmed. I was pleased to see her. She was wheeling a ridiculously old lady in an old-fashioned wheelchair. I was surprised the woman was still alive; she looked ancient. A few wisps of white hair remained on her head, and the veins on her hands stood out starkly through her paper-thin skin. A strong gust of wind and she'd be blown over.

Jenny kept her voice low but urgent. "I've come to see you late in the week because I want to be discreet even amongst ourselves. I hope you can help." She turned to the woman. "This is Isabel, she is currently staying with me and Malc," she said, and my mind went strangely blank as she continued, "Isabel has lived all her life in a cottage in the grounds of the Manor House. Nobody knew it was there, she lived there undisturbed for many years until social services got involved."

"Isabel?" I said faintly.

Jenny nodded, and for the first time, the woman in the chair stirred and looked up at me, I'd thought she was blind because both eyes were so clouded, but incredibly the clouds in her eyes cleared before my own eyes, she looked directly at me and smiled gently. "Ellie?" she said. "I thought I recognised you, your aura hasn't changed. You visited me when I was but a child."

I groped for a chair behind me and sat down suddenly, my legs had gone weak, this couldn't possibly be the Isabel I met over 400 years ago! Nobody lived for that long, not even a witch. We were still only mortal, weren't we? But as I opened my mouth to ask questions, Isabel had already slumped back in the chair, mumbling to herself, unseeing, unhearing, the moment of clarity gone.

Jenny shook her head, "She comes and goes, I'm afraid. I've had some incredible conversations with her, but then she slips back. She must have mistaken you for someone else, I know you've never lived round here."

I paused. Could I trust this woman? I decided to risk it. "I don't think it was a mistake; I went back in time. After leaving your tour, I went to take a quick peek at the cottage, and I went back to 1615. There was a child in the cottage with the same name, but surely this can't be her."

Jenny put a hand on my arm. "Ah, now I understand, and I know it seems impossible, but I believe she is the same person. It seems her body has just kept going, it's like she simply forgot to die. But now she's been taken away from the cottage she's deteriorating minute by minute, I don't think she will last that much longer. I wonder whether there was something magical in the water. They had their own spring, I believe. I have tried to get there – to the spring – but there are always builders around, and they seem to have capped it ... but Ellie," – she looked around the room to make sure there was no one there who could overhear – "right now, I need the spell. As you know, we're living through terrible times. The Purge is ready to explode around here again, and the vigilantes are the worst. It's not the law we fear, but what's going on under the radar that's so much worse. I've so far been able to hide in plain sight, doing my tours, but I'm convinced I'm living on borrowed time."

"Of course," I said, responding to her obvious anxiety. "Let me just lock the door, we're nearly at the end of the day anyway." I had so many questions I wanted to ask, but Jenny was here for a purpose, time was short, and she was still speaking.

"We don't know what the future holds for Isabel, but after surviving for this long, she deserves our help. During her lucid periods, she's been able to tell me so much, and I have found out I'm actually a descendant of Jennet Device, who once was Isabel's friend." I gasped, delighted to hear Jennet had got away and had a family of her own. I was pleased that my theory about Jenny was correct. "Apparently, after her early traumas, she lived a long life and had several children."

I was desperate to talk to Isabel and find out who else had travelled back in time, I needed to know, but Jenny was equally intent on getting her back home again as if exposing her to the outside world might speed her demise. Unfortunately, the old lady had slipped back again, and it was clear I couldn't get the answers I wanted right now, she was all of her 400-plus years. Jenny placed her hand on my arm.

"Ellie, if you share the protection spell with me, I can use it to help Isabel too for her remaining time." Her sense of urgency was infectious, so I slipped back into my role of teacher, and in no time, she had memorised the incantation, thanked me and grasped the handles of the wheelchair to turn it and leave.

"Wait," I said. "I understand they found a body in the secret room."

Suddenly, Isabel returned to life, almost as if those words flipped her back into focus. Her voice was so soft Jenny and I had to lean in to hear.

"My mother." A tear trickled down the creased skin of her cheek. "She was hiding there, terrified by the second purge. It was so cold, I tried to get her back into our living room, but she refused to leave the safety of the secret hiding place. But sadly, she was old, and so weak, she couldn't even drink the water from our spring. She didn't last long." Isabel sighed. "Once her soul had left, I couldn't bear to disturb her. I never used the room again. Firmly shut the door, and forgot it was there." Jenny and I glanced at each other. Her mother had been decomposing all those years with poor Isabel in the next room. "I sealed it up," murmured Isabel, as if she'd read our minds.

I pushed my luck. "Isabel, who else came to see you when you were a child?" She gave a slight look of comprehension, then, in the next instant, I saw the clarity vanish, her eyes cloud over, and her head dropped to her chest again. Maybe this would be the last time I saw her, and I'd never know who she had met. She'd probably take that secret to the grave. Jenny was keen to go, visibly twitchy now, so as I held the door open for Jenny to wheel the chair away, I felt I was bidding goodbye to an incredible link from the past, and my present.

CHAPTER 17

Three months into the roadshow and, if it wasn't such a serious situation, some of the things witches were being blamed for were laughable. In the twenty-first century, a supposed age of reason, anything and everything was being blamed on witchcraft, and history was repeating itself. There were so many parallels with the witch hunts from the past, it was bizarre.

Life for us had never been so hectic, a whirlwind of activity, spinning us from place to place around the country. I'd had little time to reflect on what had happened during that first visit to Lancashire, I hadn't had any more past life experiences, and even my dream life had gone to sleep. The truth was I had neither the time nor the energy to get into trouble. I'd rather spend my free time winding down in the luxurious spas that were always on my wish list when I booked a hotel. The other reason, and this was by far the most important, was that Sandy and Alice had come down on me like a ton of bricks after my latest time travel episode. They weren't in the least bit amused. They'd threatened a verbal warning. Yes, you heard right, they thought about sacking me! They were concerned I was being too flippant, calling attention to myself. I was effectively grounded, although I promised myself that I'd do my own road trip one day, return to some of the more interesting places, and do all the tourist stuff. Maybe in the future, we could do a girls' trip – wishful thinking. For now, the most important thing was helping the witches and getting as much spa action as I could. We had earned our downtime because the stories we heard were so disturbing. It was getting out of hand; even those without a magical bone in their body were being accused. On some days, it felt as if we'd been doing this forever, hearing one dreadful recounting after another, but in reality, it was the tip of the iceberg and then, twelve weeks after we started, we were heading home to the Cotswolds for a well-earned rest before we started all over again.

Safely back at Wood Barn, it was good to get back into my scruffs and get out in the garden, although it wasn't easy to get the stories I'd heard out of my head – some stuck more than others. One such story came from a lady called Samantha, she'd moved to a village in Warwickshire, the sort of place where everyone knew each other. She was a newcomer, an outsider. Purely coincidentally, there had been problems with internet coverage in the village. Things had got worse when Samantha moved in, and then the rumours started – how the TV connection would suddenly inexplicably play up as she passed by a particular house. She didn't know who first suggested she could be a witch, but plenty were willing to jump on the bandwagon. There was gossip about kitchen gadgets that suddenly stopped working or, on one occasion, caught fire. It seemed Samantha was the common denominator linked to all these technical issues. Although no one had directly threatened her, she lived in a circle of suspicion and felt vulnerable and scared. She was so relieved when I explained the spells to her, said she felt like she'd suddenly been given a suit of armour.

From what we were hearing, it seemed technology was the most common theme in some areas, phones connecting randomly when the person hadn't even touched them, radios and TVs changing channels and stations randomly, and spooky sounds coming through, car and house alarms going off, that sort of thing. Repeated accounts from around the country. More stories about a spate of car damage, deflated tyres, scratched paintwork and broken windows at one time would have been blamed on vandals but not now! There was no rational explanation, so minds turned to the irrational. There were even bizarre tales of cats and crows following those under suspicion and dogs behaving weirdly when they were around as if they could smell evil. In rural areas, lambs and calves born with defects, or milk curdling, even on a cold day, were again seen to be down to witchcraft. The world had gone crazy.

But the spell was starting to have an effect, I'd heard back from some of the women I'd helped that they had subsequently survived vigilante attacks. It was also reported in the press that the suicide contagion was subsiding across the country, although according to the media, there appeared to be no obvious reason, they couldn't understand what had changed. Were women getting happier again? There were also reports of women vanishing just prior to an arrest warrant being issued. I chuckled when I read these news stories. Our mission was succeeding – yes, gruesome things were still happening, but we were gaining a huge following, and the word continued to spread. The momentum was like a tidal wave, an unstoppable tsunami.

The first night back at the barn, I slept like a log, and for the next few days felt like I was coming back down to earth, a more normal life at least until we were back on the road again. But after a few days to my surprise, I found I was getting bored. I'd had enough of reading and gardening, and my fingers were itching to return to technology. I'm the sort of person who relishes the idea of just doing nothing for a while, but the reality is I'm a doer and happiest when busy, and right now I felt I'd watched as many films and Netflix series as I wanted, at the same time managing to avoid news programmes and any fictional dramas that might have included anything witchy. I decided I needed to reorganise my wardrobe – exciting times – and maybe drop into the town for some goodies for tea and a little retail therapy. There was a newly opened boutique that looked interesting, perhaps I'd pay a visit. With that in mind, I cleared some clothes I didn't wear, and then, just before I was tempted to turn on my phone, I noticed a note had come through my letterbox. We'd been keeping ourselves to ourselves, so *Come over to the farmhouse this afternoon at bang on 3.00 pm, we have a massive surprise for you!* sounded intriguing.

CHAPTER 18

What was the surprise? It obviously wasn't an away-day or even a retail therapy trip as they wanted me there at 3 pm, an odd time to organise anything. It was unlikely to be anything strenuous either. No hikes for me! Maybe a night out on the town, with afternoon tea before, or a visit to the theatre, although they hadn't asked me to spruce up. I was so tempted to switch my phone on and message Alice right now and try and coax it out of her, but I'd made the decision to switch off all my technology until we went back on the road; after three months, my sore brain needed a break if nothing else. Much as I love the witches, I'd had my fill of the horrendous stories and I knew Alice, and especially Sandy, didn't rely on technology in the same way I did. As for Mike, he still had an old brick for a phone, it didn't do anything apart from make calls – those were the days! They had much stronger willpower and had no problem putting their phones aside.

Five minutes before 3 pm, I made my way over to the farmhouse. I couldn't wait to burst through the door and see what was planned. After all the anticipation, I hoped it wouldn't be an anticlimax. Maybe I'd built it up too much. I noticed a couple of hire cars on the driveway, back window stickers giving them away. Odd, we didn't have that many visitors to the house apart from tradespeople, and they never parked here. Was this the surprise? Who was here?

The door was unlocked, and I heard excited voices as I headed into the kitchen. Alice, Sandy, and Mike were in the room, and they had been joined by a tall, willowy woman with her back to me. She was standing next to two other shorter women. Did I hear an American accent? Then the woman turned and looked straight at me, I screamed, "Lizzie, oh my God, oh my God!"

She nearly hugged the life out of me, the biggest bear hug! Both of us laughing a bit hysterically as, dishevelled, we released each other.

"Honey, what have you done to yourself? Is it really you?" I grinned as we took each other in. She hadn't changed a bit. "Wow," she said. "If I passed you in the street, I'd walk right on by." We laughed again then went back for another hug, I couldn't catch my breath, and tears mixed with the laughter.

"I've missed you so much," she said. "I was so worried when Sandy and Alice lost contact with you. Didn't know what had become of you." So they had been in contact with Lizzie all this time. I knew it! By now, I was properly sobbing and slobbering in the most unladylike way.

"I thought I'd never see you again," I said, turning to Alice sternly. "You've been in touch all this time?"

She grimaced. "Sorry, Ellie, it wasn't the right timing. Just savour the moment now and don't over-analyse, there were reasons." Typical Alice, that told me, didn't it? I knew there was no point arguing with her; after all, she'd organised this for me, hadn't she? I'd take her advice, go with the flow, live for the day, enjoy every moment. I couldn't believe this was the surprise, and I wouldn't swap this moment for anything right now.

Lizzie said, "I've been keeping a low profile living in the USA – good timing coming back over now, especially because of how well you're doing over here." So she even knew what we were doing; I really had been kept in the dark. Reading my thoughts, Lizzie said, "So sorry to keep this from you, I know you were dealing with your own shit, but it felt safer." She obviously also knew about what had happened to me. "Anyway," she turned to the other two women, "these are my friends in the US, they know everything, they're bona fide witches too, Leah and Daisy. We met in New York, but we've all since relocated to Massachusetts, not far from Boston. I still do lots of work in New York, but easier to fly in for jobs." I gasped, so on my trip to the US, I'd been just down the road from Lizzie without realising it. Maybe it really had been my Lizzie that the weird witches near Salem had seen? After my experiences were they a risk to her too, or just me?

The only person missing now was Sarah. Alice had been vague every time I'd asked, saying she was also living overseas like Lizzie, although, to be fair, I'd kept my own share of secrets from them too, so I couldn't be too judgemental.

"OK, where are you hiding Sarah?" I asked now. "Or is she due here but late as usual?"

I saw the looked that passed between Alice and Lizzie, and Alice said, "One thing at a time, Ellie, you always were too impatient." I felt a frizzle of excitement. Did this mean I would be seeing Sarah as well tonight? Was she, too, coming from overseas or wherever she was now living? Had they hidden her somewhere, was she just about to jump out on me, scare me half to death? It was the sort of thing they might do.

Changing the subject, Lizzie said, "While you were chilling this afternoon, I was being hypnotised with the protection spell, and learning how to disappear. I'm fully protected. I feel a whole lot better now, I can tell you. My friends are too." She looked over at Leah and Daisy. "We are going to see what we can do to help over in the States, like you are doing over here." She gave me a twirl and then disappeared.

"Oh my God, are you trying to tell me you're a witch too, Lizzie?" It crossed my mind that maybe she'd been hidden from me until they could fully trust me.

She reappeared, grinning and shaking her head. "No, of course not, but I am a sympathiser and part of the undercover movement, just like Alice." She frowned, changing the mood. "You know, things in the US are going much the same way as here. Where I live has a strong history linked to the Salem witches, and I have an awful feeling about it all kicking off again." Tell me about it!

Her friend Leah continued, "We want to learn from what you are doing over here, see how we can help our friends be prepared. From what Alice has told us, it's gone amazingly well over here, exceeding expectations, you've done an awesome job."

I nodded, maybe now was the time to let them into my secret. I had to tell them about my own Salem experience; I needed to warn them to avoid the weird witches with their mind-bending powers.

"OK, you guys, there is something I haven't told you. I was waiting for the right moment. This is too much of a coincidence, you living around Salem, Lizzie. A year ago, I went on a tour of Massachusetts with two friends from Hampstead where I was living at the time, Tess and Laura. We went to Salem, Cape Cod, Nantucket, and Boston. It was a holiday to remember for several reasons. Beautiful place, but some weird stuff went on around there." I paused for effect. They were all listening intently, my mother included. "I think we must have just missed you, Lizzie. We got talking to some women just outside of Salem, we stopped off for some food. They said they'd met a woman from England, and the description was too coincidental not to be you, although I couldn't be certain because I had no idea where you were living."

Lizzie interrupted. "Do you remember the name of the place you stopped at?"

"Sorry, I don't, but I do remember the name of one of the women we spoke to; her name was Em – Em Corey, the same name as one of the Salem witches. A very odd woman, too familiar, we all got a bad vibe from her. She didn't say, but I was sure she was a witch."

My mother had gone very pale. "Why didn't you tell us this before?"

I gave her an exasperated look. "Err, you haven't shared everything with me, have you? Where Lizzie was living, for example! I'm telling you now, it didn't seem relevant before. I had some truly odd experiences while I was there. I think someone was out to get me, I didn't want to alarm you guys, but now I know where you're living, Lizzie, you must be vigilant."

Alice made some coffee, and we sat around the table while I gave them an account of exactly what had happened, about Em, the women with her, and how it felt like she was almost extracting our thoughts. I told them about the three near-death experiences, attempted murder by burning, drowning, and garrotting, although, thankfully, I survived all of them to tell the tale. I told them about the cosmetics company Tuttuba and how Em Corey had been over in England when I was working in advertising, specifically to find me, but missed me as I'd given my notice in by then.

"She wanted me to help on some campaign, which was crazy, I had no idea why she thought I could add value to their multi-million-dollar company, they seemed to be doing pretty well on their own."

My mother hadn't regained her colour; she looked like she had seen a ghost. "Tuttuba and Em Corey!" she said. "I know all about that woman and her company. It's a front for a clandestine group of witches – bad witches. They spread malice and harm by subliminal messages through social media and advertising, and rumours are they might be putting something harmful in their cosmetics, some sort of influencing spell." She gave me a grim look. "Without a doubt, my darling girl, without the protection spell, you would have been bumped off. How horrendous, you'd have died a terrible death, and we might never have known what happened to you. It sounds as if that evil woman used a mind-reading spell. I can show you how to repel that. You must understand they will have known all about you, Ellie, and your link with me. I've had a brush with these women in the past. It didn't go well."

"I knew there was something about her. She set all my nerves on edge the moment I set eyes on her." I thought about how repulsed I'd been by her strong perfume masking a putrid smell and added, "I worried if I told you, you'd say I was being overdramatic."

My mother shook her head. "You really should have told me. Your instincts were spot on, you were dealing with the most dangerous of witches on a poisonous mission. You know, one of the reasons I wasn't keen on you moving to the Whitby area was because of its history. The women we're talking about are descended from the Whitby whaling witches – they were known as the Whitby Wailers. They were banished in Victorian times, taken forcibly and sent to Boston, expelled from England."

It was my turn to be shocked. "I had one of my past life experiences at the Waterside in Boston and I think I must have actually seen them arriving. The Whitby Whaling Company owned the ship they disembarked from."

"You have an amazing power," Sandy said. "What else did you see?"

"Not a lot more. It was during my garrotting experience – I slid back in time, saw them come off the ship, but then they disappeared into the crowds. Why were they banished from Whitby?"

"For doing exactly the same as they're doing now, spreading hate and vitriol within their community. They were arrested, tried, and deported. Rumour has it their families have been causing trouble ever since, even on the other side of the Atlantic. If these women were on the hunt for you, Ellie, your life was truly in danger." I felt nauseous. Not only had I witnessed the arrival of the women deported in disgrace from their communities, but I'd tangled with their descendants.

Sandy was speaking again. "They took the names of the original witches of Salem, but we are well aware of what they're doing, and once we are all protected, they cannot harm us. But they must have been disturbed by you, felt threatened even though you didn't know the extent of your own power. They would have known who you were without a shadow of a doubt, hence trying to hire you. This is the only time, Ellie, I will agree that you did the right thing by resigning. This also explains the supposed accidents you had – you were at the mercy of toxic witches." A chill ran down my spine, we were working against dark forces and I wondered how many more lucky escapes I could get away with.

Seeing the fear on my face, Alice tried to lighten the mood and came over to Lizzie and me, embracing us with one of the biggest hugs ever from someone usually so undemonstrative. "OK, let's not have any more secrets.

We have to trust each other like we've always done, it's the only way to protect each other." We all nodded, although I had my fingers crossed behind my back. Of course, I still had one guilty secret I hadn't shared. How could I admit I'd had a relationship with a major witch hunter, Professor Seb Williams? But why did my heart skip a beat whenever he entered my head?

And then, just when I thought they'd sprung all they had to spring, Alice said, "Ellie, someone's dying to speak to you." I could see she had a FaceTime call, and then I had to sit down because my legs had gone weak.

"Sarah?"

"Ellie! Yes, it's really me." she grinned, "God, I've missed you!"

"I've missed you too, and why aren't you here tonight?"

"Bit of a way to come. I'm living in a commune in Goa, working on a cooperative for sustainable fashion, living my true life off the grid these days. We employ local people to make the clothing. We don't have any technology in the commune, so I visit the local town's internet cafe once a month to catch up. You do not know how happy I am to know you're healthy and still alive. I feared the worse for so long."

"I thought exactly the same about you," I said. "Alice and Sandy kept me very much in the dark. I feel so much better now talking to you, and you look so well. Life must be good." I felt like a weight had been lifted from my shoulders, just seeing her face. "Why did you leave the Cotswolds, though? It's so beautiful here."

She shrugged. "Just needed a total life change and boy

does life over here do that, it's an amazing place, an assault on the senses. You will have to come and visit when you've succeeded in your mission to save the world." She knew all about it then. I couldn't understand why it had taken them all this time to put me back in the loop. Why hadn't they trusted me? We continued chatting for what seemed an age until Sarah had to go, her time on the internet running out, she promised to come back to the UK for a visit soon, or we could go out there to see her. I wasn't sure a commune was quite my scene. We'd have to find a top-class hotel nearby. I felt complete for the first time in ages, now I had reconnected with Lizzie and Sarah.

We kept chatting for a while, until Lizzie said we'd have to go as she'd booked a table in one of the local bistros for all of us, her treat. We continued ten to the dozen for the rest of the evening, hardly coming up for breath, and then into the night when we got back to the farmhouse after realising the bistro wanted to close for the night. Everyone else had already left, and they started to hint heavily, cleaning tables around us and then putting chairs up on those tables. We had so much to catch up on, including the revelation that Sarah was living as part of a cult, not just a commune. Would she be allowed to leave it, or would we be able to visit her when things over here calmed down? But I told myself she looked happy and healthy and could freely talk to us, so maybe it wasn't all that bad. At least she wasn't caught up in the Purge. She was off the grid and as safe as she could be.

CHAPTER 19

Six months later
Travelling from place to place was tedious, and yes, I know we were helping humanity, but I was bloody knackered. I'd never worked this hard and played this little. Even the novelty of a luxurious spa each evening had lost its sparkle. I just wanted to sleep for a year. At this stage, we'd been to all four corners of the British Isles, every single place on my list, apart from two.

Our last but one stop was Hampstead. It didn't seem that long since I was living there. I hoped they were faring well. I felt less scared going back knowing I was protected and had the invisibility spell in my repertoire so I could always disappear if I got into a hairy situation. So what if I bumped into Seb? What could he do to me? I had to embrace the power I knew had seeped through my veins, have the confidence to know he couldn't touch a hair on my head even if he and his cronies tried. Bring it on, see if

I care. But even just thinking of seeing him again made my heart beat double time, and I'd changed my look again, just in case he was sniffing around. Even my friends from around here wouldn't recognise me and I planned to stay incognito if and when they came to see me for the spells.

I couldn't believe our mission was nearly accomplished. We were already seeing early signs that the tide was turning. They'd soon realise there was no point dragging us through the courts. What would it achieve? Then, breaking news – the suicide contagion was officially over. I was glued to screen and print, picking up all the latest news. Of course, however sensational the headlines, none of them told the real truth, the one we all knew. If I'd been writing news stories myself, it would have been along the lines of "Witches revolt, you can't touch us now!" or "Witches murdered for their beliefs, heads must roll!" At least now, we knew that our work was paying dividends. Put that in your pipe and smoke it, witch hunters. You can't eradicate, demonise, or dehumanise us.

When I lived in Hampstead, it had been a pretty peaceful place, I hope it had remained so during my time away, and my friends had been left alone. They were such an amazing bunch of people. I hoped they hadn't been harmed. Then I thought back again to Seb, and his meeting with the officials, sniffing around, too close for comfort. Why would he have been around here other than for sinister reasons? Did they have their suspicions about what was going on locally? Protected or not, I wasn't keen on bumping into Seb or any of his crew. But I'd done enough surgeries now to know to keep my head down, and since that experience around Pendle, I hadn't been out on any more adventures or had any other past life incidents. I was just here to help the team. I had a job to do, an important one at that.

So far, Hampstead seemed a breeze, a breath of fresh air, and everyone appeared to be still unscathed. Although they were not taking any chances, and were more than happy to ask for our help as a precaution. How had they got away with it when other areas hadn't? It was hard to explain, especially as I knew from personal experience there was a thriving magical community. Maybe they were better than other areas at keeping it underground. After all, I had warned Matt when I fled the area that the witch hunters were in town. Maybe they'd gone further underground or forgone their magic for the time being.

However, as it turned out, when Tess and Laura came in together, I couldn't resist. I had to tell them it was me.

"Ladies, you might not recognise me, but you both know me very well!" They looked at each other.

"Your voice is certainly familiar," said Tess. "But no, I don't think I've ever seen you before."

I laughed. "It's me, Ellie. I've done a transformation spell. I've come back to help you all!" Laura squealed out loud. "Sshh," I said hastily.

"Sorry, Ellie, it's just amazing to see you, you left in such a hurry!"

"It's a long story. Someone from my past turned up around here. I knew I couldn't stay. Sorry to leave without letting you know."

Tess said, "We spoke to Matt, and he said something

had troubled you. He was so sad you left. He loved you so much, he was heartbroken."

"I know he did, but I just couldn't risk staying. But I'm back right now and here to help you!"

"We knew you were a powerful witch," Laura said, "but this! How on earth did you find out how to do the protection spell?" I chuckled. "Oh Laura, that's another very long story, and if I tell you, I'd have to kill you!"

They laughed. "But can we catch up after you've finished here?" Tess said. I nodded; I couldn't see the harm in going out for a quick drink with them.

"But only on the condition you will have done the spell by then."

They nodded. "Absolutely, we'll do it when we get home, then we can go out this evening if you are free." I agreed, I needed a break, and went through the spell with them – by now I was a pro – and they both hugged me and left saying how excited they were to catch up.

On to the next few women and a couple of guys, some of whom I recognised as having been in our group, although they of course didn't know who I was. There may well have been others I'd have known had they not also used transformation spells. Then Matt came in, looking tanned and handsome. Holy shit, I should have expected this. I hesitated, then reasoned Tess and Laura would let him know, so I'd better come clean. "Hello, Matt." He looked puzzled. "It's me, Ellie!"

He shook his head. "No, I can't believe it. It can't be."

"Don't you recognise my voice?"

"Yes, yes, of course I do, but you've done a bloody

fantastic job, I didn't have a clue. You do look amazing, though!"

I smiled. "You too. Have you been away?"

"No, just working outdoors, still doing the same job." He grimaced, then took a moment, stared deep into my eyes, deep into my soul, and nodded. "Still the same beautiful eyes, it is you! How have you been?"

"I'm doing OK, and you?"

He gave me a mournful look. "Still missing you, you broke my heart you know."

I changed the subject so he'd know I wouldn't get into anything deep and meaningful. "How are things round here?"

"Still pretty much the same," he said, and frowned. "I can't understand why we've been left alone, it's so odd. But it feels like something is brewing."

"Yes, but look," I said, "we need to get down to business." He nodded, knowing I had others to see.

When he left a while later, he kissed my cheek. "If you are ever around here again, promise you'll look me up."

"Of course I will." I put a hand on his arm. "Please make sure Lily gets the spell. I hope she's OK. And how about Kat? I haven't seen her either."

"Lily's doing well, thanks, and Kat is too." I didn't like to admit I'd be seeing the girls tonight, maybe it wasn't such a good idea, would he feel miffed if I saw them and not him? Oh well, I'd not be around here long enough to worry about it.

I had an incredible night with Laura and Tess, although I felt a little worse for wear the following morning. Sandy and Alice had been stern before I set off, they knew I was catching up with some old friends. "Don't you go getting yourself into any trouble," Alice warned me, and Sandy added, "Just watch what you drink, we need you in good working order tomorrow." I didn't need a lecture, I knew to be careful, and just for extra security I did a transformation spell, as did Laura and Tess so we looked like an everyday trio of yummy mummies meeting for a well-deserved break from the little brats. We went to one of our usual haunts, just like old times, except they weren't, were they? Nothing was like old times. There was always an undercurrent.

Working with Sandy and Alice had been an incredible experience, but as we saw off the last person in Hampstead, I was revelling in the thought that there was just one more stop. The icing on my cake had been that I'd seen Kat, she'd been one of the last to come over. An intuitive witch, she'd seen through my disguise immediately.

"Ellie, I always knew you were much more powerful than you let on but what you're doing is incredible, and I can see that it's working all over the country, just amazing!" She looked just the same, and I wondered why she hadn't used a spell or two on herself. "Just a personal decision, the transformation spell is popular around here; some guys are constantly changing their look, but not me." She continued, "You do know you broke Matt's heart when you left?" Not again, I'd already heard this from Laura and Tess. I must admit I did feel a little guilty.

"I know, and I'm so sorry. I had my reasons. But you know, if I hadn't moved on, I'd have never been able to work with my mother and best friend to help the witches. It must be fate." There was so much more I could have told her, but to be honest, I didn't have the inclination or the time, it had to be onwards and upwards. I think she understood.

She squeezed my hand. "Look, I know you're about to finish and move on to your next stop, so we'd better get on with the spells, then I'll leave you in peace."

I smiled. "It's been lovely to see you, and I'm so glad everyone is good around here."

CHAPTER 20

We arrived at our last venue, ready to start on Monday morning, knowing that by Friday at 7 pm, that would be it, our job done, finito, and I couldn't wait! I had to pinch myself. Was this it? Mixed feelings, to be honest; joyful to have finished, but what an incredible experience too. We'd heard some pretty horrific stories, and being able to make a difference was awesome, a legacy to pass on and hopefully help generations of witches in the future. What we had done was powerful, a collaboration of past and present, all thanks in part to Hettie and her magical book, Cassie for the part she played, and Sandy, one of the most powerful witches of our time. Our own personal troubles put firmly behind us; we really were kindred spirits these days.

This was the end of the road for me. My big news was that I'd officially resigned, leaving the firm, and Sandy had said there was no point in me going on beyond the end of the week. All on good terms, of course, but it had only ever been a made-up job for the duration of the road trip. I could have stayed on and helped with the marketing and advertising, but they already had a fantastic marketing team.

I had to think of myself now; I'd noticed my skin was getting a little dry again, even my beauty spells couldn't help with this, and I'd tried a few different ones, picked up on the way. I'd tended to drop into bed some nights without due care and attention to my beauty regime. I knew the answer: rest, hydrate, and sunshine. I hoped Sandy and Alice would do the same, and take some time out, although they still had to get on with the day job, so there was probably no chance, even though Sandy had recruited a new team of lawyers who were looking after the family law side while Sandy and Alice were on their mission. But they were keen to return to the day job, itching to get back to the office once they knew we'd done our best, they weren't ones to twiddle their thumbs. They'd still represent individual witches from their office, but they hoped this work would dry up; that would be proof – if we needed it – that we'd done our job, done enough. As for the firm, it seemed that everyone wanted to work with us; we had lawyers knocking on our door, we even had a waiting list, but no one wanted to leave once they were with us. We were sure that before long we would be opening offices in different areas of the UK to keep up with the demand.

We couldn't be in every single place, but it had been my responsibility to pick venues and I hoped I'd chosen well.

Right now, we'd arrived at the estate where the Maharaja kept his elephants. Any guesses? You will know exactly where if you've been paying attention! Whitby was our last stop, although I was returning with a strong sense of trepidation. What would I find here? Did they still need our help, or was it too late for the Mystical Ladies? The Mulgrave Estate in Lythe, just outside Sandsend and Whitby, is a fascinating place ticking all the boxes, despite no spa this time. On the plus side, we had the privacy we craved and plenty of space for our surgeries, and this place had coastline, acres of woodland, and beautifully manicured gardens. I could get out in the fresh air if the weather was good rather than being stuck indoors. Incredibly it had been in the same family since 1743; the grand-sounding Marquis and Marchioness of Normanby lived there now. Hettie would have fitted into this time frame, as would Lavender Cottage, come to think of it. How amazing that generations of one family had lived there all this time; it made me think of the Manor House in Lancashire, the home of Alice Nutter, a similar background. So many other places had similar histories, housing the same families for centuries. I found that fascinating.

The week started quietly, strangely so. On Monday and Tuesday just a trickle of people, and no one I knew either, no sign of the Mystical Ladies. Maybe I'd made a big mistake coming back here and it was too late, after all, this place had been the first place to experience a lockdown when the Purge first took hold. What the hell had happened around here? How had my friends fared?

Maybe this lack of response had given me the answer I didn't want to hear; the witch hunters had eradicated the witches around here before we had a chance to save them. Or maybe, just maybe, some of them knew what was going on and fled, safely living elsewhere, far away from Whitby. I hoped and prayed this was the case.

It turned out we needn't have worried. It was just Whitby time, something like Sarah-time, a slow start. By the middle of the week, we had a rush on our hands; maybe they felt a little nervous to begin with but realised they didn't want to pass on the chance of being protected. I was still mortified that there didn't seem to be a sign of the Mystical Ladies, where were they? I felt guilty, we should have come here first, maybe we were too late. Then a thought: they wouldn't recognise me. I looked different, maybe they did too, they were a skilful lot, perhaps they too had transformed. Perhaps they were doing better than I thought and had managed to weather the storm. Then, a very recognisable woman came and sat down; no transformation here; she still had the hippie look, tie-dye T-shirt, long skirt, Doc Martens boots, and lank grey hair that looked like it needed a good wash and a brush. Susan from the Mystical Ladies! She'd been the group minute-taker, we all laughed as Lottie always offered the job to everyone, but Susan was the only one ever to rise to the challenge. At first, I had been a little intimidated by her, the one I wanted to impress the most, but I found out her bark far worse than her bite. We got along well; she was a wise witch so it surprised me she hadn't bothered to change her look. Perhaps it was because, like Cassie, she could hide in plain sight, one of those people who could live invisibly in society, and always the sensible one, she wouldn't have done anything remotely witchy to bring attention to herself. I was so happy she was alive and kicking and had come to me for help. She smiled politely at me, at first not recognising me until I said, "Susan, it's Ellie from Lavender Cottage."

She gave me a quizzical look then nodded. "I thought I knew the voice. What an amazing job you have done transforming yourself. I must admit I've never had to use one; no one seems to notice me. I live on the periphery of society. No one bothers me."

"You don't know how happy I am to see you," I said. "How has it been around here?"

She looked away. "Horrendous, Ellie, so bad since you left. You did the right thing, others have gone too. Still, at least you've come back to save us – better late than never, I suppose." I felt there was more than a hint of sarcasm; did she realise this area was the last of the roadshows? I'd had my reasons to stay away, hadn't I?

"It's been difficult for everyone, Susan, I've had my issues too, but I'm here now. I hope it's not too late?" She shook her head. "I understand. I always knew you had talent, but this spell. How on earth did you discover it. I'd never even heard of it before now."

"Susan, it's a long story that goes back to the past, maybe for another time?"

She nodded. "Of course, I know you're busy, let's get on with it then." She'd never been a great conversationalist.

Before she left, I wanted to know about Lottie and Bella but she shook her head.

"I'm sorry, my dear, Lottie disappeared in the early days, at the start of the Purge, and hasn't been seen since. Luke was bereft and sold the business soon after. From what I heard, he left the country and is now living in Berlin. There's a big music scene over there, apparently."

"Is anyone else running Breeze Records?"

"Yes," she said. "Some older guy. I think he might have been a known name once upon a time. I haven't been in myself, haven't met him."

"And Bella, from the Black Rose boutique?"

There was a pause before she said, "Bella was found dead in the river, it was put down as a suicide. They said she had money troubles – at least that was the official reason. But we all knew. It wasn't suicide. I'm afraid others suffered the same fate, although not always by the same methods, that would have raised too many suspicions."

I felt sick. "That's horrendous, poor Bella." Then I thought about my magical cleaner. "Cynthia?"

For the first time Susan smiled. "One of the lucky ones. She used her magic to get out just in time. I think she is somewhere in Norfolk, with family I believe."

"Hazel?" I asked. "And Emma?" Both active members of the Mystical Ladies.

Susan didn't spare me. "Hazel was what they call a jumper – the train from Whitby to Middlesbrough. Emma threw herself off the cliffs adjacent to the Abbey in Whitby."

I gasped. "Did someone push them?"

"What do you think? Not one of these women was in the least depressed or suicidal, make your own mind up."

This was all so painful and personal; I'd spent time with these wonderful women. Emma cast her spells to make us look our best, and with her biting honesty, Bella ensured we were beautifully dressed, while Hazel was old-school, never one to keep her opinions to herself, but would do anything to help the other witches. By this time, I was aware we'd been talking for too long; I had to get on, running out of time for others that needed my help. I'd never heard Susan so animated.

"Dark times," said Susan grimly. "For our kind, maybe the worst in history, none of us has fared well and of those living, many are currently in custody or being dragged through the legal system, but we've lost some beautiful souls." And that was her last word, she hurried away, promising to send in the next person waiting.

As the week went on, how brilliant it was to see the lucky few who'd made it, and as soon as they administered the spell, they would be safe at last. For now, they could rely on the invisibility spell to get out of there if they wanted to. They all had one thing in common, they were the quieter ones; some were loners who kept their magic to themselves, and they didn't say much. I hadn't met any of them at any Mystical Ladies meetings; now I realised they were the wiser witches who knew advertising wasn't good. They didn't do anything to raise suspicion and they kept their heads down, simply getting on with their lives. Their spells were as subtle as they were, with nothing to suggest from the outside that they had a magical bone in their bodies. They had survived because of this, unlike many of their livelier, more gobby sisters who'd thrown caution to the wind.

As the rest of the week went on, some were more forthcoming than others in recounting the horrendous stories of what had been happening around there since that fateful day when I fled the area. The Purge had started here, and sadly I was right, we were too late in some ways. I felt guilty that I had left them to it, but staying wouldn't have helped them. I'd never have found the spell if I'd been arrested or worse. I suppose there's an element of survivor's guilt; I was one of the lucky ones. Thankfully there were a few inventive witches like Cynthia who'd had the foresight to escape, using their magic to get out of town before they were discovered.

We were just about to shut up shop for good, with just one minute to go, when a latecomer squeezed in. Although I was exhausted, I wasn't mean enough to turn anyone away while the door was still open, even if we had little time with them, and from our experience, there was always one! Oh my days, I recognised this young lady, Victoria. I smiled as I remembered her argument with the sadly deceased Hazel, one of the bossy older witches who'd labelled Victoria a snowflake. I wondered if she knew Hazel's fate.

This argument had been totally out of character for Victoria, as she rarely joined us for meetings, and when she did, she was never one for rocking the boat, but she'd raised the subject of how ethical a love potion was, compared it to spiking a drink in a bar. Like Susan, she didn't recognise me until I put her right.

"Ahh, Ellie, you look so different."

"Still me underneath." I smiled. "How have you been, Victoria, how have you managed to stay under the radar?"

"I have quite a repertoire of spells, but I want to add your special one, it will make me feel so much safer." Her nerves were evident in her voice, so I showed her the spell as quickly as possible. I, too, wanted to get away. I knew I'd shed a few tears tonight for friends now lost. I'd drink a toast to them. There was no doubt this, for me, had been the hardest surgery by far. It was personal.

CHAPTER 21

Three months later
Well, doesn't time fly when you're having fun! I didn't follow Sandy and Alice back to the Cotswolds; I had other plans. No, not another job, heaven forbid, I was officially unemployed, and money wasn't an issue; I had more than a penny or two to rub together. I didn't want a job, and I didn't need one. The salary from Sandy's firm had been nice, a bonus, but not a necessity. Sandy and Alice had left shortly after the last surgery, leaving me to finalise everything, and I was more than happy to do that, especially because I had time on my hands. They couldn't wait to escape; they had to return to their day job on Monday and wanted to savour as much of the weekend as possible. As they'd been away so long, Sandy felt they both needed to meet with the staff on Monday to see what state the firm was in; they couldn't afford any more time off, so there were no holidays planned for either of them.

Before they left, Sandy, not usually one for demonstrative behaviour, had come over and given me the biggest hug, saying, "Ellie, never in my wildest dreams did I think we would work together. You have proved yourself over and over, I'm very proud of you."

I nodded and said, "It all seems like a dream. Have we done this? I keep asking myself."

Alice looked exhausted and more than a little downcast as she hugged me. "You've been amazing. I'll be glad to return to the day job, but I'll miss working with you every day, Ellie." A part of me knew this was not true; spending so much time together, we'd all started to get on each other's nerves. There was nowhere to escape from working in such close contact with each other.

It was good to be a free agent again, not having to answer to anyone. I was gasping to travel; somewhere hot and exotic would be nice, I could go anywhere in the world. I'd seen enough for now of the British Isles, and nice as it was, I wanted to go somewhere far-flung. Perhaps a cruise, I'd never been on one, but Jane McDonald made them look fun. A luxury one, of course, maybe in the Caribbean. I always saw them as something for oldies, but they had been catching on with my age group, and happy with my own company, I'd have no qualms going on my own. A fantastic way of seeing the world in luxurious surroundings – only the best for me, my darlings! Or should I relax and go and sit on a beach somewhere, the Seychelles or the Maldives, or what about a singles' adventure tour somewhere like Australia and New Zealand? Or a US trip and stopover to see Lizzie; she could show me round New York – but perhaps I should have an Indian adventure, dropping in on Sarah in Goa. God, I missed that girl. We'd been in touch, and I knew I was permitted to go, I just had some doubts. Was there a risk of getting drawn into the cult Sarah was part of?

For the time being I'd made the decision to stay at Lavender Cottage while I made some choices about the next chapter of my life. After all, I hadn't stepped foot in the place since I had fled, what seemed a lifetime away, not in the most brilliant circumstances, and there was no need to rush back to the Cotswolds for anything. To be honest, a break away from Sandy and Alice would be good.

The disbanded Mystical Ladies were secretly checking up on each other; the lucky ones left unscathed. They had wasted no time administering the protection spell around here and were already causing mayhem with the invisibility spell. Susan had also shown us all how to do a protection spell around our homes, something like Isabel's mother did over 400 years ago, and that went a long way towards making everyone that much safer. Our confidence grew, we were empowered and courageous, knowing the protection spell had spread around Great Britain like a virus. We had enough magical power up our lacy sleeves to face our enemies. If they dared show their faces around here, they would surely know the tide had turned and they were now on the back foot. A big part of me wanted to scream and shout at them, batter down their doors, and then disappear right in front of them, goad and spook them out, and make them fearful for a change. But that wasn't me. I was a peaceful person, revenge was a dish best served cold, but I'd do it in a way that was non-aggressive. I wasn't even fearful of Seb; he no longer scared me – what could he do? We were protected, and there was no harm in me staying for a while in my beautiful cottage, savouring the moment.

I'd known it would need some care and attention; I certainly hoped the vermin hadn't moved back in. The front garden was in a state, weeds had taken over and I was sure it'd be just the same at the back; it looked like an overgrown, tangled mess. If I stayed awhile, I'd maybe have a chance of finding out more about what had happened to Lottie, my newfound half-sister. Nobody had seen hide nor hair of her, but had she realised something was going on and had got out in time? Then there was my birth mother, Anna, where was she? Dare I wish that they were both together, safe and sound? I'd see if I could do any detective work, maybe someone around here would know. And what about Luke, he'd apparently left the country and was living in Berlin, but was he innocent, or had he been involved in the Purge – was he one of the bad guys too? A dreadful thought crossed my mind, had he done away with Lottie, and her body lay undiscovered somewhere in an unmarked grave? Was it possible that Seb, my old friend Will, the ghost tour guy, and Lottie's boyfriend Luke had been in on it together? I recalled the cryptic message on Seb's phone, something had been going on, had they indeed sorted Lottie out, especially as she was the queen bee around here? On the other hand, if Luke had been as innocent and bereft as he had reported to have been, should I feel guilty that I had ignored his desperate message? Perhaps I'd never know for sure whether he was innocent or complicit, I'd made the only decision I could at the time. I had no one to fear; even if I saw Seb right now, it wouldn't bother me; he couldn't touch me, and I had no fear of reprisals. But maybe I was just kidding myself, thinking of the last time I'd seen him in Hampstead when I'd been petrified. Or perhaps the thing I feared most was myself, scared that if I saw Seb, I'd fall hopelessly back in love with him.

I spent the next few months quietly, sorting out the garden which I'd chosen to do myself rather than get help as there was no heavy work involved, simply lots of pruning, tidying, and digging out of weeds. I was aiming for more doing and less thinking, and nurturing the garden was therapeutic and peaceful, other than the odd wasp or bee sting, stinging nettles, and rose thorns. I even thought about chickens and a beehive, but I really wasn't planning to stay so where had that thought come from? I still hadn't booked that luxurious break in the sun; I couldn't decide exactly what I wanted to do and every time I thought about booking something, I couldn't quite summon up the right enthusiasm. Something was keeping me here. The cottage felt at peace, like it had given a great sigh of relief, protecting its legacy. Hettie herself could rest in peace too. I'd released it from its heavy role of hiding centuries of old secrets; there was nothing left to find. It felt like it had its own personality, and we were perfect companions. It didn't ask anything of me except the odd vacuum, dust, and polish, and I, in turn, didn't ask a thing from the cottage apart from a place to shelter.

I'd soon got it back to its best, inside and out; it looked pretty much as it had when I'd left. I'd even taken to venturing out on a sunny day to the riverside when I'd finished my toil. I'd take a folding chair, my thermos coffee cup, and a good book, and that was it; I was content and serene until the sun started setting, the air felt a little chill. I'd then shiver and head back to the house. Facing my fears was cathartic. The house had just needed a good clean and thankfully there had been no sign of any furry friends moving in, and the alarm system had successfully kept unwanted human visitors out too. I'd become a bit of a domestic goddess, going onto all the websites and podcasts to check the latest product to get a good shine or any tricks of the trade to keep the house sparkly and, as I cleaned, I put on some familiar tunes, humming as I worked. Yes, I know I had the cleaning spell, but this was good exercise and kept me occupied. When I'd finished for the afternoon, I took a look around me, a satisfied smile on my face. It was good to be back.

CHAPTER 22

I hadn't had any weird or wonderful experiences since Lancashire, and my dream world was pretty calm. Not sure if I was happy or sad about that. Perhaps something was keeping me grounded. The vibe had changed around here, I could feel it in my bones. Without realising, I was settling back into calm, country life. I kept getting messages from Alice, When are you coming back? Missing you. I sent back a smiling emoji and Still sorting things out around here. She wanted to know if I'd booked my sunshine break yet and I told her I'd sorted a holiday out, nothing too adventurous. I'd settled on an all-inclusive break at an adults-only hotel on the Greek island of Santorini. Maybe I'd leave the cruise for next year.

Lavender Cottage was the only fly in the ointment; what the hell to do with it? I was meeting with the agents to get an idea of how much the cottage was worth, and they could also arrange viewings of the apartments I'd bought in Whitby. The dilemma was whether to sell everything, or rent out the apartments while leaving Lavender Cottage just for me. Decisions, decisions. I did like it around here, and some of the Mystical Ladies had started creeping back for informal meetings. We'd also contacted some other witches, the loners doing their own thing. Not originally in our group, but they now seemed to feel far more comfortable about mixing. Would I decide to stay permanently? I couldn't say, but what I could say was never say never.

That morning I'd woken in a glorious mood, lightheaded and euphoric as if anticipating something exciting. I'd had a refreshingly dreamless sleep, and although I'd got up with the lark at sunrise, I didn't feel tired. Instead, I felt full of nervous energy, a tightly strung elastic band. Using this energy fruitfully, I tidied the house, although it didn't need it, and then went into the garden to pick herbs for the kitchen. Back in the house I had a quick shower and changed into skinny jeans, a floaty blouse and comfy loafers, then sprinted out of the house to the shops, wanting to get there as soon as they opened for some fresh produce for breakfast and lunch. I loved the divine smell of freshly baked bread and croissants at the deli. Most days, I'd be a little more relaxed, going online to do my usual scan of news stories before I did anything, but this morning as I walked through town I had a satisfied smile on my face. I'd recently undone the transformation spell, as I no longer felt the need to hide behind a disguise. Now I was the same Ellie who had left Yorkshire all that time ago. I was no longer skulking in the shadows. Bring on our enemies, what will they do about us witches now?

There was a new owner at the deli; they were less friendly and not really into conversation, but that was fine. I picked up a basket, filling it with tasty goodies I fancied, then moved on to pick up a few treats from the soap shop, a couple of paperbacks from the bookshop, and some delicious chocolates to munch on this evening with a glass of wine – yes, I know it wasn't exactly good eating but who cares, grapes are part of my five-a-day, right? My final stop was at the newsagents for the papers – sometimes I tired of simply getting my news by scrolling.

Back at the cottage, I made a strong coffee with the deli's recommended coffee of the day, a rich dark blend, and added some creamy raw milk after rudely glugging some straight from the bottle and wiping away a milk moustache. Thickly buttering a flaky croissant and adding a big glob of lush strawberry jam, I added a few fresh strawberries, that's now two towards my five-a-day, and life felt good! Taking the steaming mug and laden plate into the garden, I sat at the wooden garden table, spreading out my selection of papers. I was drawn to a compelling headline; I wanted to see what was going on. I'd picked both the highbrow papers with an allegedly objective news story and the tabloids where sensationalism was what sold, as well as a couple of the locals.

The news in the past few months had been all about the previous prime minister. There had been some serious allegations of sleaze and, finally, he'd been given a vote of no confidence by his party and been forced to resign. So, for the third time in history, we had a female prime minister. Would she be more sympathetic towards us? I didn't expect too much from anyone in power, but my feelings of anticipation had been spot on – my sixth sense, or maybe my witch's intuition – had been trying to tell me things were about to change. But boy, I hadn't expected it so soon!

I couldn't believe the breaking news, and on one of the only days I hadn't scanned the news apps first thing. As I picked up paper after paper, I read different variations of the same headline; I'm so glad I bought one of each. They all seemed to be running the same story; it looked like we had changed the world in such a short time. We'd read about the first signs of change, the reduction of suicides; sadly, there would never be a time when some poor soul didn't feel that this was the only way out, this wouldn't change, but the suicide contagion was another matter. The mass murder – in the guise of suicide – and persecution of witches had subsided. But what I was reading now took my breath away. The new prime minister had already reviewed some of the current laws and was particularly horrified by the Witchcraft Laws. Declaring it not a law for the twenty-first century, she had immediately made it illegal to persecute anyone for their beliefs, whatever they were. She apologised to the witches and ordered those going through the legal system and those already languishing in the many prisons around the UK to be immediately released and pardoned. She also apologised on her government's behalf for those who had already lost their lives or been incarcerated. Could she be one of us? Wow, that was a turn-up for the books; she could wreak havoc. She looked familiar; had I seen her at one of the roadshows? I went onto my phone and did some research, googling her name. Yes, I was right. I knew it! Now she'd herself been protected; she had nothing to lose. Oh my days, things were going to change drastically around here.

She didn't give a solid reason for the change of heart in the official statement, but I knew. She was one of us, and protected against malicious death, and potentially could disappear if she wanted to. Imagine the chaos in Downing Street when she faced the protagonists, giving them a taste of their own medicine with a spell or two. As I read further, she was quoted as saying, "Blaming innocent women and men for all the ills happening in society takes us back to living in the dark ages. Persecution, scapegoating, and, in many cases, misogyny, must stop. I will stamp it out. I have never been presented with any hard evidence that they have done any harm. If anything, we should all embrace our magical side and work with those more gifted than others, not persecute and degrade them." Oh my God, she was giving the green light, we could practise magic without repercussion. The statement went on, "For the reasons I have stated, I am ordering the immediate release of everyone currently in custody accused or tried of witchcraft-related crimes. I will also pardon all witches in the UK from the past and present murdered for their beliefs." So that covered the Pendle witches, like Jennet and Isabel. Then there was Hettie, and all the beautiful Mystical Ladies I knew who had perished, centuries of sisters. One hundred per cent, she was one of us; I was even more convinced now. She gave a scathing review of the previous prime minister and his scaremongering. I laughed my most wicked laugh; what have you unleashed,

Hettie, with your spell, oh to see you once more and thank you, that would be my dearest wish.

The tide had already started changing, though. Even without the changes in the law, there was no point in persecuting witches who had regrouped and become stronger. I knew for a fact, havoc was being wrought with the invisibility spell; there was fun to be had dodging the police, or anyone else who wanted to arrest them. The law change was the icing on the cake, justification, and exoneration. The vigilantes were themselves now running to the hills, scared they'd be targeted. As we got stronger, it would be a case of if you can't beat them, join them. I suppose this was what was already happening. No point going after them or trying to incarcerate them – they were indestructible. Better to have them on side than off. As I read the papers, the stories were incredible, and the headlines made me laugh out loud: Witches Revolt, Prime Minister on the Dark Side, and Pointless Purge! Never in my wildest dreams did I believe this would ever happen, be so successful. I had expected a trickle of change, but this was a tsunami, and I knew the witches were safe in the hands of the prime minister while she was in power.

I suppose there followed a bit of an anticlimax; there were no big celebrations, parties, or anything else like that. Life just went back to normal, or as near to normal as it ever was. No massive wave of magic was being flaunted, most of us wanted to reflect and keep our magic to ourselves. Life for Sandy and Alice was back to normal, and they had their heads down with their work, plus of course they were still involved in the environmental aspects of their magic. Having met up with Lizzie, and spoken with Sarah, we'd kept in touch when we could. Alice never told me why she hadn't told me about them from the get-go, but she must have had her reasons. Anyway, that was now water under the bridge, and I'm certain they all had my best interests at heart, so I wasn't going to over-analyse. Hopefully, someday soon when Alice was less busy, we could get together for a good holiday, and reunite with Sarah if she was allowed out from the commune, or cult as we knew it was. Maybe Lizzie would come home, too. I was just thankful all my friends were unscathed and protected although Lizzie had said there were still challenging times ahead in the States, they were behind us in the protection game. Lizzie had even asked Sandy if she fancied branching out to the States, and she was considering it.

Over here the tide had turned; everyone wanted our spells, especially now they realised that we'd had a bad press, weren't evil or in the least bit scary. Everyone seemed to know someone who was a witch, and now they wanted our help. Now that we were popular again, there was a great interest in what we could do, particularly transformation and love spells as an alternative to dating sites or beauty treatments. Was this really what we wanted? I wasn't sure, but popularity was sure as hell a darn sight preferable to a purge.

CHAPTER 23

After my early start and taking in the momentous news, I felt pretty exhausted and, because I didn't have to answer to anyone other than myself, I decided on a nap. I'd found a great sleep app with mesmerising music to lull me to sleep when I was finding it particularly difficult, but today I had no such problem.

I was still in the cottage, unsure if I was awake or asleep. The place looked just the same, but I felt a presence, someone else was here. As I looked around there were subtle changes. I moved into the kitchen, and food I didn't remember buying was on the counter. I didn't buy this sort of thing, did I? Maybe I had but had forgotten. There was more as I moved through the cottage – what or who was I looking for? There was music on, "Night Porter", that spooky, dark tune from Japan, the 1980s band. In the bedroom, as I glanced in the mirror there was movement behind me: a black figure, a man. Who was he? What was he doing here? I felt fearful, my heart beating fast. There was a leather jacket hanging up on the door hook, it wasn't mine and laid out on the bed in the other room was an outfit – not something I'd wear. Increasingly panicked, I searched for the figure I'd glimpsed, but every time I saw movement it was on the periphery of my vision, when I turned there was no one there, only an oddly familiar scent of cologne. Then there was a loud bang, and I woke.

I shot out of bed, knocking over a glass on the bedside table. I laughed as I realised what had seemed so loud was simply a bird at the window. It had caught a reflection of itself and was trying to intimidate its rival. But there was no doubt my strange dream had unsettled me, and I did a quick check around. Nothing was out of place, it was just another dream, but the uneasiness I'd felt for most of my life was back like an old foe.

I wanted to get out of the house and decided to go and pick up some kippers from Fortune's. I didn't buy them often as they stunk the place out, but I fancied some today, and I'd noticed when I got home from my earlier trip that I was getting short of jam for my croissants, so I could pick up a new jar. I'd go to Botham's, the divine bakery over the other side of the bridge, and maybe get some cake to have with a cuppa later. I wasn't being that good with my food now; I craved carbs, and bread and cakes were my downfall. But my metabolism seemed to have changed and I found it quite hard to put on weight.

I found a space easily in the car park and ignored an opportunistic seagull waiting to see if I'd throw it some food. No chance. They'd become a bit of a pest around here, especially if you were a young child carrying ice cream or had an unwrapped fish and chip lunch. It had drizzled earlier, but now it felt nice and fresh. It was earlier than I thought, still early afternoon, although it already felt like I'd done a full day. I decided to walk over the swing bridge and head to Skinner Street before returning to Church Street and finally on to Henrietta Street to pick up the kippers. I didn't think it fair to waft the fishy smell in all the other shops.

Strange, Skinner Street was buzzing with people dressed in full-on Victoriana. The biannual Goth Festival was mixed with everything from goth, steampunk, and Victoriana but I didn't think there was another festival being held, maybe I hadn't got the memo! Whoever they were, they looked amazingly authentic, so gracious and glamorous. I grimaced, I knew from experience how uncomfortable it was to look this good; I wouldn't be joining them. The men were resplendent in their funereal-looking outfits: long coats with starched shirts, silk waistcoats, and black silk top hats. The women, their stunning dresses similar to those Sarah had made for us in shot silk – I shuddered as I noticed their nipped-in waists – the outfits finished off with tiny hats on their swept-up hairstyles. There were a lot of children although I'd have thought it was a school day. They were dressed more simply, the boys in sailor suits, the girls in lacy white dresses with straw hats adorned with ribbons, and several of the women were pushing babies in ornate prams.

What was unusual was the absence of cars and vans parked on this narrow road, often blocking the pavement, ignoring the double yellow lines, and putting on their hazard lights as if that made it better. Maybe traffic had been stopped for whatever was going on. As I made my way to Botham's, the day started to get weirder. The French restaurant was no longer there; instead, a thriving greengrocer was displaying fresh fruit and vegetables on the pavement in wooden pallets. I passed a chemist shop I hadn't noticed before, can't think how I'd missed the old-fashioned scales and shaped bottles with different coloured liquids in the window but then I'd not ventured to this side of the bridge since I got back here, and a lot can change in just a few years. With sadness, I wondered how many previous shop owners were forced to leave, businesses changing hands since the Purge. I thought about poor Bella, and her beautiful Black Rose boutique, now closed.

But something wasn't right, Botham's was split into two businesses, the bakery and a pub called the Hole in the Wall – I remembered reading that it had been an original business on Skinner Street; had it opened again, and why had the bakery downsized? I'd always thought business was booming. After all, who didn't need cake? The shop was opened in 1865 by the enterprising Elizabeth Botham, who'd somehow found time to have fourteen children. She'd started by selling her baked wares in the marketplace. Incredibly her great-grandchildren and even her great-great-grandchildren are still part of the business. Today, though, it looked like they'd sold part of the business to a brewery, and the smaller shop had a fresh coat of paint, and the signs looked different.

Mercifully, though, there was still a sizeable display of cakes and pastries in the window, Yorkshire curd tarts among them. I'd also pick up some more croissants and maybe a date and toffee cake, perfect with my cup of tea. Inside was a queue of mainly women, not as finely dressed as the women promenading up and down the road and apparently more stressed, I thought they looked as if they belonged below stairs in Downton Abbey, dressed in black dresses with white aprons, as were the women behind the counter. A grander-looking woman was supervising the younger servers, issuing instructions. She was dressed in a simple velvet black dress with a white collar. Whitby was certainly embracing its Victorian past with enthusiasm for the current event and there was so much history to draw on. I joined the queue; it was particularly busy here today. Finally, I got to the counter, and it was my turn. I'd had quite a long wait, each person had a long order, and by now, I knew exactly what I wanted. I'd also spotted a small granary loaf, I'd add that too. I smiled at the girl waiting to serve her next customer – me – I wondered if she was a descendant of the founder, but as I started to speak, she looked straight through me as if I was invisible and addressed the next customer.

"Excuse me," I said, "but I think I'm next in the queue." She didn't react in any way and with a sinking feeling, I turned to the lady now being served instead of me. "Hello, I think it's my turn." Nothing. She continued with her long order. I couldn't believe she was just being plain rude, but by now I had an inkling of what might be happening. Yes, I was invisible and no, it didn't look as if I was going to get any cake.

I smiled to myself; I'd go and test out my theory in another of the shops. Walking further up the road, I spotted a traditional butcher's shop; this looked new, too, I hadn't noticed it before. Not so busy here, would they see or hear me? I waited my turn and got to the counter, maybe some chicken to put in the freezer or treat myself to a sirloin steak. The same thing happened. Try as I might, I couldn't get their attention; they looked straight through me like I was a ghost.

I'd try just one more shop to clarify. There was an old-fashioned-looking cobbler, I'd always used the one on Baxtergate, and I hadn't noticed this one before, but that's not to say it hadn't always been here. The door had one of those bells that chimed, giving the shopkeeper the nod that someone had come in, important in this sort of shop where there was a lot going on behind the scenes. The cobbler was behind the counter, and other people were in the shop. They all looked around, hearing the chime, all looking like a ghost had just walked in. I walked back out again, not stopping to see their reaction as the bell chimed once more.

There was no need to test it out in any other shops. I knew without a doubt I'd gone back in time. There was no Victoriana festival as I'd first thought, I was back in Victorian times, and that's why everyone looked so authentic. As this was such a historic place, some of the shop fronts hadn't changed that much, which is why I hadn't realised straightaway, and there were so many festivals where people dressed up in weird and wonderful costumes. Strange, though, the transition to Victorian

Whitby was smooth, no fuss; I'd not had that familiar frizzle of electricity or anything similar. There seemed no rhyme or reason; every experience was different. This was more like the Hampstead Cemetery experience, although then I'd only slipped back ten years. I was sad I couldn't communicate now with the genuine Victorians, although I could hear and savour the atmosphere. I wasn't going to get freaked out, but rather consider it a gift. I had no idea how long I'd be here in this time, but I wanted to see as much as I possibly could.

At uni, I'd always found the Victorian era a little spine-chilling, children's toys especially, eerie china dolls with creepy, staring eyes looking as if they were watching you. Intricate doll's houses with the small Victorian-dressed figures and furniture, so faithfully reproduced, they even had rocking chairs and cots that moved – as if the tiny inhabitants came alive at night. You already know about the death pictures I found at the cottage, but the general use of sepia photography in this era, with its soft brown tint, made everything look surreal. Look, if you dare, at Victorian children celebrating Halloween; that will freak you out. But now I was actually back there, it looked and felt far more ordinary, in fact, not that different from the Goth Festival. Most women wore black, the colour taken on after Queen Victoria's husband, Albert, died. I wondered if Hammond's jewellers would be open; I knew they dated back to this era. I'd go and see as by now I was resigned to the fact I wasn't going to be getting my kippers any time soon.

As I walked, I could see shopping seemed to be very

much a pastime for those with disposable income, much as it is for us today. Nobody seemed in a hurry as they browsed the shops, emerging with parcels. I noted the sweet shop looked pretty much the same and was just disappointed I wouldn't be able to get my hands on such delights as toffee bonbons, pear drops, and chewing nuts.

With delight, I saw that Frank Meadow Sutcliffe, the famous photographer, had a studio on this street. I'd never asked, but now wondered if my old friend Will, the ghost tour guide, was a relative, sharing the name as he did. I recognised in the studio window how well he was able to capture the very essence of the people he photographed. Portraits of strait-laced, unsmiling Victorians in their finery, the men standing, women seated, in their Sunday best, and children in sailor suits or pristine white lacy dresses as seen walking about. A far cry from other everyday pictures of the working classes, of fishermen and their families, children playing, and women with wicker baskets full of shellfish. The pictures brought to life the chaotic conditions in the real Whitby where many were in desperate poverty. Even though these were contemporary, the sepia made them feel nostalgic, giving an eerie glow.

Further back, I could see a display of the death pictures, you couldn't avoid them. I didn't look too closely because once seen it was impossible to unsee those images, as I'd found to my cost with the ones I'd found at the cottage, which were still giving me nightmares. I shuddered and walked away quickly.

I reached Pier Road, on my way to the beach – I wanted to see how the Victorians holidayed. I knew wealthy families loved the seaside, as much for health as for leisure; the benefits of bathing in the sea were well-documented. As I walked past the building which, in my time, was the famous Magpie fish and chip shop, the evocative waft of deep-fried fish and chips mixed with vinegar was missing, instead there was what looked like an admiralty building. Also gone were the loud and brash arcades full of people feeding money into hungry machines, then feeding in more, trying to win it back, and there was no souvenir shop selling tacky souvenirs.

During my uni course we'd toured around here with one of our tutors, visiting Barry's Square, part of the area known as The Cragg in Victorian times. Around 120 fishing families had lived here. In my time few of the original houses had survived, but now there were numerous cottages, most not in a good state of repair. I knew there had been massive overcrowding, and unsanitary conditions with shared bathing and very few privies between families. There was a disgusting stench from the open sewers I could see running into the sea, and to my horror I saw a number of rats near children who were playing in ragged hand-me-downs. Unsurprising that there were so many childhood illnesses, the kids in front of me were continuously scratching heads and bodies. I knew nits, scurvy, and bedbugs were endemic as must have been rat bites. We often hark back to the past and think it's better than the present, but I was thankful to live in my time, purge or not.

I'd seen the Sutcliffe picture of Barry's Square, right where I was now. In the pictures, they looked happy enough, but I imagined that hid the truth. I could see chimneys covered in soot, with ladders for the residents to climb and hang up their washing, although it probably came back not much cleaner and stinking of smoke. The washing facilities were limited and shared. It seemed the women took turns to mind the children while others washed in tall tubs using mangles to squeeze water out of the clothing before it was hung out to dry.

Even in the slum-like conditions of chaos and squalor, it was apparent people were not work-shy. They didn't have time to feel sorry for themselves, there was too much to do, and they seemed a tight-knit community, all helping each other. The noise level was appalling – babies screaming, children squealing, and men and women shouting at each other above the din. There seemed to be no privacy or peace, but the shouting wasn't aggressive, just a way of being heard. The bearded fishermen, dressed in long leather boots, navy blue, roughly knitted jumpers, and well-worn hats, seemed to have finished for the day and were enjoying a beer or two while the women, in long, shapeless, dirty dresses with once-white pinafores, shawls and headscarves, were still fully occupied. Looking at the children, I knew many of them wouldn't make it to their fifth birthday. I was finding the stench hard to bear and needed to move on before I retched, and I wondered how the wealthy could pass by these squalid living conditions without some guilt.

Heading towards the Pier and Tates Hill Beach I saw beachgoers, men, women, and children, were wearing much lighter clothes in both colour and weight, much less formal than those promenading, but still modest for a seaside break by our standards; they certainly didn't strip off to sunbathe. Many sat on the beach in stripy deckchairs with their family and friends but kept their day clothes on; they must have been sweltering. They protected their skin against the sun with umbrellas; it wasn't fashionable to be tanned, pale was the order of the day. Good job it was a fine day, they would have been useless in the rain. Looking around me, gone were the brightly coloured beach huts, obviously a more recent invention. Instead, there was a raft of what I can only describe as sheds on wheels, being pulled to the water's edge by horses. I smiled at their modesty as the exquisitely dressed woman would enter the hut, climbing down into the water on the other side still modestly dressed but in a bathing suit, more like a dress with matching trousers. There were certainly no glamorous swimming costumes or thong-bottomed bikinis, leaving nothing to the imagination. The men were slightly less modest, not always changing in these bathing huts, but they still wore a one-piece suit covering their chest and down to the knees. There wasn't a speedo or sports short in sight, or, as often seen on stag dos, a mankini. These were the braver souls, though, many holidaymakers were happier sitting on the beach than going into the cold North Sea; even on a sunny day, the water was freezing. These children were doing pretty similar things to children today. They had wooden buckets and spades and just seemed to splash about in the sea, dodging the waves, not worrying if they got wet; maybe they had spare clothes to change into. There were donkey rides, little ones were laughing as they were taken up and down the coast, their older siblings keeping an eye on them, and the grins on their faces said it all. Other children were sitting around a traditional Punch and Judy show.

I was struck by how pale the children were and knew that even those from the wealthiest families could succumb to some of the many diseases, there were no vaccines in those days. Nevertheless, they were infinitely healthier than their counterparts I'd seen at The Cragg. For a moment, I thought about these children and what they would have given to have this seemingly carefree childhood; most of them were already working. Such different sides of the coin.

The pier and the East Pier Lighthouse looked the same, and it felt like the fashionistas of the time were keeping up with their neighbours and showing off to their peers; they all looked fabulous. I could stay and watch these wonderful creatures forever, and although they wore their outfits effortlessly, I knew from experience they were anything but comfortable. Even the elderly were out in force, dressed in long black dresses with fancy headgear, the more infirm pushed by their nurses in bath chairs, taking in the sea breeze as the doctor had ordered. I'd never seen the pier so busy. On this glorious sunny day, it was buzzing.

As I walked further down the road, I passed a pub that looked particularly crowded, with many of the patrons, mostly men, raucously the worse for wear. It was a mixed crowd, fisherman and other trades and there was a strong aroma of stale beer, fish, and sweat. One elderly man, who looked like he was still working, wiped foam off his long beard and then lit his pipe with satisfaction as he savoured that first inhale. A roughly dressed woman passed by and started hustling a group of men; she was obviously a local character. She went up to one of them, and he shouted, "Go home to your bairns Maggie!"

She smiled, her remaining teeth black. "Come on, love, you know you want it, you've never said no before."

He shook his head amiably. "Not today."

"You don't know what you're missing," she said. She knew these punters wouldn't give her a penny for her services and now she did no more than lift her skirts, turn round and give them what today we'd call a moonie, before shuffling off.

There was still a swing bridge over to the other side of town, but it wasn't as ornate as the one I was familiar with. I had reached Church Street, and instead of battling the cars over the bridge, it was now horses and carriages. The cobbled streets looked very similar but with no road signs, telephone boxes or double yellow lines. Like Skinner Street, this looked not dissimilar to the buildings I knew because many of the cottages and shops predated Victorian time. What was remarkably different were the living conditions in the many Yards, Sanders Yard, Kiln Yard, and Argument Yard among them. In my time, these were pretty places with old cottages, many used as holiday homes, but now they were crammed with run-down housing like those at The Cragg and known locally as "ghauts". The yards were shortcuts to other streets but doubled up as living areas that were both squalid and unsanitary so strolling past the quaint and busy shops on Church Street, you couldn't avoid sights, sounds, and smells from a very different life just yards away.

Sanders Yard, one of my favourite places, no longer looked inviting; the cafe, with its outside seating and glorious abundance of potted flowers, had gone. Instead, numerous tiny dwellings were crammed together, housing many who had migrated from the country to find work. No indoor bathrooms for these residents, and you could smell the toilet facilities, or lack of them. It struck me that they didn't seem to be miserable. Maybe that was a first-world, modern problem; we had too much now and didn't realise how lucky we were. Many women were chatting amiably over the washing and while they bathed their children – up to half a dozen sharing the same greying bathwater. Maybe they were happy with their lot because they knew no different. I was happy to move on; I hoped this was an isolated pocket of poverty; the quaint historic Yards full of their old-fashioned charm were not so attractive in these times, crammed with human misery.

CHAPTER 24

Although I'd effortlessly slipped back in time to Victorian Whitby, I was aware I hadn't felt the usual electrical current when it happened, and I was starting to feel uncomfortable. Although I told myself that didn't always happen, I wasn't usually in the past for so long. My experiences in the main had been short and sweet. But I wasn't going to panic, I didn't think I could get stuck. Could that even happen? Unfortunately, I didn't know anyone with similar experiences to mine so there was no one with whom I could swap notes. The truth was, I was starting to get tired and a little bored. I'd got the gist of the times, and it was a relief that things had improved since then.

Maybe I'd transition back as seamlessly as I'd arrived. I knew everything would be OK if I saw my car in the harbour car park, familiar sights and sounds would surround me. Perhaps if I willed it strongly enough, it would happen. I stopped, closed my eyes, and concentrated, determined to get a handle on my alarmingly erratic time travelling, but then, as I neared the harbour, my heart sank. There was no car park, just a well-used slipway with fishing boats moored up. I realised I longed to smell diesel smells from modern boats, despite the indisputable pollution. I'd even welcome seagulls raiding bins for discarded fish and chips and equally rowdy hen and stag parties outside the pubs further down Church Street.

I could see a couple of ships boarding, and one looked uncomfortably familiar – it bore the name Whitby Whaling Company. I'd last seen it in Boston. No, it couldn't be. Unbelievably, it seemed I was witnessing the start of the journey of the Whitby whaling witches, the Whitby Wailers, as my mother called them. Well, this was even weirder than usual, seeing the women in better condition this side of the journey, fresher, less unkempt, and more aggressive, before their exhausting journey across the Atlantic. Now, shackled together, they were hurried onto the ship, the last passengers to board.

One of the younger women was fighting back, kicking and then spitting in the face of the man restraining her. He gave her a sharp slap on the face and shoved her hard against the other women, where she received scant sympathy, they merely sneered as she was dragged to her feet and pushed brutally onwards. I shivered as I remembered meeting their future descendants still living around the Boston area – Em Corey and her pals Beatty and Blanche, bad witches with evil intentions. Sandy knew them of old, and she was relieved I was protected by the spell. She was convinced that otherwise my "accidents" would have proved fatal. When I first told her about my encounter, and she'd got over the shock, she was a bit vague, telling me they were on a poisonous mission, making it plain that they weren't in any way after my help. They already knew of my connection to Sandy and how the protection spell would present a disastrous stumbling block to their plans. Maybe Sandy felt I couldn't cope with the whole horrifying story in one go - ever the protective mother - but what she went on to tell me about these women was beyond terrifying.

I sort of knew she was hiding something, but she finally crumbled, admitting that the toxic witches were developing the ultimate serum for women prepared to pay an exorbitant amount to slow signs of ageing. When I'd questioned her further, she'd been snappy. "Must I spell it out? This serum can only be produced from the blood of young witches. Those who are used are never the same afterwards. Many have even died." I'd answered, "Why didn't I know this?" She'd shocked me rigid, but I immediately grasped the implications of how the spell we were so busy teaching would scupper their plans. I'd been in far more danger than I imagined. With this in mind, I kept well away from the ship and the forebears of the women I'd already met and thwarted – bad blood through and through.

One of the men herding the women handed a wad of money to a crew member. I couldn't believe the whaling ships habitually took deported prisoners. But it looked like the captain was taking a backhander to relieve Whitby of a somewhat troublesome problem. I was shaken and scared, would these women be able to see me, could they curse me? I hurried away swiftly, I didn't want to take any chances, past or present. I felt I'd overstayed my welcome in Victorian Whitby. If only I knew the return-to-my-own-time formula. I was sure there was one, but it remained frustratingly out of my grasp. What if I truly was stranded this time? I couldn't communicate with anyone, so where could I turn for help? Where to go next? I needed to distract my mind from my rumbling stomach. I wracked my brain, thinking what I'd learnt in my history degree and remembered being intrigued by the Whitby Union Workhouse, situated in an area called The Ropery. It was a place of last resort, redolent of stigma and shame, but at least it gave me a focus while I waited to be hurled back to the twenty-first century.

As I arrived in front of the vast 1794 Georgian building it was as sinister and intimidating as I'd expected, more prison-like than a refuge. How would I feel if I was arriving here with nothing? Could I put myself in the shoes of those desperate souls? Were the inmates cruelly treated or was there kindness for the poor and infirm behind these four walls? I knew Charlie Chaplin had spent some of his childhood in a workhouse, as had William Golding, the Lord of the Flies author. I'd always been fascinated that creativity could flourish in such circumstances. I walked through the gates and down the long pathway. They may have tried to make it as appealing as possible with the strong aroma of roses growing profusely in the borders, but what I did notice intertwined with the roses, as if intentionally planted, was deadly nightshade, perhaps better known as belladonna. My gardener at Lavender

Cottage had pointed out the fatally poisonous plant with bilberry-like berries and he'd taken no time to rid the garden of any trace of it. How odd it should be growing here as if nurtured.

I suspected there was a pauper's entrance around the back of the building, to which new inmates or patients would be directed instead of the rather grand entrance welcoming visitors and officials. I knew from the 1881 census that behind the imposing wooden door in front of me were 121 patients and a few staff and I couldn't help but reflect on the lives of blacksmiths, seamstresses, postmen or quarrymen who found they had no other choice than to check in to this hotel of last resort. There were also the many unmarried mothers who ended up here, shunned by society, as were the widows with no income. But the saddest records of all were of orphans whose mothers died in childbirth, and unwanted children, abandoned when families could no longer afford to feed and clothe them, one too many in an already large family.

At the time of the 1881 census, it was run by a Master and Matron who had two daughters. They lived in staff quarters in the workhouse and, I presumed, fared better than their charges. The other staff were two nurses – I imagined they worked shifts, one on and one off – a teacher and a porter. I wondered if they were still here, it'd help if I knew the date. The imposing front door was open a little, and I slipped in, finding myself in an impressive entrance hall with flooring similar to the tiles at Wood Barn. There was a strong aroma of beeswax mixed with the waft of carbolic soap, and they'd tried to make the space appealing with mahogany furniture and exotic jardinieres with luscious aspidistras and huge ferns. An imposing stag's head on the wall stared at me with his glassy eyes. If you'd walked through the doorway into this entrance hall, maybe you'd think it wasn't so bad. But I was all too well aware this was for show and didn't bear much resemblance to the areas the paupers would see.

The first door I came to opened into what appeared to be the living accommodation of the Master and Matron. It was a typically Victorian room with dark furniture, a piano in the corner, and a vast rug protecting the parquet flooring. The chaise longue and buttoned plush velvet sofas looked surprisingly opulent and would have been at home in a posh hotel. They'd certainly made themselves comfortable here with a number of botanical pictures on the walls and a collection of taxidermy – creepy dead animals – the one that caught my eye was a group of tiny rabbits having a tea party. An oversized clock ticked loudly on the mantelpiece, and there was a bookcase crammed with books on the opposite wall.

I left this room and tried one of the other doors which led into an office. Like the living accommodation, it was spick and span. A large mahogany desk and leather-backed chair made for a formal, professional setting. I took a deep breath – there was a strong smell in here of tobacco, a pipe smoker, maybe. Rows of bookshelves held important-looking files and there was a neat pile of papers on the table. I couldn't resist – the bills were mainly for everyday stuff – payment for provisions, wages, that sort of thing, and then further down the pile, an invoice from a pharmacy. A massive order for laudanum, arsenic, and morphine. I knew in these times such items could be bought over the counter, but who the heck was using such a large quantity of drugs, and was it for personal use or to subdue the patients. The next sheaf of paper was receipts, and even more shocking, they were for huge barrels from a local factory and then, to my horror, details of receipt of various body parts from London hospitals which I could only assume were sent from the workhouse for medical research. Then I froze as the door handle turned. I wasn't going to take any chances and moved swiftly behind the velvet, aubergine-coloured curtains. Heavy footsteps followed by lighter ones, and I caught snippets of conversation – "the doctor was on his rounds, so there would be bodies to move tonight ... Albert, the porter, was on standby ... after dusk at the graveyard ..." The voices moved away as they left the room and, mercifully, they hadn't spotted the untidy pile of paperwork I'd left on the desk. Something was obviously happening tonight, and I had a dreadful feeling it might link to the receipts I'd been looking at. I came out from my hiding place, tidied up the paperwork, and left.

As I moved away from the quiet, pristine hallway, comfort receded and my surroundings became more as I'd anticipated with narrow, dark, and dank corridors, the noise increasing with every step, a constant din coming from all directions. I investigated a few rooms, initially apprehensive that I might be seen, but it became obvious I was invisible. It felt prison-like, although nobody appeared to be locked in, but it certainly hadn't been built for comfort, and decor was non-existent. In every room, productive activity was taking place, and different aromas met my nose, not all of them pleasant, an amalgam of disinfectant, cabbage, and sewage. It wasn't an environment that encouraged people to stay long, although some of the inmates I'd read about had become institutionalised and never left.

Sleeping was in communal dormitories, row upon row of metal beds, all neatly made up. Each bed had a chamber pot, so it looked like it was at full capacity, and there were toilet cubicles in one corner of the rooms, concealed behind a screen. The washing facilities were basic, although I suspected the inmates were expected to keep as clean as possible. In most workhouses, they had a weekly bath, which again was shared with others, but there was no disguising the smell of too many people crammed into too small a space.

Men and women were housed in different parts of the building and exercised separately, and there was a hospital wing with patients overseen by a lone nurse. I knew only two nurses were employed; they must have had their work cut out. I came across a functional laundry, full of women doing various jobs. It was damp and steamy with the vile aroma of soiled clothing, bed linen, and dirty cotton squares obviously used as babies nappies, although the workers seemed unaffected by the smell. I stayed to watch for a while; two middle-aged inmates were barking orders, allowing no slacking, and most workers looked exhausted, ready to drop. Two extremely old ladies were sitting in a corner knitting, oblivious to what was going on around them, their needles clacking, adding to the noise. The vilest job by far in this room was separating the soiled items for washing, it was the younger women doing this job, and I noticed an increasing pile of bloodied rags, makeshift sanitary towels to be washed for reuse – how gross!

I needed to get out of this room, the vile stench was making me queasy. I found my way outside into the fresh air, I took a few breaths and looked around. It was a hive of activity, everyone was working hard, the men doing manual work, chopping wood for fuel or breaking stone to be sold for road mending, while young boys were being taught these skills, so they'd leave with a trade. The men wore loose shirts, trousers, and waistcoats, and everyone wore heavy black boots meant to withstand hard work and last. One of the most hated jobs was oakum picking, where old ropes were unwoven, and the fibres were separated to be sold back and mixed with tar to make a waterproof sealant. The older residents were tending the kitchen gardens, weeding and digging, and others were pulling out vegetables, including large cabbages and potatoes, ready for the kitchen. Everyone mobile was put to work. The workhouse had profitable links to the outside world, although I was prepared to bet the inmates earned little for their hard work other than bed and board. It was almost slave labour.

Timekeeping was regimented, everyone downing tools when a bell rang, and they headed to the communal dining rooms, women and children still separated from the men. I followed the women, who wore long shift dresses with white aprons, a mobcap, and some with a woollen shawl;

maybe these were what the old women were knitting in the laundry. Hands had to be washed first, with a staff member inspecting them before people were allowed to take a place at one of the lines of tables and benches. Once everyone was seated, grace was said. There were many similarities to the canteen at my boarding school, the same level of regimentation, and aggressive or antisocial behaviour punished with extra chores and little food for the day.

It wasn't a surprise that the food being dished out didn't look appetising. Boiled cabbage with meat scraps added, it looked watery, like some sort of broth. Not much nutritional substance but they were eating it gratefully. Plates were wiped clean with rough-looking crusty bread, not a morsel left in the bowl. Once they'd finished, they went up to collect what looked like tapioca – frog spawn, we called it at school – accompanied by a choice of beer or weak tea. Water wasn't an option unless it had been boiled.

The workhouse had its own chapel and a mortuary; this in particular was well-used, but it was one area I really didn't want to see for myself. I'd read the stats and listened to the lectures, I knew of the high child mortality rates here, and wasn't sure I could bear seeing a child's dead body. But how incredible it was, to see all of this first-hand, like an immersive experience, the sounds and smells of history. It was clear that here no one had time to feel sorry for themselves, and I was reminded of the old saying, *Busy hands and idle minds have knitted many a sweater. Busy minds and idle hands have knitted many a brow.* I wondered whether people were better off here in the workhouse or in the slums hidden in the lanes just down the road. The jury was out on that one.

Children were housed in a nursery where the noise was indescribable, a cacophony of infants crying for attention from their wicker baskets on wheels. A nursery nurse was taking a surreptitious glug from one of the baby's bottles, and I wondered if she'd smuggled some alcohol in. She seemed increasingly inebriated as she moved around the room, picking up a crying baby, shoving a bottle of milk in its mouth, and then doing the same with the next one. There was no love for these poor little mites. I'm not the most maternal, but this made my heart weep. I wanted to pick up and cuddle each of them.

I made my way down a corridor that led to the classrooms. I knew education and religious instruction were important to keep children on the straight and narrow and prevent them from following in their parents' footsteps. Boys learnt practical skills, suiting them to a trade or farming. The girls were taught domestic skills with a view to nursing or entering service. Many would want to get away from the area once they left here, moving elsewhere so the stigma of being in the workhouse didn't follow them.

I sat at the back of the boy's class, listening to the teacher running through the times tables; they learnt them by rote, just as I had done at boarding school. The boys were surprisingly quiet and well-behaved, only speaking when the teacher asked them something. Perhaps they knew that misbehaving meant a punishment far more severe than the crime. Each child had a small chalkboard and chalk on their wooden desks, and when work on times tables was done, the teacher asked them to copy from the blackboard. "This will be your homework. Take your boards with you and learn these words ready for tomorrow for your spelling test." The schoolmistress looked quite kindly, something like my beloved Miss Honey, Roald Dahl's character in Matilda, although I did notice she had a cane on the table. She was presumably employed by the workhouse, as teaching was one of the few jobs an inmate couldn't do.

I kept my place at the back as the lesson finished and, as they filed out of the room, each boy helped themselves to a small bottle of milk which looked as curdled as those I remembered from my own school days. As the boys left, the girls were already lined up, they all looked similar, with short hair to keep nits at bay and save time when washing. They all wore a version of the heavy black boots, many of them a poor fit and passed on from those who'd outgrown them, left the workhouse, or died. When the girls' session ended, the schoolmistress tidied up her books and wiped the blackboard with a heavy sigh. She was ready to go home for the day, and she wasn't the only one! I sighed, too, and she turned, startled, looking straight at me. "Who are you?"

CHAPTER 25

I'd not been too careful as I'd made my way around the workhouse convinced no one could see or hear me, but I wasn't expecting this. This woman was different, and I didn't want to freak her out.

"I'm Ellie. What's your name?"

She looked me up and down. "Do I know you?" I could see her puzzlement at what I was wearing, I was still in my twenty-first-century garb.

"I don't think so, but please don't look so worried, I'm not exactly a ghost."

"Not exactly?" She seemed even more alarmed.

"Well, I was in Whitby, minding my own business," I explained, "when I was taken back in time. I've been here longer than usual, and I feel there might be a message here for me."

She relaxed then and smiled. "Ah, I think you should meet my mother, she might be able to help."

I smiled back with relief. Thank goodness, someone who could see me, knew what I was, and could offer help. "What's your name?" I asked again.

"Florence, Flo to my friends, Miss to the children. But we have to leave right now, they'll be coming to clean soon, and if I'm seen talking to myself, they'll lock me away with the others!"

"The others?" I hadn't seen evidence of anyone being locked up, even in the infirmary. I opened my mouth on a question, but she gave me a teacher's stare.

"Come, follow me, but don't say anything until we arrive. I have something to show you." As I followed her down the dark and dingy corridors, I wondered why such a beautiful young woman would choose to spend her days working in this environment; surely she'd be far better off teaching in a private school or becoming a governess and living in a grand house.

As she breezed through the corridors, everyone smiled when they saw her, inmates and staff alike, and when we entered the infirmary, it was apparent she'd been here many times before and seemed to know every patient.

"I visit them after I finish teaching," she explained. "I make sure they're being cared for. They tend to get forgotten, not prioritised, as they can't work." I nodded, looking around me. Most of the patients looked to be in a sorry state. "We haven't got long," she murmured. "Follow me. The doctor will have finished his daily rounds by now." She led me swiftly through the infirmary and then out through another door into a narrow corridor which was in a worse state than anything I'd seen so far. I heard a low moan from one of the rooms.

"Why aren't they in the main infirmary?" I asked.

"This is unofficially known as the asylum, where they bring particularly troublesome inmates. Sadly, there is a very quick turnover in this section."

"What does that mean?" She didn't answer, just gave me a grim look. I tried another question. "Why on earth do you work here? Surely you could have an easier life as a governess or regular schoolteacher?"

"I must be here to support my mother, who's incarcerated. I'm not supposed to be in this part of the building, but I stole a key." As she pulled it from an overall pocket, she confirmed my suspicions that patients were regularly dosed with highly addictive laudanum, a solution of opium powder in alcohol. I'd seen the invoice earlier.

"What about arsenic and deadly nightshade?" I said.

She nodded. "Those too. Life here can be so unbearable. But I just want to care for my mother."

I had my reservations; I didn't think that being taken to see a madwoman would help me. Florence read my expression. "My mother isn't mad, you know, just troublesome. They don't know what to do with her, so they lock her up. Of course, they don't know she's my mother. I came here to teach and be near her, but I'd be tarred with the same brush if anyone discovered the connection. In fact, I only found out that she was my mother recently. I lived with my grandmother, but it was only on her deathbed that she told me the truth." She sighed. "But it is too late now."

Wow, this sounded uncannily like my own life story. "What was the truth?" I asked.

"No time for questions. Rose, my mother will be able to tell you more, but just as important is that you have a means of getting away from this godforsaken place. There may be others who will be able to see you, and not all sensitives mean well." I nodded, and she continued, "This workhouse was originally built by a wealthy landowner with a finger in some murky pies and an ulterior motive. He bribed the architect to include a secret underground tunnel to bypass the 199 steps and exit in the St Mary's churchyard. Only a trusted few know about the passage." She handed me a scrap of paper. "Follow these directions when you're ready, but be cautious, the tunnel is in regular use – for highly dubious purposes." She handed me the key to Rose's room. "Once you're inside, lock the door behind you. If the doctor turns up, hide. I'll go back to the infirmary and try to stall him."

She turned back the way we'd come and I unlocked the door and entered. I wasn't prepared for the filth and squalor that greeted me. How awful for Florence to have to see her mother in this condition. There were no toilet facilities in the room, so she was lying in her own filth. Her hair, once fair, was peppered with grey and long and unkempt, as were her filthy fingernails, and her skin was sallow as if she hadn't seen the sun for a long time. How long had she been here? She seemed almost inhuman. Why was she not looked after like the others? What had she done to be incarcerated like this, and why didn't Florence get her the care she needed? Maybe she couldn't.

"Hello, Rose," I said softly.

She stared at me, a moment of clarity. "Ellie, is it you?"

She knew my name, and then I saw the telltale heart-shaped mole, identical to mine. Oh my God, another past life? I knew I didn't have long, I had to compose myself.

"Rose, can you tell me why you're locked away like this?"

"Hysteria, I'm in here for hysteria, but my only crime is being a healer. Flo can't get me out, but she does what she can. She would have the same treatment if they discovered her visits. She comes and sits with me before the doctor comes to sedate me. Be careful. He will be here soon. You must lock the door, so he doesn't suspect anything. He's the only one to come in here, plus one of the trusted nurses and my darling daughter."

"Do they not clean you, change your bedding?" I asked.

She shook her head. "As you see, not often. The nurse occasionally does it, but that's not her job." She gave a wry smile. "But the doctor never forgets to sedate. That's as regular as clockwork. He's building up the dose now. I can tell, my mind is less clear after each dose. I keep forgetting things, although I try hard to hold on. I'm sure the next dose will be the lethal one."

"Why would they want to kill you?"

"Oh, Ellie, look at me properly, past the dirt and grime. You must know Flo and I are the only people to see you." She nodded her head downward at the mole on her chest.

"You're witches," I said. "But that's not illegal now, right?"

She cackled, gaining energy from somewhere deep inside. "Legal or illegal, we'll always be persecuted. There are other witches here too. I was doing no harm, only healing. But right now, I'd like to put a curse on them all." Despite the harsh words, she had a serene smile, she knew her days were numbered, and there was nothing she could do. "All I will say is be careful in your own time, trust your instincts and look out for the wolf in sheep's clothing." Where had I heard this before? Holy fuck, Hettie had issued the same warning about Seb.

I was so sorry I couldn't help this poor soul, but I knew in my own time I was protected. I didn't need the warning. She continued, on a roll now, "Once I'm dispatched, they'll move in another poor soul before my bed is cold, and they'll sell my body for cash – the hospitals are crying out for cadavers to dissect. The trade in bodies from the workhouse to the big teaching hospitals, especially in London, is rife."

I nodded slowly; this only confirmed the invoice I'd seen in the office. Men, women, and children were dehumanised for a gruesome and lucrative trade. I yearned to get back to my own, more civilised times. I was feeling increasingly anxious, I hadn't stayed so long on any of my previous time slips, and was horrified by the Victorian poor. I felt for these poor souls hopelessly trapped with no way out. Most of the inmates were likely to spend the rest of their lives institutionalised. The only hope was that the children, at least, were getting an education. Maybe some of them could pull themselves out of the quagmire of poverty.

Would I ever return to my own time? Once again, I thought, was I stuck here? That was not a thought I wanted to entertain. Living in a time where few people could see or hear me would be purgatory. Surely now I'd seen Rose and sort of got the message from the past, I'd go back. I wish I knew how to control my travelling. There was no more time for questions as I heard heavy footsteps outside the door, the key turned in the lock, and the doctor was about to enter the room.

Even though it was unlikely the doctor would be able to see me, I wasn't taking any chances. I threw myself under the bed, dragging a heavily stained blanket with me and tried not to gag at the smell of the material over my face. Above me, Rose knew what was coming and lay back down on the bed.

The doctor strode in; he meant business today and was in a rush. "So, Rose, have you been behaving yourself?" Did I recognise that mellow voice, and from where? Rose didn't answer until he repeated his question and then she mumbled, "Yes."

"Good, good, it's time for your medication. You'll feel you're gently slipping into sleep, all your problems solved." Did he really say that? Was she going to die here tonight by lethal injection, with me as a silent, helpless witness?

I had to do something and started to creep out from under the bed. Could I knock the needle from his hand? But what good would that do? He'd only come back and finish the job. Rose wasn't going anywhere. There was no way she'd be able to escape in her state, even if I opened the door right now, and anyway, where could she go? They'd cart her off to one of the formal asylums, never to be seen again, and I wasn't even sure she'd survive the journey. I heard him fumbling around, unsure what he was doing. Then I nearly jumped out of my skin as she pounced on him like a vicious alley cat, shrieking,

"Don't you touch me, you bastard. You'll pay. I swear you will, I'll curse you for eternity." He picked himself up and roughly pushed her back on the bed, struggling to get a straitjacket on her, but she was twisting and bucking so much he could only manage to shackle her arms and legs to the metal bed-posts. "Damn you, you bitch, you will pay for this." He slapped her hard across the face and went to get the needle. "You'll be packed off to London for the medical students to have fun with in the name of medical science, not that I think for one minute they'll learn anything worthwhile from your scrawny corpse – but by then, you'll be rotting in hell."

I couldn't help myself, I had to do something, and I rolled out from under the bed and sprang to my feet, screaming at the top of my lungs, "No, no, no. What the fuck are you doing to this poor woman?" He turned, the needle clattering to the ground – he'd heard me! With horror, I looked deep into his wicked eyes and recognised them. How could I not? They were ingrained in my soul, all of my souls: Seb's eyes. I had to get away.

CHAPTER 26

I scrambled out of the room as quickly as possible, locked the door and pocketed the key. It would buy me a little time, but only until someone realised the doctor and Rose were locked in together. I had to escape from Seb's past life and put the asylum, the workhouse, and the horror behind me. I shivered; I'd only just avoided witnessing a lethal injection being administered. I was certain Rose would be dead by now, and an uneasy thought wormed its way in. Would the protection spell protect me in this time? I couldn't know for sure and didn't plan to stick around long enough to find out. There was nothing I could do to save Rose; no way I could change the past. I could only learn from it. But I couldn't avoid the fact that she was yet another victim of my soulmate Seb's past. So sad, and yet again, our paths crossing in time. Was this going to keep happening, an endless repeating loop through time? I'd had the sense to flee from him in my era, but right now,

I was too close to him for comfort. I knew he couldn't touch me in my time, but was I safe here? I couldn't be sure. I needed to get away and damn quick.

I headed swiftly to the back of the building. Florence had given me directions to the tunnel created at the same time as the workhouse and used for the smuggling of contraband and to transport bodies out of the workhouse away from prying eyes. The tunnel entrance was off a cellar area accessed via a steep, narrow stairway. The cellar was deathly quiet, dirty, and neglected, with sour-smelling mattresses lying around and bundles of stained sheets amongst which, incongruously, were abandoned opened boxes of what looked like alcohol and tobacco.

It took me a little time to find the trapdoor and the smell hit me as I opened it. The lack of fresh air and the stench made me want to retch. As my eyes adjusted, I could see lit hurricane lanterns attached to the wall at regular intervals, getting smaller and dimmer towards the end of the tunnel. Someone had been here recently, and perhaps was still here, I'd have to hope they couldn't see me. I felt claustrophobic, and the flickering light wasn't helping. It was spooky, but at least there was light at the end of the tunnel. I'd been told that the tunnel would take me to the churchyard, bypassing the steps – a means of escape.

I moved forward, trying not to trip or stumble along the well-used route. There was a heavy, damp smell tainted with tobacco, paraffin, stale alcohol, and a strong chemical smell I'd smelt before. Then it hit me like a bolt of lightning, it was the embalming-fluid stink of the horrendous witches in Salem, which they'd been unable to disguise. I'd known instinctively then that the scent was the smell of death, and now it was flooding my senses again.

Trying to avoid breathing too deeply in the eerie silence, I hurried on. Where the tunnel broadened out, it was being used as a storage area, with digging equipment and rolled canvases and ropes. What the hell were they doing here? When I reached the exit trapdoor and climbed up and out into the churchyard, I was startled to see the sun setting in a stunning red sky. I hadn't realised how much time had passed. Hearing rough male voices, I darted behind a gravestone. I couldn't risk anyone seeing me. My head said run for the hills, nothing good could be going on in a graveyard at dusk, but there was a morbid compulsion to stay and see what was happening with my own eyes. I moved forward cautiously so I could get a better view.

I recognised one of the four men as the porter from the workhouse, one of the few employed there. I'd noticed him earlier because he was wearing his own clothes, not the paupers uniform. Tall, heavily built, he was obviously in charge, barking orders, bottle of beer in one hand, clay pipe in the other, the smoke spiralling into the ever-darkening sky. He was swigging nonchalantly while the others, in dark brown baggy trousers, uniform of the working man, followed instructions. I knew this guy worked hard during the day, you could tell from the rippling muscles bulging his tight, stained shirt, and what he was doing here was increasingly obvious.

In the light of hurricane lamps the men were gathered around a newly dug grave as someone else came into the flickering circle of light. The vicar!

"Albert, my bottle if you please, and the promised donation." he demanded. The big man passed across a bottle, and the clergyman took a hefty swig, then the big man peeled some notes from a wad in his pocket. With a satisfied smile on his face, the bribed clergyman took the notes and hurried back to the church, not even glancing at the desecration in his churchyard. The grave was so fresh there was no gravestone to indicate who lay there, but amongst the men there was an unmistakable buzz of intense excitement.

"Young, I heard," commented one of the men. "TB it was, wealthy family, should be a fair haul."

Albert nodded. "There'll be more than a drink in this for you." He divided the remaining notes and handed them out. "Bonus from the Master." The men sniggered as they pocketed the pay, and one muttered, "Undertaker said she was buried with jewellery."

"Get on with it then." Albert gestured, slopping liquid from his bottle, and they set to. They had picks, spades, axes, rope, and a tarpaulin. I was witnessing a grave-robbing and feared I might vomit. I wanted to leave, get far away, but remained rooted to the spot. I'm ashamed to say since finding the death portraits at Lavender Cottage, I'd had a morbid fascination with death in Victorian times and the rich/poor divide, with wealthy families hiring black-clad guards to guard the house until the dead were buried, usually one or two days later.

The gravediggers moved with stealth, Albert chivvying them on. "Make haste. We need to get her into the storeroom, ready to send to London on the piss ship, then we've got barrels to move. Master wants 'em on the ship too, to get money's worth." I wasn't surprised; I'd gathered the Master was in on every angle of death and corruption, even if not all of it was illegal. If those who died in the workhouse were unclaimed by family within seven days, their remains could legitimately be sold to hospitals. What a gruesome business. Everyone was involved in the trade, undertaker, vicar, Master and Matron right down to the porter and gravediggers. And not only would they profit from her remains but from the jewellery haul too. I wondered how they were able to keep all of that hidden at the same time as they were actively working to get funds from benefactors and charities.

Two men had now attached ropes around the coffin and raised it. I knew the wealthy were not generally buried directly in the earth but on a brick construct which allowed for more than one coffin. The poor, on the other hand, went straight into the ground, often without a coffin, although depending on family finances, they might be wrapped in discarded sailcloth from the shipyard. The men had opened the coffin. I could see the silk lining and the small bell attached to the underside of the cast-aside lid, just in case she'd been buried alive.

As they lifted the body, the shroud fell away, and I saw her face. The undertaker had done a good job, she looked serene, the traditional coins, a gift for the ferryman to take her across safely to the afterlife, resting on her eyelids. As they tossed her unceremoniously on the tarp, I saw she was dressed in her Sunday best, a long black dress, sleeved and stiff-collared. It even looked like she was wearing a corset, her waist was impossibly tiny. She wore rings on every finger, Whitby jet jewellery, and, incongruously, the nursery rhyme sounded in my head Rings on her fingers and rings on her toes. She shall have music wherever she goes. There was additional jewellery at ears and wrists. She could have been going to an opera instead of eternal rest. The men were reaching into the empty casket, grabbing silk bags, each one I imagined filled with jewellery.

"Master'll not know if a couple of pieces go missing?" said one of the men.

Albert paused, then nodded. "One item only." He wasted no time in appropriating one of the bags and selecting something I couldn't see for himself before putting that bag in his pocket and waiting for the men to hand him the others. "Now wrap her up and fill in the grave, we need to get out of here." In no time, the earth was replaced with almost no sign of disturbance and the body of the poor woman bundled in the tarp was put in the wheelbarrow they'd brought, dirtied shovels and pickaxes piled on top of her. She would be sold to the teaching hospital, her family completely unaware, confident she was at peace. I was shaking with anger, then nearly jumped out of my skin as the clock in the churchyard chimed, nine strikes, the sound bringing me back to my own dire situation.

As they disappeared down the tunnel with the wheels of the barrow squeaking with every turn, the smell wafted back to me. I thought of Florence, trying to plan Rose's escape before she realised there was no hope. I wondered what had caused their many years of separation. I probably wouldn't ever find out. In different times, though, I felt she and I could have been good friends. Now I'd seen the past, surely I'd go back to my own time? Could I use the force of my own willpower? I yearned for the comparative safety of twenty-first-century Whitby. I'd seen enough of Victorian life, both sides of the coin, rich and poor, and neither appealed, really not for me! It had become clear you couldn't change the past, just learn from it, but I continued to feel haunted. It seemed I couldn't get away from Seb, either in my mind or in the past and I shuddered as I remembered the evil glint in Dr Death's eyes. Would it ever end? Probably not, and what other horrors would I come across along the way?

I followed the path towards the Abbey for a few moments. It was fully dark by now, and I sat down on overgrown lush grass that hadn't been mown for a while. I needed a few minutes to get my thoughts together. There was a breeze, and it was chilly. I'd have to move on. Just then, and with an unspeakable sense of relief, I felt the familiar lightheadedness, the world began to spin beneath my feet, and everything went momentarily black.

CHAPTER 27

I came to with a rush of excitement. I knew I'd travelled and, in many ways, didn't care what era I was in as long as it was far away from the body snatchers, Dr Death, and the dreaded workhouse; I'd need some time to reflect on the horror. I'd seen more than enough of misery, poverty, and madness, and it was evident that even the sanest of individuals would end up institutionalised in that place. Despite rose-coloured nostalgia, the truth was, it was a brutal era if you were poor. I thought fleetingly of Sandy and her poverty-stricken beginnings; if she'd lived in these times, how on earth would she have risen above her circumstances?

Time to acclimatise, get the cogs of my brain in gear, take it all in, process where and when I was, and observe those around me. Was I back in my own time? It took a few minutes to register, I was still on the field near the Abbey, but things looked different. The previously lush, overgrown grass was now worn down in places and straw-like, and there was a glorious, high summer sun beating from an azure blue sky, not a cloud to be seen, the height of summer, and certainly no longer early evening. I could do with a bottle of water, I was parched. I stood up and dusted myself off. Listening intently, I smiled because amongst the cacophony of noise ahead was the unmistakable sound of a fair in full swing.

I heard tinny organ music and a booming, "Roll up, roll up, all the fun of the fair!" My girls and I always loved it when the fair came to our university town. We'd fill up on hot dogs and candyfloss, then go on a spinning, high-octane ride. It was always a wonder we kept the candyfloss down! My mother would have been horrified if she'd known; she'd done her best to protect me from what she'd called riffraff. I remember her reaction when a fair came to our nearest town. I was always grounded, not allowed out, and so jealous of friends recounting all the fun they'd had. To spite her I'd made sure I sneaked out more than once at boarding school. Unfortunately, one time, I was caught out, and my furious mother told me scary stories about young girls who'd fallen in love with fairground life, who moved on when the fair upped sticks and then were never seen again. Some days when our relationship was particularly fraught, that had seemed an attractive option. There were so many things that she disapproved of – fun in particular!

The music was familiar, you know my obsession with 80s music. I made out what sounded like "Waltzinblack" by the Stranglers. Watch the YouTube video if you dare, it's set in a graveyard with skeletons partying, one of the spookier songs I listen to, and you know I like my gothic. Was I in the 80s? I'd be more than happy if that were the case, although I was getting a little fed up with being away from my own time, like being on a holiday that had passed its sell-by date.

Time to investigate. A group of people advanced from the 199 steps, past the church and onto the field, and I tagged along. From the way they were dressed, I assumed the Goth Festival must be in town. But something wasn't right. The festival was held in spring and autumn, and I saw the group were dressed as fashionable summer-clad Victorians, whereas goth festivalgoers were usually clad in heavier and darker fabrics. The women's dresses were made of cotton and fine white silk, with deep-coloured silk ribbons around their waists and deliciously over-the-top decorated straw hats adorned with flowers. Teenage girls were dressed in simpler white dresses with straw hats, similar to the ones I hated at boarding school, little girls wore oversized hats and frilly white dresses, and the boys wore sailor suits, or a jacket, shirt and smart shorts. The men were in bowler hats or straw boaters, and lighter suits, their summer holiday gear, I assumed, but I noticed no one was showing an inch of flesh; there was no chance of a tan for this group. Some of the women even had parasols and white gloves.

These guys looked well-behaved and well-dressed, not in the least bit rowdy; in fact, they seemed pretty stiff and formal, even melancholic. They were certainly playing their parts well and looked brilliant, but they didn't seem to be having fun; they had little interaction. There was always something going on in Whitby, maybe this was a steampunk get-together or Tomorrow's Ghosts with a summer vibe, but something wasn't right. I felt unsettled, I couldn't put my finger on it, but these guys looked too authentic in their costumes.

There was only one way to know for sure, I had to ask someone. I caught up with the group. They didn't look friendly or approachable; even the children seemed to stick to the "seen but not heard" rule. But I had no choice. I made for one of the older women; she was head to toe in black, wearing what looked like mourning dress.

"Hello," I said. "Weird question, I know, but could you tell me today's date?" She ignored me and kept her eyes straight ahead, ignorant cow. I tried one of the smartly dressed men with an impressive handlebar moustache, but once again, nothing. Then I touched the arm of one of the children. Surely this would get a reaction, but nothing apart from a fleeting quizzical look.

Holy crap, it began to register that, although I'd travelled, I was still in Victorian Whitby. Perhaps on a different day, or maybe a different year? I felt completely deflated, this was not the result I'd hoped for. On a positive note, there was a seventy-year stretch of Victoria's reign, so hopefully, Dr Death was either still in medical school, retired, or dead. Looking around at the unnaturally, probably arsenic-lightened white faces of the women, it occurred to me that maybe that explained the order of arsenic at the workhouse – not for use as poison but for the upwardly mobile matron's gentrification. I was cross with myself at my initial elation – I should have spotted right away that I hadn't travelled many years.

It was also obvious that nothing had changed as far as people being able to see or hear me. Resigned to that, I decided to see what was happening and continued following the crowd heading for the fair. As I passed a tree, I saw a flyer for the fair; it was running for the whole month of August, but no year was given. I should have asked Rose the year when I was with her at the workhouse. The garish poster promoted attractions that would certainly be banned in the twenty-first century, and I winced as I scanned it. Human curiosities and oddities, Princess Ruby and Prince Louis, Esmeralda the Bearded Lady, and conjoined twins Frank and Alfred.

It was the heyday of the travelling fair, each competing to be the best, the most popular. I made my way into the midst of this one and looked around at the throng. The popular rides were getting busy, with queues of people waiting patiently for the Carousel, Steam Yacht, Ghost House, and Crazy House of Mirrors. It seemed people let their guard down and forgot themselves once they were enveloped in magic far from their normal lives. There was laughter coming from the red and white striped wooden helter-skelter slide and a snake of people holding mats and climbing the spiral stairs for second or third goes, squealing with delight as they slid down.

A crowd of noisy children had gathered around the brightly painted Punch and Judy show booth. Punch, out of favour in the twenty-first century, was his usual violent self, and the youngsters were splitting their sides as Punch used his stick to repeatedly hit Judy on the head while the bottler, who worked with the puppeteer, went around the crowd, banging his drum, collecting payment, and encouraging the audience to hiss and boo ever louder.

It was a refreshing change seeing people enjoying themselves, if I'd been born into this era, this is where I'd want to be, although you could keep the tight-fitting corseted outfits. I moved on, taking in all the brightly painted side stalls and the delicious, mingling aromas. My stomach was empty and rumbled at the sweet smell of brandy snaps and toffee apples, and I looked longingly at glass jars full of chocolates, liquorice, and boiled sweets. The stallholder was weighing the confectionery into bags, and as a small boy ran up with his coin and asked for a quarter of chocolate mice, I was reminded of the leaving do Ollie had set up for me, with stripey bags full of sweets – that seemed a lifetime away.

A drinks stall was selling ginger beer, lemonade, and cream soda, the bottles sealed with a suitably sized glass ball to avoid spillage. There was even a stall selling snuff made from blended tobacco leaves with different flavours added; I caught whiffs of coffee, chocolate, cinnamon, and peach. I didn't associate Victorian times with ice cream, but there was a wooden contraption selling "penny lick" glasses filled to the top, although there were no 99 flakes. There was a mile-long queue for this stall, although I had my doubts about hygiene as the glasses were handed back, quickly wiped and refilled for the next person. Another stall was attracting a crowd as it was selling bottles of gin – mother's ruin – and there were some enthusiastic tasting sessions going on as well as shot glasses refilled over and again with brandy, sherry, and whisky. This was familiar, the girls and I had partaken at many a similar session.

At the Hoopla stall and Tin Can Alley, people were putting in a lot of effort to win tacky prizes, and it was clear there was plenty of money changing hands. I was impressed that everything looked freshly painted and well-maintained. I also noted there was no litter, so although the scene was familiar in many ways, there were differences. The rides were mainly powered by steam, which drifted like a misty cloud above the site, adding to the heady atmosphere. I smiled as a man showed his strength on the High Striker, raising the heavy wooden hammer high above his head and bringing it down with a mighty thump to impress the young lady he was escorting. Shrieking caused me to look up to where people were being swung round in rapidly rotating chairs under a canopy.

Moving to a quieter area, I spotted a painted wagon set back from the others, deep maroon, with brightly coloured flora and fauna edged in gold leaf; it looked brand new. Either side of its wooden steps there was an abundance of flowers, and herbs in pots, and the hum of bees sated on the sweet nectar could be heard even above the hubbub of the fair. On an old-fashioned wind-up gramophone, a scratchy 78 record softly played some classical music. A sign on the door announced that Eliza – World Famous Clairvoyant would connect you with loved ones and tell your future – appointments not always necessary. There was another sign stating that palmistry, crystal gazing, tea leaf reading, and tarot cards were also available, this was obviously a woman covering all her options, and if she was the real deal, she'd be able to see me straightaway, although I had my doubts. I was sure there were some genuine clairvoyants, but I knew it was big business in these morbid times, and there were charlatans taking advantage of the newly bereaved and vulnerable.

It was just possible this person could not only see those from the afterlife, but a kick-ass witch from the future. Sarah was always into the supernatural and one time she thought it would be fun for us to join a group messing around with a Ouija board. We declined, which turned out to be a wise decision as she returned looking like she'd seen a ghost, and for more than a few days afterwards, she'd been very quiet. She never spoke about what had happened, but she never participated again. I knew Queen Victoria had been at the forefront of the spiritualism obsession. The royal couple often arranged séances at Windsor Castle. Following Albert's passing, a thirteen-year-old from Leicester, Robert James, attended a séance and passed a message to the Queen from her husband using a pet name only she knew. From then on, he was regularly invited to Windsor Castle to participate in séances.

With all this going through my mind, I climbed the wooden steps to the wagon. A note on the door said a reading was in progress. I knocked politely but received no answer. I knew it was rude, but I wasn't sure time was on my side, I opened the door and looked around. This was obviously the luxury model of its time, and like the Tardis, felt far more spacious inside than out.

It wasn't quite the luxury motor home I'd lived in while renovating Lavender Cottage, but the plush parlour area was neat and spotlessly clean. A mixture of lavender and incense wafted over me, and I could see everything had been polished to within an inch of its life, the shine of soft wall lights reflected in gold-framed mirrors. There were fresh flowers in vases, pictures on the wall, and fitted mahogany furniture with gold leaf embellishment. Built-in seating was upholstered in deep burgundy velvet, with storage underneath, cleverly designed to utilise all available space. A rug in muted colours was set before a fireplace, and a copper pot was simmering on the cooking range. An intricate glass chandelier hung from the surprisingly high ceiling and a chart on the wall showed hand palms labelled with the elements earth, fire, air and water, while another named the palm lines – head, life, heart, sun, and fate. On one of the shelves was a white pottery head, its glaze crackled, PHRENOLOGY written on the base. A small dressing table backed by a mirror was decorated with rows of beads, and the table crammed with an assortment of crystal balls of all shapes and sizes, and a pottery palm with a painted eye in the middle looking at me knowingly. A burning candle gave an eerie glow.

Two women were sitting on either side of the mahogany table. They didn't seem to sense my presence as I walked towards them, so I called out, "Eliza!" She didn't respond, so I tried again, but it was disappointingly clear that neither of the women could see or hear me. Eliza had an unruly mane of dark hair tamed by a scarf with beads worn across her forehead like a bandana.

Dark eyes, heavy makeup, and deep red lipstick lent her a dramatic appearance, although olive, weather-worn skin made it hard to tell her age. Opposite her, dressed in white and with fashionably lightened skin, was a young woman. She looked to be in her early twenties, and it seemed their session was just beginning. Eliza was doing a cleansing ceremony, wafting sage around the table, setting her intention. The young lady was looking increasingly intimidated.

"We will start with a palm reading. Please remove your gloves." The younger woman laid her white kid gloves neatly beside her silk purse and sweet-smelling nosegay she'd put down earlier. Eliza nodded solemnly. "Now, cross my palm with silver, and we can begin." She accepted the proffered coins and began to gently stroke the hand she held. "So smooth, my dear, the only blemish a needle prick – embroidery, I imagine?" She closed her eyes, and even though I didn't think she was aware of me, I stifled a laugh – talk about stereotyping. She remained like that for a full moment before opening her eyes and bending forward over the young lady's hand.

"This line, my dear, is your life line. It is strong and means you will have a lot of luck and a good long life, and a sign your guardian angel will be always with you."

I scoffed silently. Was it really this easy?

The young lady had regained her composure and was completely invested in what Eliza was telling her. "What else can you tell me?"

"I can read the tea leaves for you if you wish." And, as the young lady opened her purse, Eliza rose to fetch a fine china cup – one she'd prepared earlier, I thought to myself with amusement. It looked like a load of quackery to me, but I moved closer. I was intrigued to see how Eliza would play this.

"Have you had the leaves read for you before?" The young woman shook her head. "Well, you must think of a question while sipping the tea, then hold the cup in your left hand and swirl it round three times." Having followed instructions, the younger woman leaned forward eagerly as Eliza gestured for her question.

"I want to know why I haven't met my own Mr Darcy. My mama has tried her hardest with introductions, but it must be a love match for me."

Eliza pored over the leaves which she had decanted onto the saucer, then did the closed-eye routine again before smiling benignly. "My dear, I can clearly see you will meet your intended very soon. Just have a little more patience." Well, that was pretty much a non-answer, but the young lady sat back in her seat, obviously delighted. Everything I'd seen convinced me I was watching a not-very-convincing fraud.

I'd seen enough and was about to leave when I noticed a sudden chill in the air, and a breeze rippled through the room. Had I left the door ajar? Eliza also looked up; she must have felt it too, but the young woman seemed oblivious as she prepared to leave. I hadn't noticed before, but there was a pack of tarot cards on the table next to Eliza, and something very strange was happening. The cards were being spread as if by an invisible hand – Eliza wasn't touching them – and then one of the cards was taken from the pack, rising slowly and held in the air. I called out in alarm, "Who's there?" but there was no response. The young woman had seen what was happening. Her whitened face turned even paler, she was terrified, and I couldn't say I blamed her. The floating card descended slowly to the table where it lay face up, and even I knew enough to see this wasn't a good one. It was the Death card. Was this a message for the now horrified woman? Eliza swiftly swept the card from the table, grabbed the deck and slipped it into a drawer, but by then the young woman had fallen to the floor in a dead faint.

Eliza went into full panic mode, as terrified as anyone in the presence of what could only be a real spirit. She rushed to a cupboard to fetch smelling salts and raised the woman's head to hold them under her nose. As she began to regain consciousness, Eliza helped her back onto the chair and brought a cup of water, encouraging her to only take small sips. When she turned to fetch a damp cloth, I saw the young woman shakily take a vial from her purse and raise it to her lips. I smelt rotten plums; the unexpected turn taken during the session had scared her rigid, and she'd resorted to laudanum. After that she didn't want to hang around, gathering gloves and purse and leaving with a muttered farewell.

I felt I could also do with a little something to calm me down, but with no Rescue Remedy to hand, I had only myself to rely on. As I followed the stricken lady out the door, Eliza put up a closed sign. I couldn't blame her.

CHAPTER 28

I made my way from the heart of the fair, curious to see where the fairground people lived, and came across a group of wagons, smaller, older, and less glamorous than the one belonging to the clairvoyant. Horses, used to pull the wagons, were grazing nearby. Outside the wagons, a noisy group were playing cards around a table, and it was apparent this wasn't just any group, this was the cast of the freak show on the poster. The smallest man and woman I'd ever seen were seated on the knee of the tallest man I'd ever seen, and they were stunning – Prince Louis and Princess Ruby. Both were dressed exquisitely in the height of fashion. It was a lively game, with much laughter and a fair amount of joshing – these people knew each other well and were comfortable in each other's company.

I knew they performed the closing ceremony of the fair in the evening and that their appearance was considered not for the sensitive eyes of children, although of course they weren't in the least bit scary. There was a well-dressed man in the group and I wasn't immediately sure what he was doing there until I noticed, moving in his lap, the withered body of his conjoined twin, kept alive by his healthy body. They must be Frank and Alfred; I wasn't sure who was who.

Walking up to the table, I coughed to see if anyone looked around, but it didn't appear anyone heard me, until a tall, well-built individual with a long bushy beard rose from the table. Nobody seemed concerned that the game was being abandoned. The person who stood was wearing a long gown, but every inch of flesh I could see was covered in soft brown hair. There was a hissed "Follow me!" as they passed. I obeyed without thought and was led up the wooden steps of a nearby wagon. The tall figure opened the door and ushered me in, closing it behind us, then turned and we contemplated each other.

"You can see me?" I said unnecessarily.

"Well, that's obvious, isn't it?" With a giggle, she held out her hand. "Esmeralda, the Bearded Lady."

We shook. "I'm Ellie," I said, and she nodded as if this was something she knew already. I looked around, the wagon was neat and tidy but nowhere near as luxurious as Eliza's.

"What year is it?" I asked.

"1895." She didn't bat an eyelid. "You're not the first time traveller I've met, you all seem to like the fairground experience. But I can't be too long, questions will be asked, and I have to get ready for the show. The Major will be round soon."

"You've seen others like me? And who's the Major?"

She smiled. "I'm the only one out of our group who can see, and yes, I've seen others from your time. And he's the Showman – owns and runs this show."

"He's good to you?"

She nodded. "Of course, we're his biggest attraction. Tickets for our show are sold out the minute they're available. Princess and Prince, as we call them, have a high opinion of themselves, they may be tiny, but they pull no punches. They're our voice when we are unhappy with anything. When Princess speaks to the Major, he knows he'll have a mutiny on his hands if he doesn't comply with her demands, and Prince adores her, so he'll go along with anything she says. When she wants a new outfit," she'd gestured to the sewing machine in the caravan's corner, "I have to put everything else to one side and create another stunning outfit. The crowd love her too. You know, their real names are Mary and Stanley, but all of us have taken exotic-sounding names – image is important." She grinned. "My real name's Ada, and I've told very few people that fact." I'd stifled a laugh, she didn't look like an Ada. Esmeralda suited this amazing woman so much more. "And," she added, seeing my expression, "don't forget, if it wasn't for this, most of us would be languishing in an asylum." I nodded slowly; I hadn't thought about it quite like that before. When I started to tell her about my experience at Eliza's reading, she snorted a laugh.

"Eliza, huh! Her real name is Louisa, and she's married to the Major. She's no psychic, and she's certainly not a sensitive. She's got a great business going on there, people are so gullible."

"But," I said, "she certainly summoned something." And I recounted what had happened with the tarot cards.

She shook her head thoughtfully. "That woman is no more able to summon a spirit than I am. I suspect it was you who inadvertently called it." She saw my face and hastened to reassure me. "The Death card doesn't always mean what you think, it shows an ending, but that can just mean transformation and new beginnings ahead." She laughed again, her whole face lighting up. "I'll wager Eliza was horrified – got more than she bargained for."

I agreed, I couldn't forget her look of pure horror, but I wasn't completely happy, I wasn't sure whether Esmeralda was being truthful or simply kind.

"Look, I have to go, it was lovely to make your acquaintance Ellie, and you shouldn't worry. I'm sure you'll return to your own time when the time is right. In the meantime, come and see the show later, although I should warn you, the crowd see us as less than human – and we act up to that. We do have challenges, but we're as intelligent and articulate as any other group of people; in fact, we all have superpowers – after all, I can see you, can't I?" She sighed. "Fact is, just being ourselves doesn't bring in the money. You know, maybe you're here longer because your power is getting stronger."

"Hope so, although I must confess, I've seen some brutal things. My times aren't perfect, but I want to go home."

"My dear," she said, her lovely brown eyes full of understanding, "I've never ever known any traveller to get stuck permanently out of time; just go with the flow and trust in the magic." And she drew me into a warm hug.

As I left her wagon, I wondered about her back story, no time to ask questions now, but there was always a story. Maybe I'd google her when I got back. I had one more question, I turned halfway down the wagon steps. "What happens to you when you get older, too old to work?"

"Ah, my love, don't you worry about us; we've been putting money away for a long time. We'll buy a big house by the coast, somewhere remote where we're not bothered by the 'ordinaries'. We plan to live out our lives in peace and harmony." I smiled back at her; it was good to know they'd have the last laugh and that it wasn't only the Major who would gain from their years of work.

I decided to follow her advice and enjoy the rest of my time at the fair. I watched a group of roughly dressed boys working in couples, weaving in and out of the crowd as they bumped into people and apologised, one distracting the victim while their friend skilfully raided their pockets before disappearing into the surrounding crowd. No judgement from me; I'd learnt that people had to do what they could to survive.

I made my way into the House of Mirrors. I'd done one of these years ago with the girls, and we'd found it hysterical, but now, unnervingly, I wasn't seeing my distorted reflection in the mirror but another woman, shrouded in mist and in Victorian dress. I whipped around but there was no one behind me and then, when I checked back, the mirror was blank, not even my own reflection – worrying! But as I moved among the mirrors, different desperate women stared at me, each of them mouthing an urgent message I couldn't hear. I was starting, even in the heat of the hall, to feel chilled to the bone.

It was with a deep breath of relief that I burst out of the House of Mirrors and headed towards the Carousel. The crowd had thinned and there was no queue, even though other rides were still busy. Here, the painted horses were still, and no one was seated on them waiting for the off. Then I saw the operator wasn't in his box, there was a barrier up with a closed sign. The horses were gorgeous, all newly painted and each bearing their name on a beautifully written plaque. I knew that, other than Esmeralda, people couldn't see me, so I climbed onto one of the most beautiful animals, Oliver, with horsehair mane, leather stirrups, and a golden pole to hold on to. Memories of my work friend Ollie made me smile, I hoped he was OK, but for the moment I felt exhilarated as if Oliver could take off any moment bearing me on his broad back.

And as if thought provoked action, I felt a jolt, and with the distinctive sound of steam hissing from the engine, Oliver, along with all the others, started to move to a tune – "Waltzinblack" again; maybe that was an original waltz tune from this time. I had to hang on tightly as the horses began to move up and down. This was freaky; no one else seemed to notice the ride was working, and I couldn't see the operator back in the booth. By now, we were circling faster and faster, I felt I was flying, the music increasing in tempo and Oliver surging up and down beneath me. Perhaps I could stop the ride, maybe there was some safety switch on the horse, but I couldn't find it, and just when I thought I couldn't hold on much longer, we began to slow, and I saw with horror that there were mirrors surrounding the sturdy column at the centre of the ride. From each of those mirrors, women were screaming at me. Was I really seeing them or was it just my overstressed imagination?

As the ride slowed and stopped there was an orderly queue waiting to get on. The odd thing was that they were a completely different crowd, wearing an assortment of clothing from different eras. Were these other time travellers? But before I had time to ponder, I felt a familiar electrical current stronger than usual, I knew what was happening and then I was spinning out of control, further and further into the dark vortex before blackness descended.

CHAPTER 29

Once again, I had quite a crowd around me as I came to. Sod's law, wasn't it; I'd been desperate to return to the twenty-first century, but what bad timing, making a scene as usual. That was assuming I'd really left the Victorian era this time. Where were the smelling salts when you needed them? I'd seen Seb again but as a killer doctor, which wasn't great. Rose's lethal dose was now many years ago, and I thought with sadness of poor Florence, doing what she could to care for her mother. I couldn't think why Seb hadn't carried out his murderous plan immediately. I shuddered; maybe he had other designs on the poor woman, keeping her captive to have his wicked way before dispatching her. What a sorry tale and horrifying experience Victorian Whitby had been, the grave robbers and the poor unfortunates in the workhouse, the only consolation was Esmeralda and her friends; they seemed to have a good life travelling with the fair. I was infinitely grateful to be back in my own time. I was still feeling queasy, but once I'd sat up and brushed myself off, the crowds had dispersed. One of them was an off-duty policeman, and he took over, shooing the onlookers away. Thinking of Matt, I smiled as yet another handsome policeman checked me over, ensuring I was OK. I told him I occasionally fainted; it was nothing serious. He seemed satisfied with my answer and left me to it. He looked a little weirded out when I asked him for the time, date, and year but shook it off because I'd had a bump on the head.

I headed towards the car park; I needed to get out of there, return to the cottage and digest what had happened. I looked at my watch; hours had passed since I'd driven into town, and I wasn't even sure what had triggered my return. I wasn't taking it for granted that I'd find my car; I just hoped it was where I'd left it and, to be honest, I didn't take it for granted that I was back; I had to test it for myself, smiling and saying a friendly hello to anyone I passed. I got some odd looks, but to my immense relief, a couple said a cheery hello back. I passed a newsagent, picked up a paper – double checking the date – and a bottle of water, plus something sweet, good for shock. Thankfully my car was still there, there was a big fat parking fine slapped onto the windscreen, but that was the least of my worries. I finished the water and munched on the chocolate flapjack; it gave me a sugar rush but didn't do anything for the dull headache I had.

I had embraced my magical journey so far, but I just wanted to live an ordinary bog-standard life at times like this. Was that too much to ask? Would I, should I, have been able to stop another of Seb's past life incarnations, and save Rose? I'd probably never know. I felt he was haunting me again, bouncing through the years in different roles but with the same ending each time. I was relieved to think this timeline would put a stop to it. Even if our paths crossed, he couldn't touch a hair on my head; I was protected. If I repeated that in my head enough times, maybe I'd completely believe it.

My most recent experience had firmed my resolve. I wanted to return to the Cotswolds and the relative safety and security of living near Sandy and Alice, at least for the time being. Of course, I was well aware I didn't own Wood Barn, and it did feel a bit like I had moved back with my mother, even though we had our own properties. But, I reassured myself, I also had the penthouse apartment in Richmond by the Thames; I now knew that Sandy had been the mystery buyer and was holding on to it for me. I loved that apartment, and maybe I missed London life – after all, Hampstead had been fun while it lasted. I knew that although I loved Lavender Cottage heart and soul, it was time to say goodbye to this side of my life. I felt I should start the next chapter, whatever and wherever that would be. There was an agent whose boards I'd seen around, and their properties seemed to sell quickly. I'd call them first thing in the morning.

I drove onto the cottage's driveway, turning off the ultra-secure alarm system as soon as I unlocked the door and discarding my shoes into the basket by the door. I paused; there was something about the atmosphere, I couldn't immediately put my finger on it, but the air around me seemed to shift. I shook my head; it was likely my brain was still scrambled after the trauma of what I'd seen and heard. As I walked into the cottage, I was sure things had been moved from where I'd left them, but perhaps I was just becoming paranoid – after all, the alarm had been on. I turned on the news to check the time and date – still good! But I couldn't shake that unsettling feeling that something was off-kilter. I switched the lights on, and one of the bulbs flickered – surely not, they'd not long been changed. I hoped I wasn't about to have another experience. I couldn't handle it so soon after the last one.

It didn't take long to set things in motion, and within a few days, there were regular viewings of the cottage and I was delighted to learn how much it had gone up in value – buyers were keen on the area because of the Whitby witches, and the cottage had its own reputation. The agent told me to hold my nerve and sit back if a bidding war occurred. I did suspect that some of the viewers weren't genuine buyers but determined to do their own bit of witch-hunting. They whispered to each other as they went round the rooms and into the garden. I soon realised who was serious and who was not but left it to the agent to weed out the serious offers. I couldn't help but compare the situation now to when I'd first purchased the cottage – nobody had wanted to touch it with a barge pole then, but of course, I had spent a packet restoring it.

I'd put my latest journey back in time to the back of my mind. I felt desperately sorry for Rose but knew I could have done nothing to save her. Over the past few years, I'd done my fair share of zipping through the centuries, but now I was firmly back in the twenty-first century and wanted to focus on the future; I'd had enough of the past.

CHAPTER 30

Having driven into Whitby one bright sunny morning, I decided to chill with breakfast at Sanders Yard, although, as I took a seat, I couldn't help thinking of its past, poverty-stricken residents squeezed into slum-like housing. Today though, I just needed some carbs, so what better than a full English; bacon, eggs, sausage, hash browns, beans, black pudding – I'd put that to one side – and toast, just what the doctor ordered. I added some strong coffee to the mix to make the perfect meal. When I'd finished, I dropped into the deli, picking up a few cheeky goodies and a few bottles of my favourite Sauvignon; the brownies looked particularly delicious. I promised myself I would start healthy living once I returned to the Cotswolds.

Back at the cottage, I put my key in the door, leaving it open so I could pick up the shopping from the boot of my car. Carrying the bag in, I went to put it on the table and turn off the security alarm, but something wasn't right. This time I didn't imagine it; the cottage looked different inside. For pity's sake, this was not what I wanted. I didn't want to go back in time again; totally inconvenient, but I knew without a doubt that either this was a bad joke or I was back in Victorian times. The big clue was the pictures on the wall; I recognised them all, the images of death. I'd given them hastily to the museum at Pannett Park, wanting to unsee the images, and I'd even had a bad dream about one of the dead girls coming to get me. I did not want to see them up on my walls! There was also an embroidered sampler in a wooden frame, the words *Every House Where Love Abides Is Surely Home Sweet Home,* dated 1858. The floor was covered in old-fashioned lino, no longer the luxury covering I'd chosen, and the open fire told me someone was home. Bloody hell, how long would I have to stay this time? This was not my favourite era – too much human misery.

There was someone in the house; I could hear movement upstairs. I'd wait for them to come down, and hopefully they wouldn't be able to see or hear me. With luck, this would be just a quick blast to the past, but why the Victorian era again? I moved around the kitchen with curiosity, opening the dark wood cupboards. The butler sink had an old curtain ruched up under it, and a large mahogany table with a bowl of fruit on top was in the middle of the room. My beautiful, bespoke, fitted kitchen had disappeared, along with my high-tech gadgets and well-stocked cupboards. I wondered who lived here and hoped they wouldn't mind me helping myself to a drink.

Knowing they didn't have safe drinking water back then, I found some beer stored in a covered wooden container. That would do.

The stairs creaked as someone descended. A tall man came into the room, not wearing Victorian clothes. Was I dreaming? I pinched myself. The guy was smiling at me; those eyes, oh my God, it couldn't be.

"Ellie," he murmured. "I've been waiting for you to come home." I wanted to run; I wanted to get back in the car and drive hell for leather then I realised the car wouldn't be there. He came over and pulled me to him. Oh boy, I was in trouble. Was I even protected in this era? Could he harm me? I felt a panic attack coming on, my heart beating ten to the dozen, fear rooting me to the spot. Where was the fight-or-flight response everyone talks about?

"It's OK, Ellie, you have nothing to fear. Here, sit down." I felt sick; maybe I'd throw up, and that would put him off. I sank down on a chair. I had no choice, there was nowhere to run, and I couldn't deny that however crazy and dangerous, there was a part of me that felt a frizzle of passion. I was still in love with him, even if he meant me harm.

As I composed myself, I couldn't understand why Seb was dressed in his everyday gear, not Victorian garb. He wore his trademark dark skinny jeans and black T-shirt; his leather jacket was draped over another of the chairs. He looked a little older, hair a little greyer, some crow's feet around his eyes, beard and moustache peppered grey like his hair. But he was still the most handsome, alluring guy I'd ever met. He gazed at me, and I couldn't help but stare back into those ice-cold wolf eyes as if hypnotised.

I couldn't get my mind to work properly; my head spun as he tenderly wiped my face with a damp cloth.

"Ellie, darling, sorry to give you such a shock. I can't believe you fled from me before. I have so much to tell you. I'm afraid I haven't been completely honest." Well, that had to be the understatement of the year.

"Are we in Victorian times?" I asked.

"We are," he said. "You're not the only one who can time travel. The difference is I can do it intentionally. I know for you it's purely accidental." I had no idea how he knew that, and seeing my face, he continued, "You must be so confused, but can you just be patient and listen? I have so much to tell you." He took my hand. "And people I want you to meet."

I pulled my hand away. "Who? And why Victorian times?"

"I knew the only way you'd believe me would be if I met you back in time."

I grimaced. "But you're a doctor in these times. I saw you ready to murder Rose."

"I'm so sorry, Ellie, it's not always like that. You have to believe not all my past lives have ended in the same way." I didn't reply, I knew what I'd seen, and I also knew darn well that in my time he was a witch hunter; how was he going to wriggle out of that?

"How did you know I was here?"

He shrugged. "I didn't for sure, I just hoped. It's been so frustrating that it took you so long."

"Well, excuse me! You didn't find me a few weeks ago

when I got stuck in Victorian times, and I seemed to be there forever."

He didn't rise to that. "Please don't over-analyse. I know it's a lot to get your head around, but you first need to know that I didn't mean you any harm in our time. Maybe I came across as too overbearing, but I couldn't understand why you ran off. I was looking forward to starting our new life together. I loved you ... still do."

I wasn't falling for that and laughed with no amusement. "All well and good," I said, "but you were one of the hunters. I saw your message about the Purge."

He shook his head. "You honestly thought I was about to murder you?"

"The message from Will, 'Have you sorted E out yet?' What else was I to think?" I asked.

"That's why it's always best not to look at other people's phones; you misinterpreted." He went to touch my arm, but I shook him off.

"I don't think so. I know you've been working for the government, advising them. I'm not stupid, I saw the headlines. How many red flags did I need, Seb? Then I saw you in Hampstead, huddled up with the men in grey suits – official business – right?" Worm your way out of that, I thought. I had nothing to lose.

"Ahh, Ellie, there's so much you don't know about me that I couldn't tell you then. It would have been far too dangerous. All I ever wanted to do was protect you, my love. I, too, am a witch, a very powerful one. I knew you were powerful too, but you still had much to learn, you are still reaching your full potential. I was forced to work with the government, but I was feeding them disinformation. They thought I was one of them, but I was doing everything I could to protect all of us. Then I heard what you were doing, that you'd mastered the spell to save us."

"You know about the spell?"

"I even came along to one of your surgeries in disguise!" Surely if he meant me harm, he could have done something then, couldn't he?

I shook my head; how was it possible? Surely I'd have known him. "So, you are protected?"

He laughed. "Indeed, and I can disappear too." He promptly did, then reappeared.

"I can't believe it, where was it? Which surgery did you come to?" Then before he could answer, I suddenly knew – "Hampstead?"

He nodded and smiled. "But Ellie, you are a very powerful witch; you must know there is no way I could harm you," – he gave a wicked look – "even if I wanted to."

I wasn't in the mood to be charmed. "But the Purge, the lockdown in Whitby, you didn't stop that, and the murder of the witches around here." Tears were rising. "They were my friends."

"I'm so sorry I couldn't do more. I was surprised and didn't know the hunters would move as quickly as they did. I thought we had longer." Could I believe him? I wanted to, and he read my mind. "I know it's a lot to take in, but I know about your journey. I've been working with Sandy and Alice. We share a past." That's all he would say on the matter. He knew Sandy and Alice – what the hell? They had never said anything to me about Seb.

But then, why would they? I hadn't told them about my relationship, it was the only secret I had left.

He took advantage of my silence. "Look, I don't want to give you a heart attack, but I need to convince you I'm one of the good guys." I knew he hadn't hurt me in my time, but he had history, didn't he? Lots of it!

"OK, what else have you got up your sleeve, or is there a rabbit to pull out of your hat?"

He gave me a grin, and for a second, I thought I could easily jump up and kiss him before reason kicked in.

He'd sensed my softening. "Wait here," he said, "I'll bring my guests down to meet you." I wasn't sure I could cope with any more as I looked towards the stairs. I couldn't believe my eyes; this was beyond surreal. Lottie and Anna, my half-sister and birth mother, were alive and well, and here, in Victorian times. Could they both time travel? Was that how they managed to disappear off the face of the earth?

I was across the room like a flash and fell into Lottie's arms; then it was Anna's turn, and now I knew beyond a doubt that what Seb said was true. Why hadn't he told me more when we were together at the cottage? Surely he could have trusted me. It'd have saved me so much grief. Again, he read my mind. "Too dangerous, Ellie. I was trying to keep you out of it. I knew bad times were coming. I had planned we'd all move away from the area when I returned from London. But by then, it had all kicked off, and you'd disappeared into thin air. It took me some time to track you down. I found you in Hampstead, and you did another runner before I could explain."

My feelings were all over the place; after living in fear for so long and my experiences, how could I return to what we had before? I realised it would take time for my head to trust him, but my heart was already there; the flame had never gone out. I didn't know what to think, but seeing these two amazing women who meant so much to me and hearing their stories was amazing; I was immensely thankful they were safe and sound, the lucky ones, and when they insisted that everything Seb was telling me was the truth, I had to believe them. Seb interrupted.

"Ladies, there will be plenty of time to catch up." Then, giving me a knowing look, "Take up where we left off." Oh boy! "Right now, though, we need to get back to our own time and show you how to control this time travel talent, Ellie."

I nodded slowly, probably about time I learnt how to avoid falling in and out of different centuries, it had only ever ended in tears. Maybe now I had something to stay firmly in the present for, a flutter of hope.

CHAPTER 31

Back in our own time, the next few weeks passed in a whirl. Seb moved in, and we carried on from where we'd left off, but this time with honesty on the table. I knew the moment I saw him again, I'd already fallen back, hook, line, and sinker, with the love of my life, my soulmate. Even if he was one of the bad guys, I didn't stand a chance. But please don't worry, I'm not stupid. I'd quizzed him to death on so many things, his bad attitude for one thing, and the way he'd isolated me from all my friends, the Mystical Ladies, and Lottie, my best friend – and, of course, sister – around here. He had a convincing answer for everything; it made sense that he'd felt the need to keep me sheltered. At the time, I'd felt I was drowning, slowly suffocating, but I understood now it was for my own good. I wish I'd known what was happening in the background; it would have saved me a lot of grief. But maybe, if I had known, I wouldn't have taken off and found the protection spell; everything happens for a reason. The remaining elephant in the room was the WhatsApp message talking about the Purge, although he'd given me a satisfactory explanation for that too. I had a sneaking suspicion he'd wanted me to see the message as he never usually left his phone lying around, maybe me fleeing was the plan after all? He'd never admit it, but I knew that had I stayed at the cottage instead of getting safely away, something would have happened. It was almost as if I'd had to live this life and experience for my safety, my magical journey, and my destiny.

I already had a buyer for Lavender Cottage. We needed a fresh start, making our own magic together. Once the sale went through, we'd decided to move to London. It was the most convenient solution for both of us. I had my awesome riverside apartment in Richmond and could start running again along the Thames. Seb was more than happy too as he'd just secured a book deal with a major publisher. It hadn't been titled yet, but think Confessions of a Male Witch, a dark novel based on his experiences and obviously semi-autobiographical. He was working under a pseudonym as obviously he couldn't take risks with his identity being discovered, think of him as a literary Banksy. Writing wasn't new for him, he'd published factual history before, but this would take the literary world by storm. The publishers were already looking at film rights and a Netflix series. This was a big deal, but as usual, he was unassuming, it wasn't about the money, he just felt he needed to tell his story.

There was one more thing to do and I approached this with trepidation. Time to tell Sandy and Alice about our love affair, I wasn't sure what they'd think, he was officially a witch hunter, after all. It was time to tell, the final secret divulged. I'd already had a conversation with Sandy letting her know that I wouldn't be returning to Wood Barn, so if she wanted to rent it out for income, that would be OK. I didn't give a reason, and she didn't ask. Maybe she was pleased to see the back of me. "Don't worry, darling," she'd said, "I'll keep it for whenever you want to grace us with your presence. Don't be a stranger."

I'd spoken to Alice too and, unlike Sandy, she questioned me. "So where are you going to live, Ellie? What's going on?" I told her I was planning to stay at Lavender Cottage for the time being while I decided what to do. I wasn't lying. She seemed sad that I wouldn't be her neighbour but understood when I said, "You and Sandy are working 24/7, and all work and no play makes Jack a dull boy! You'll be happy enough with your surrogate mother." I didn't realise how close it was to the mark when I said this. I was to find out soon enough why they had such a close relationship.

I'd kept the visit a secret from Seb. I wanted the element of surprise for all parties. We'd set a date for them to come and stay at Lavender Cottage and holy moly, they were on their way. I couldn't believe it when Sandy had agreed to come and stay, if you remember her horror when I'd bought the place. Seb knew something was up, but I kept smiling mysteriously. I was excited and nervous, I so hoped everything would go well. But I reminded myself I was an adult and no longer needed her approval.

I did an extra special magical clean and added vases of roses from the garden – I usually bought lilies, but

Sandy hated them, the funeral connection. I fluffed up the cushions and throws and lit my favourite candles so the room smelt divine. I'd also picked lavender and herbs from the garden, dotting them around the house. I felt a little tense, as you know, I'm not a domestic goddess. Seb was a better cook than I was, but I was learning and quite enjoying putting together some easy dishes, nothing too complicated, I was too impatient. This evening it was a no-fuss dish. You couldn't go wrong with Nigella's Spanish chicken. It consisted of chopped-up peppers, onions, mushrooms, baby potatoes, and chicken thighs; add some paprika and seasoning and bung it into the oven, job done – a one-pan delight. I'd put on Kate Bush's Sensual World; the title track always got us going – we even managed a quickie. We couldn't keep our hands off each other.

The wine was chilling, Seb had picked up a New York cheesecake and our favourite honeycomb ice cream for afters; we'd be stuffed. He knew we had friends coming, but not who, he hadn't even enquired. I was so nervous, but he was the opposite, totally chill. When I heard a car pull onto the driveway, I flew out of the front door as Sandy and Alice emerged from Sandy's latest luxury car; she'd ditched the orange one, and this was a brand-new metallic grey Range Rover Sport, more subdued, and perfect for the Yorkshire Moors. Sandy handed me a bottle of champagne. "Hello, darling." Alice was also laden with goodies but immediately clocked my nervous energy and raised her eyebrows. I smiled as I saw Seb had come to the door.

"I want to introduce someone," I said. "This is Seb."

They both shrieked. "I can't believe it," said Sandy. "You're together?"

Seb looked as shell-shocked as they were. "Sandy and Alice, I had no idea you were coming." He put an arm around me. "So these are our surprise dinner guests."

I think I was still in a bit of a state of shock as they brought me up to date on how Seb had been working under the radar with Sandy and Alice. They rarely met in person, but he was a key source of information. They hadn't confided in me about his involvement because of the importance of secrecy and had no idea of our relationship. I could understand the logic but couldn't help feeling things would have been simpler if I'd been kept in the loop. At least now all the skeletons were out of the closet. I didn't know then that there was one more to go – it wasn't long before I found out what it was.

The evening went well – and everyone complimented my culinary skills – with a carefully chosen playlist in the background, a selection of my cherished vinyl inherited from Anna. Seb had sorted the music, so there had to be a few tracks from Japan, Siouxsie and the Banshees, and early Duran Duran, but the evening wouldn't have been complete without something from Kate Bush, even Alice was now smitten! She requested Sensual World, and Seb and I exchanged glances and grinned. Anyone looking through the window at us would have thought we were just a normal family enjoying each other's company.

Once I'd got over my initial shock, I realised it helped enormously that Sandy and Alice already loved Seb and for once, my mother approved of a boyfriend. "Seb's been pivotal," she said. "You can trust him completely, we do, and he has amazing magical powers." Was that a wicked smile she sent my way? I smiled to myself, I knew only too well about his magical powers, in more ways than one!

The next morning, after a leisurely breakfast prepared by Seb and taken out in the garden, my peace shattered when he commanded our attention. I hadn't noticed before, but he looked a little worse for wear, as if he was worried about something. I glanced over at Sandy and Alice; they shrugged, as intrigued as I was.

"It's OK, Ellie," Seb reassured me, "I just need to share something. It affects all of you, or rather it affects your past lives. We need to go to the river. It will be uncomfortable, but you should know."

Sandy took the lead. "Come on then, sooner we go, sooner we'll know what he's being so mysterious about." She linked arms with me, and Alice followed. I had a flashback to Seb's fascination with the river when he first visited the cottage. He'd had a strong urge to spend time there. He knew what had happened in the past with Hettie and her lover Abe – Seb's past life – but how were Sandy and Alice involved? I didn't understand, but he was obviously well-prepared and had even brought a few camping chairs to set at the water's edge.

Having arranged the chairs, Seb faced me gravely. "It's time, Ellie. We need to return to when Hettie drowned as a witch."

"I've seen that," I said. "I don't need to see it again."

"But you've only seen up to the drowning. You need to see more so we can move on, create our future together, and learn from the past. You need to know the truth; after this there are no more secrets, total honesty and full disclosure as we go forward." He held out his hand to me and we went back in time with ease. We were observers of a scene I'd seen repeatedly in my nightmares. I shivered, and Seb tightened his hold on my hand as we watched Hettie dragged to the river on that bright autumn morning, the stunning red, copper, and yellow of the trees framing the horror. Her hair was matted, hands and feet bound; she'd given up struggling, there was little point, she knew her fate. I saw her silently praying, turning her face to the morning sun. I wanted to cry out, but knew Seb and I were merely observers. We could do nothing, yet this was a scene ingrained in my DNA. One of her captors shook her roughly. "Don't struggle, witch." Then she was hurled into the water.

When they were satisfied she was dead, her body was hauled from the water.

Seb whispered, "Are you OK?" I wasn't but squeezed his hand in response. Having done their job, the men didn't stick around; they left Abe on his own. He was silent, the eyes I knew so well cold and unyielding. If he regretted the murder he'd set in motion, he showed no remorse. Did he truly believe Hettie was a witch, or was this a convenient way of ridding himself of an unwanted lover? I wondered if he understood the strength of her curse forged by betrayal and hate. If he didn't now, he would in the future.

The silence was broken as two women approached the river with bundles of linen. They looked like a mother and teenage daughter. He turned and spoke, "The witch is dead; I did this for you. Now sort her body and make haste."

"Abe's wife Mary and his daughter Catherine," Seb said. "Look closely." Shock jolted through me. "Sandy and Alice's past lives?" I gasped.

He nodded. "I was certain when I first met them that they had been mother and daughter. Abe married Sandy's past life and Alice was his daughter."

Abe walked away as the women began to work on Hettie's body, Mary cursing continuously. "You witch, you seduced my husband, cast a spell, gave him a potion. Fucking my husband, bearing his bastard child, you've got your comeuppance you slut." They were rough with Hettie's body, showing no respect for the dead. I turned away, it was unbearable to watch, but it explained the special bond between Sandy and Alice. I had to remind myself this wasn't them, and I wasn't Hettie.

Seb understood how I was feeling. "Time to go?"

"Do they know?"

He shook his head. I trusted him, and he'd proved himself worthy of that; after all, why show me something that didn't show anyone in a good light? I couldn't blame present-day incarnations for past evils.

Once both Sandy and Alice had understood and digested what I'd seen, they came swiftly to terms with it, and our mutual mantra grew stronger – You can't change the past, but you can learn from it, right wrongs and do better.

CHAPTER 32

You'd think that I'd had my fill of surprises, but as we waved Sandy and Alice off after the weekend, Seb commented, "Well, that was intense." An understatement if ever there was one. "Now, get dressed in something nice, I'm taking you out tonight." I frowned, I thought we were having a cosy night in, I'd already changed into my scruffs, and after all the revelations, I wasn't sure I was ready to put on my glad rags and head out.

"Why don't we just put on some chill-out music, light the candles, crack open a bottle and watch something light?" I was thinking of Sex and the City or its recent update. But Seb wasn't having that, and because he was so insistent, I gave in. Don't judge me, or him for that matter, he'd redeemed himself. True his head was often in a historic cloud, and yes, he could be a bit moody and melancholy, but that's just who he was, and it was his Heathcliff persona I'd fallen for in the first place.

He drove. Was that a sign that I might need a drink? I was sure that was right as he led me into the White Horse and Griffin, the pub where I'd met Will and his friends, a lifetime away. I immediately spotted Lottie sitting with a group. We hadn't had a chance to catch up properly since we were reunited in Victorian times, so we'd had no opportunity to discuss just how Seb knew Lottie and Anna; that was for another time!

She came over to hug me. "Hey, sister, come and join us!" With a pang of guilt, I realised I hadn't asked her about Luke, and I remembered his last text message when she'd disappeared. As she led me over, I realised the handsome fellow next to her was Luke, he'd changed his hairstyle. It turned out he'd been away touring but was back for a few weeks before going off again. Lottie would join him as they conquered the world, so they were only in Whitby temporarily.

Talking quickly, interrupting each other as long-marrieds do, they explained that he'd finally learnt what was going on after Lottie's disappearance and was convinced she'd been murdered along with other unfortunate victims of the Purge, but it turned out she'd stayed safe and Anna had joined her in hiding. There was another guy with cropped hair and a familiar cheeky smile. It was Will! Where had all that beautiful hair gone? He stood and enveloped me in the biggest hug. "So amazing to see you again, Ellie, we were so worried about you!" So it was confirmed that Will was one of us, my Purgegate suspicions were unfounded. He was working undercover with Seb, which completely explained the WhatsApp message. We'd come full circle, meeting up again where it all started, just like old times, the bad days of witch-hunting forgotten.

All my favourite people were back together, but it was soon apparent that none were sticking around for long. Anna had returned to Harrogate; Lottie and Luke were going on tour; Will would travel, starting in Australia and New Zealand, and, of course, Seb was no longer at the university, having given up his professorship. There was nothing to keep any of us here. The change of government and a new prime minister had made things far safer; witches were now celebrated – at least the good ones – although that notably excluded Sophie from the advertising agency and the contingent from Salem if they ever came over here again.

It was great to see everyone, and we promised to keep in touch, but I needed to leave Hettie and Abe behind, as did Seb, neither of us needed constant reminders of our past. I had mixed feelings about the cottage. I'd got an amazing deal, but somehow couldn't bring myself to sign the final papers on the sale. I couldn't explain it to myself, let alone to anyone else, I simply knew it wouldn't be right. I just couldn't cut ties with this place. It wasn't a popular decision, and, the estate agent was royally pissed off, refusing to believe I'd turn down such a good deal. She had to smile through gritted teeth, though, because she was still selling my other properties.

I was sobbing as we left for London, it was the end of another era even though, as Seb pointed out, we could return for holidays. We'd decided for the time being to let the place, there was no point leaving it empty and unloved. As the cottage vanished in the rear mirror, I silently thanked Hettie for all she'd given me. We headed to the apartment in Richmond and planned exciting, fun things to do. Seb needed a break from writing, and we planned to travel to visit Lizzie in the States and Sarah in her commune in India. Seb was interested in London's history, and we found an amazing tour guide who he hired privately. I'd never seen Seb as a city boy, but he loved our time there, and I could see how it satisfied his ongoing obsession with history.

Life was good. We were having fun, I trusted him a hundred per cent, and we were totally relaxed with each other. He had shown me his magical repertoire and admitted he knew I'd added a love potion to his drink. I could only smile – guilty as charged. He also convinced me we could have fun back in the past, and one morning I had the idea we could go to Abbey Road and see the Beatles doing that famous photo shoot. We loved the Beatles, had recently bought the whole catalogue on vinyl in an auction, and were working our way through it. Our song was "If I Fell" – get the sick bag out. Not like me to be so gushy, but I was madly in love.

So we returned on the morning of Friday 8 August 1969 to the EMI Abbey Road studios. There was a guy on a ladder with a camera, and John, Paul, George, and Ringo were laughing, going across the crossing, larking around, while a policeman stopped the traffic. They had several attempts to get the right photo, and for whatever reason, Paul decided to go barefoot, with a cigarette. John looked wonderful dressed in white; just over a decade later, he would die – so tragic. George was the most casual in double denim. As neither Seb nor I could be seen, we took turns to follow the guys across the road as they kept re-shooting. Finally, we'd seen all we needed to and went to go. Did I imagine it – excuse the pun – I'm sure that John turned round looked straight at me and winked. Even weirder when we got back to our time, I realised the crossing itself had moved. When I'd done the tourist thing with my parents many years ago, we had not crossed at the same point, they'd repainted it further down the road!

Seb wanted to see what the fuss was all about at the start of the punk era, so we went back to Malcolm McLaren and his girlfriend Vivienne Westwood's Chelsea boutique, SEX. It was 1974, and they'd just opened. This wasn't my sort of shop; fetish wear and bondage had never been my look. Outside the shop, there was a sign in pink foam spelling out its name. We didn't spend long there as it was overpowering with rubber curtains, red carpet, and graffiti-covered walls. The Queen of Punk, Jordan, glared at us in the shop; that was odd. Sometimes, people saw us, other times, they didn't. Seb also wanted to see Denmark Street, our very own Tin Pan Alley, a hive of musical activity since the 50s. We visited in its 60s heyday; The Stones and The Who recorded there, and we spotted so many famous faces having coffee at the Gioconda cafe. Seb was in musical heaven. We also took in the boutique, Biba, where Sandy had once worked. She wasn't there, maybe the wrong time, but the place was amazing; they were doing a fashion shoot with Twiggy. We went on to Ronnie Scott's for some jazz, although bumping into the

Krays was a little disconcerting. We weren't taking any chances, apologised politely, and transported back to the twenty-first century sharpish.

But that didn't put us off. I'd always loved the Spice Girls, Victoria being my favourite, even if she didn't smile – she was the coolest – so we returned to 1997. I wanted to see them before Geri left the band. Frivolous, but I loved it. Another favourite, of course, was Kate Bush. We went to the Hammersmith Odeon in 1979. I loved every minute; her stage presence was so powerful, even though she was shy in interviews. I knew she'd learnt some of her stagecraft from a mime artist, and her singing and dancing without sounding out of breath was amazing. Of course, I didn't have everything my way; Seb wanted to see some of his music, so we went to see Japan, the alternative 80s band.

Although I hadn't been keen on going back much further in time – certainly not Victorian times, I'd seen enough – I had one era that I wanted to revisit and explained to Seb that I'd seen Hettie as a child in London before she came to Whitby.

"If she'd stayed with her mother in London," I said, "maybe she wouldn't have met Abe."

His response was "Fate always finds a way." I wanted to go back to see if I could see her again in Georgian London, near where I'd had my leaving party at the Prospect of Whitby. The pub had the same vile smell as before, nothing had changed since last time I was back in this era. There were still dodgy deals, drunken behaviour, and prostitutes plying their trade. Seb followed me out of the pub as I went down shady side streets, seeing if I could find the lovely young girl to tell her we'd meet again, and she'd help save the witches in my time. Sadly, it wasn't to be. The sights and sounds were the same but there was no sign of the child I so wanted to see.

CHAPTER 33

It was a wonderful, carefree few months with the man of my dreams; I'm sure you want to puke, too gushy by far, but he was my knight in shining armour. As I've said before he could also be a moody bastard, but that was his personality, he couldn't help it. He was not a perfect human; he had flaws, but who doesn't? I'm sure there were things I did that annoyed him, too. Now and again he'd withdraw, zone out, especially when writing. I learnt what to expect and would go off and do my own thing. He was a mad professor, after all.

He'd been so patient, helping me develop my time-travelling skills, and I'd learnt how to stop random travels. We'd had fun going back in time, seeing and experiencing what we wanted to see in whatever time zone we fancied. I hadn't dwelt on the misdemeanours of his past lives, how the perpetrators had inflicted pain on me in my past. It wasn't his fault in the present day. When we'd seen when and what we wanted to, we took ourselves overseas, travelling around the States for a bit, visiting Lizzie on the way, and then over to Goa to see Sarah, who I hardly recognised as she was doing the hippie look with her hair in dreadlocks, but she was living her best life, as were we all now. It had been a brilliant trip, making our own memories, and I was delighted that Sarah and Lizzie loved Seb as much as Sandy and Alice did; they just got him. I felt queasy on our return from India, which wasn't surprising. It was an amazing trip, but we both had Delhi belly while there, and I couldn't seem to shake off the after-effects.

Now we were back in London I'd brushed it off and concentrated instead on reconnecting with those that I wanted to see again, my old buddies. I'd already told Seb all about my adventures with Tess and Laura, and the Hampstead magical crew, and I had guiltily told him all about Matt, I couldn't keep any secrets now, all the cards on the table. I must admit it felt like I'd been cheating on him, after all, we didn't officially break up, I did a runner. He didn't make a comment, just gave me a wry smile. I didn't dare say that it was OK anyway, as when Matt and I were having sex, I always fantasised about him, that wouldn't have been tactful, but it was true! He didn't volunteer any information about his love life and I didn't ask. I wasn't sure I wanted to know if there had been anyone else.

I met up with Tess and Laura again, at a restaurant of their choice, somewhere new that had only recently opened in Hampstead. It was a good choice, and we promised to keep in touch, sure I'd see them again soon now I was not too far away. Like before, we slipped straight back into our easy three-way friendship. I told them I'd love to see Matt's sister Lily again, but it would open a whole can of worms with Matt after seeing him at the Hampstead surgery. What I didn't know – they hadn't mentioned it when we met after the surgery as maybe they thought I'd be upset – was that Matt was now in a relationship, and he'd fallen madly, deeply in love by all accounts, and I didn't want to rock that boat. Tess and Laura still saw him from time to time, they moved in the same circles. Life after Ellie was OK for him it seemed, I was pleased to hear this, it took the pressure off if I bumped into him again in the future.

There was just one other person I still wanted to see, and thankfully he was still working at the advertising company I'd left a lifetime ago, so was easy to contact. We arranged to meet one evening after work at one of our regular wine bar haunts.

Ollie was gushing at how good I looked, and beside himself that I'd got back in touch. "Darling, country living becomes you, although I never thought for a minute you'd leave the city – couldn't imagine you in wellies! And I never did see that spooky cottage you bought."

"I asked you to come."

He looked guilty. "Sorry, babe, I just couldn't summon the courage to travel up north; all sorts of strange things were happening." I just smiled and nodded; there was lots to tell, but I wasn't in the mood. I was desperate for a shallow night out, nothing deep and meaningful. I deliberately changed the subject. "So who's your latest squeeze? Dating anyone serious?"

"Babe, he's even put a ring on it." He put out his ring finger, and there was a Tiffany diamond band.

"Omg, who is the lucky guy?"

"Ryan, I met him online, we've been dating for a couple of years. I tried to let you know, but it looked like you had become a hermit for a while, changed your number? Like you'd disappeared off the face of the earth!"

I laughed it off, but something had changed; I couldn't put my finger on it, but I felt there was an atmosphere, as if whatever we had before had long gone. I wasn't the same person who had left London, but it seemed Ollie still was. He droned on about office gossip, late nights out, getting home in the early hours, as if nothing had changed for him. I wasn't sure what we had in common any more. We'd started with cocktails. Ollie, with a wink, ordered a sex on the beach, and an espresso martini for me. We downed those and ordered the same again. As I picked up my second glass, my stomach lurched a little, and I suddenly felt queasy, I reached the ladies in the nick of time and threw up into the toilet bowl, the vile smell making me retch again. I slid to the floor, feeling faint, then everything went black.

I was in the office back at my old firm. There was a commotion in Simon's office and, unobserved, I went to see what was going on. I spotted Ollie, but instead of his usual office attire, he was dressed in the skimpiest of shimmering shorts, a bright top, and, bizarrely, a pink wig; he was also wearing thick eyeliner and lipstick. Even on his wildest nights, I'd never seen him dressed like this before. Simon also had a weird outfit. Was this some kind of crazy dress-down day? He wore 1960s-inspired gear, brightly patterned shirt, clashing tie, and tight trousers. Sophie was in the room, too. I remembered Sandy's warning; she was a bad witch. I'd probably always sensed that – we'd never liked each other. She, too, was dressed oddly, not in her usual smart power suit – I'd always felt she was trying to emulate me – meow! The office looked the same, but in the corner was a sweet stall like the one Ollie had organised for my leaving do. Was this some sort of works do?

I could smell a familiar smell emanating from the other person in the room, a woman dressed from head to toe in gothic, funereal black, the scent was intoxicating but vile. She was holding court with the three others and, to my horror, I saw black bile coming from her mouth; the others had cups in their hands and were collecting and drinking the elixir, gasping in delight as if it was a sort of super-smoothie. She was Em Corey, the witch I'd clashed with in Salem. The smell of death which leaked from her was overpowering, and familiar.

Sophie licked her lips. "Mmm, the taste of death, how sublime." As they drank it was as if they were imbibing new power. Em cackled. "You know what you have to do, track down that bitch, Ellie. She's given me the runaround, but you'll find her now she's back on home ground."

I came to sitting in the toilet cubicle, thankfully on my own. I must have been out for a moment or two but what a weird and ghastly vision. I needed to get back to Ollie. I had a mouth spray in my handbag, I usually carry one, and then I splashed my face with cold water. Maybe I needed something sweet to nibble, low blood sugar. Was my subconscious telling me something about Ollie? Returning to our table, I saw a smartly dressed woman speaking to Ollie and realised with shock the woman was Sophie and had to struggle to keep my composure, but the sight of her made up my mind.

"Hello, Sophie. I'm sorry, Ollie, but I'm not feeling too good; I've been a bit off since getting back from Goa, too much spicy food, I guess." I knew I was protected, but every instinct was screaming at me to get out of there and sometimes you must listen. I couldn't for a moment believe Sophie "bumping into us" was by chance. I hastily put some money down for my drinks, apologised again, and left. And I wasn't going to take any chances; I blocked Ollie's number in the taxi on the way home. When I got home and recounted the incident to Seb, he suggested my drink might have been spiked. I supposed it was possible although I couldn't imagine why, however it would certainly account for what must have been some kind of hallucination.

I'd put the nausea down to our Goa trip, but then I missed my next period. I was usually as regular as clockwork and on the pill, but having overlooked the impact a stomach upset could have, it looked like I was pregnant! I wasn't at all sure what Seb would think at his age, he'd be a mature father. I remember having the ticking clock conversation with Tess and Laura, and I hadn't planned for children; I couldn't see them in our future. We'd so much else to sort out and we'd never even discussed it. I needn't have worried. Seb was beside himself with excitement – in his own cool style, of course. We looked in amazement at the scan, where we found out we were having a little girl, the tiny beating heart incredible. After all, we had been through, this was the icing on the cake, our own fairy story. I had my knight in shining armour, and we would have our princess. I'd decided she would be called Celeste – it means heavenly, out of this world, the perfect name. I counted my blessings every day for this miracle. My textbook pregnancy was going swimmingly, and I bloomed after the sickness at the start. Pregnancy suited me!

I had planned a water birth at home. I'd read all the information, spoken to the experts, and discovered this was the best birthing option. As my pregnancy progressed so well, my health visitor signed this off for me, and everything was prepared and in place. I had been busy buying our baby's nursery gear, clothes, and equipment. One night, we'd had a curry, this was meant to bring things on – hurry up, my darling child. Over the past few weeks, we'd had some deep and meaningful chats. We knew that for the time being, I was safe and sound and, of course, protected. But there was always that doubt in my mind: who knew, with magic – could the spell be blocked by someone with more power in the future? I never took any chances, and after a particularly sleepless night, I decided to write a letter. Seb thought I was being morbid, but I wanted to ensure my baby girl would be OK.

We agreed that as I'd already had attempts on my life and more than enough weird experiences, as a precaution I'd make a will which left Lavender Cottage, the Richmond penthouse and most of my estate to Celeste when she reached the age of twenty-one. My solicitor had drafted everything, and I'd written a love letter to the daughter I hadn't met yet. Seb was not materialistic and had money of his own which he expected to dramatically increase when his book was published. So, my baby girl, you have your father's blessing that I am leaving you financially protected. In my own reverie, I smiled as my waters broke and my first contractions started.

CHAPTER 34

The contractions continued with no particular pattern, just random pains, and God, they were painful. Seb had already called the midwife. Before too long, they were five minutes apart, nearly sixty seconds per contraction.

"You're doing so well, Ellie, just keep breathing through them." Seb was so supportive as we waited for our baby to arrive. Between contractions, I thought how, in the past, midwives and wise women skilled in assisting at births were treated with suspicion, although from the past few years' experiences, it wasn't that far in the past. Thankfully, things had calmed down, and we lived a charmed life now, our fairy-tale ending.

When the midwife arrived, she confirmed our darling girl was well on her way. The birthing pool was so soothing, allowing me to sit back and relax between increasingly powerful contractions while Seb was hands-on, massaging my back and putting on relaxing chill-out music. He'd lit my Jo Malone candles to create the right ambience, then he read me short stories, and we listened to podcasts as we whiled the hours away. It seemed Celeste was warm and cosy in there and didn't want to come out. There was no need for gas or air, the water was remarkably soothing, and the pain was manageable; I was having the perfect birth. We'd been to all the classes, listened intently to the advice, and now followed it, but we had no spells in our repertoires that would help with childbirth and weren't prepared to risk using any lotions or potions.

So, too good to be true? Was it paranoia, or did I know more than the rest? Was I destined for happy-ever-after with Seb and my baby girl Celeste? You've been on this journey with me, my friend, and you know as well as anyone that life has never been straightforward. And now I was starting to worry, something didn't feel quite right; the pains had changed in strength and were coming thick and fast. I said as much to Seb and the midwife, but she reassured me. "Every new mother feels this way. We call it transition, but you're doing so well."

Seb said, "Ellie, trust her; she's delivered more babies than you've had hot dinners. Just go with the flow, you're doing brilliantly, my love." I saw the look they exchanged over my head, just another anxious mother.

The pain was becoming excruciating, and I had the strong urge to push in between trying to breathe through the pain. I'd finally been given some pain relief, which was messing with my head, and I started seeing things around the room, hallucinating; a picture on the wall was melting like ice cream, the colours spilling out of the frame, and I suddenly shouted, "Seb kill the cockroaches!"

"It's just the medication, Ellie," he soothed. "There are no cockroaches."

Then I heard a rhythmic knocking, a hammer banging nails into wood. "Seb, stop them, they're banging nails into my coffin, I don't want to die."

"You're not going to die!" But the pain intensified, and the midwife had left the room for some reason. I could hardly breathe and went into a full-blown panic attack.

"I can't do this anymore," I yelled. "It's all your fault, you got me into this mess." Seb could see my distress, and called out for the midwife. She'd only popped to the loo for what must have been a couple of minutes, but I wanted to push, and it felt like an age. When she bustled back in, she grinned.

"Right, here we go, Ellie, this is it."

My beautiful baby girl was just perfect; she fitted her ethereal name, and she'd been here before, that old, wise look of newborn babies. I delivered her at 2.06 am, I was immediately in blissful love with this precious bundle. Once I'd been helped from the birthing pool, feeling like a beached whale, I let myself be washed and dressed in a comfy leisure suit; I was impatient to hold my baby again. I know babies' eye colour changes, but she had the most striking all-knowing blue eyes. Her skin looked olive, although the midwife assured me she wasn't jaundiced, and her hair was dark brown. My skin tone and hair colour, and Seb's wolf eyes – what a combination. She was beautiful and had a heart-shaped mole just like mine and Anna's – her heritage. Seb was as besotted as me as he gazed into her brilliant blue eyes. "You know she has the best of both of us."

The midwife left once she was happy with both me and the baby. I'd had the perfect birth, and my baby had a healthy Apgar scale but underlying everything was still that uneasy feeling of foreboding.

Seb tried to jolly me out of it. "My darling, anxiety is part of new motherhood." But it was more than that, I knew; my sixth sense was on overdrive. He'd sent me for a nap after I'd successfully breastfed Celeste. She'd fallen asleep on my breast with a serene look on her face, her lips slightly open, and a damp chin, which I lovingly wiped then reluctantly left the two of them and went upstairs to rest.

I'm not sure how long I slept, but I woke with a terrible pain in my head, like a thunderclap had gone off. I felt parched, and my bed was wet. Had I peed myself? Looking down with horror, I could see the sheet was bright red; blood had flooded the bed. I screamed, "Seb, Seb, I'm bleeding!" I heard him race up the stairs and saw the horror on his face as he saw the crimson spread of blood. I heard him call for an ambulance and say "haemorrhaging", although I must have been falling in and out of consciousness.

"Please, please hurry," he gasped.

From then on, things got blurry; it felt as if fireworks were exploding in my head. The ambulance and paramedics were there in what seemed like moments, and I looked up to what seemed like dozens of eyes looking at me. Was I hallucinating? They gave me an injection, which made me feel even more lightheaded. I was unsure what was real, what was imagined, what they were doing, and where was my baby? I couldn't see Seb; I hoped he was looking after her. I tried to ask.

"It's OK, Ellie, your baby is just fine. We need to

concentrate on you now, stop the bleeding." They seemed calm; I'd be all right. But why could I smell smoke? Where was it coming from? What was on fire? My life or lives were flashing before my eyes; I saw Hettie drowning in slow motion while Seb looked on, Rose being given a lethal injection, and there were other women I didn't know, all meeting their fate in different terrible ways.

"We're losing her," I heard someone shout, and then, most painful of all the images, I saw myself bound to a stake, logs stacked around me. I was naked in the midst of a jeering crowd, their chanting growing ever more frenzied.

"Die, witch, die!" With horror, I recognised all of them. Those I loved and trusted from past and present, armed with rocks, ready to throw. Sandy, Alice, Lizzie, and Sarah, Lottie and Anna, my friends, my family, what the fuck? Menacing, full of hate I didn't understand. Then the rocks began, viciously aimed, hitting their target, and then others were throwing rock salt at me, salt in the wound to maximise pain. As the salt hit my bleeding skin, the agony was unbearable. Then, a tall man with long dark hair and black clothing parted the crowd. He wore a protective mask over his nose and mouth. He stared straight at me; I'd know those eyes anywhere – it was Seb. As he removed the mask, he spat in my face, then started yelling, "Let me finish the job." He pushed a sharpened stake straight through my heart as I screamed in shock and pain. Someone threw a flaming piece of wood onto the bonfire, flames rose instantly from the dry wood, and choking smoke filled my nose. As the fire started to take hold, I could feel the searing heat of the flames peeling my skin.

My lips cracking, I called out weakly, "Water, for the love of God." But all I could hear was laughter as the flames hungrily licked my body.

I took my last breaths as the flames consumed me; I was being roasted alive, and my life was ebbing away. In our time, Seb had done it again, this was my undoing, my fate. I was dying in childbirth because he'd blessed me with a child; I'd met my beautiful daughter Celeste, but he'd taken my life. I knew he hadn't meant me any harm, but he couldn't change it even if he wanted to. He'd said, "Fate always finds a way." How ironic, the protection spell couldn't help me now because this was a natural death. I whispered in a last moment of clarity, "Trust your instincts, watch for the wolf in sheep's clothing," then the headache exploded in one final thunderclap.

EPILOGUE

Twenty-one years later

ESTE

Was it some sort of sick joke calling me Celeste – it meant heavenly – my mother Ellie chose the name. I was the least heavenly person you could meet, and the poor soul died giving birth to me twenty-one years ago today. My father had chosen a boy's name Gabriel and I think Gabby would have suited me more, I'm a daddy's girl after all. So I've always been known as Este, from my earliest memories – easiest way to say it is S-T.

Back to my mother. I was born at 2.06 am and by 5.21 am she was dead. Apart from nine months carrying me in her womb and the brief time immediately after my birth, we'd had no time to get to know each other. Seb – I didn't call him Daddy, Dad, or any other fatherly title – had never hidden any of the gory details surrounding my mother's death from me. He certainly didn't blame me, he'd enough guilt to carry for the both of us. My poor mother bled to death, how gruesome, her life force ebbed away, so it wasn't a painful death; that was one consolation. She'd had a massive postpartum haemorrhage and cardiac arrest, one of those rare risks of childbirth. The pregnancy had been textbook, and I was a good weight, 7lbs 6oz, a healthy, bouncing baby girl. There was no sign of what was to come, it took everyone by surprise.

For most of the time my life was good, Seb had done his best bringing me up on his own – apart from a disastrous but thankfully brief relationship with Sonja. He wasn't a saint, he dated, but he kept his private life private, as did I. Don't get me wrong, our relationship wasn't perfect, we had our moments, after all, I took after him personality-wise – I didn't exactly have a bubbly personality – but as for looks, I was a combination of both, my mother's complexion, and my father's piercing blue eyes.

But I had a burden. It was the soul of Ellie, my mother. I did my best to suppress the incredible yearning I had for this woman – I'd only met her for a few hours, and I don't remember a second of it. Like a heart-shaped piece of the puzzle was missing. I didn't discuss it with Seb, we didn't really talk about our emotions, some people might even say I was cold. For one day a year it all came crashing down around me, my birthday, the day of my mother's death. I wanted to hide behind a rock, disappear, and just cry. Birthdays should be about fun, and frivolity, but for me it was bittersweet, I carried this around like a backpack full of stones, that feeling of guilt that I was responsible for her demise. So you can understand that today wasn't my favourite day, I couldn't wait for the clock to tick over past midnight, wishing this vile day away, and get on with my life until the next year. He never said anything to me, but I don't think it was Seb's favourite day either.

Over the years he'd given up trying to make this day one of celebration, even as a child I'd never wanted a birthday party, it felt disrespectful, celebrating my mother's death somehow. So we'd got pretty good at trying to ignore the day between us. But today was different. He'd persuaded me to make an appointment at the solicitors, said it was important as it was my twenty-first birthday. He was tight-lipped, didn't say too much, apart from, "Este, you're impatient like your mother, it will all become clear. Do you want me to come with you?" I shook my head. "No, it's OK, I'll go on my own. But I'm only doing this for you. You know my feelings about this date." He gave me a big hug, this wasn't like him, usually so undemonstrative, so I knew it must be important. I'd become pretty successful at putting up a fence around my heart, but I had a feeling that today would be different. I'd made the appointment with the solicitor's firm, and I was on my way to find out what the fuss was all about.

As the solicitor ran through the terms of the trust that had been set up, it soon became apparent that I was quite a wealthy woman in my own right, now I was twenty-one. I'd thought about moving out soon, spreading my wings, and now I had the keys to the door, two keys to be precise, spoilt for choice. My mother had left me an eighteenth-century cottage in the North Yorkshire Moors, Lavender Cottage, plus a luxurious Thames-side apartment in Richmond. I knew nothing about these properties! My father never discussed money, we lived a pretty frugal life on our sprawling farm. I'd been homeschooled, and we grew most of our own food, it wasn't all about material stuff in our household, and he certainly didn't flash the cash. But at the same time, I always knew money wasn't an issue either, his book had been a bestseller, and then made into a movie, and Netflix series. I'm sure he just wanted to bring me up appreciating money and had kept this from me so as not to spoil me, and so I could make my own way in the world.

I felt overwhelmed. I felt a tear creeping down my face, this wasn't like me, I usually kept my emotions firmly in check. The solicitor coughed, bringing me back into the room, he handed me a heavy brown envelope, saying, "Your mother has written a manuscript about her life." He gave me a look. "You do know her heritage, I take it?" I nodded. "Yes, I do." He neatened a pile of papers on his desk, I thought that was the end of the meeting, he gave me the impression that he'd finished, but it seemed there was one more thing. He retrieved a white envelope with the name Celeste handwritten with a beautifully fluid, steady hand.

"Your mother wanted you to have this letter on your twenty-first birthday if she wasn't around."

She was speaking to me from the grave, I thought with a jolt. This wasn't what I'd bargained for, did Seb know about it? Somehow, I think he did.

I couldn't wait until I got home to open the letter, and I didn't feel like reading it in front of the solicitor, not sure what my reaction would be. I could feel a lifetime of pent-up grief rising. I needed to read this on my own and didn't feel like going home yet. It was a lovely day, and I went to sit in the park just across the road from the solicitor's office, after picking up something sweet and a drink. Summoning up some courage – tissues at the ready – I opened the letter and sat briefly to compose myself before reading.

"My dear Celeste,

My darling girl, I haven't met you in person, but I feel I have known you forever; I love you with all my heart, my little petal; I'm smitten. This is my love letter to you, my little rosebud. I hope I am around to read this with you and that we can celebrate your 21st together over a glass of the best champagne!

But just in case I am not around, you need to know your Mama cherished you from the first butterfly flutters I felt, to the strong movements and prods as you got bigger and stronger, your beating heart duplicating my own. I have followed all the advice, eaten the right things, drunk all the juices to make you big and strong to give you the best start to thrive in the outside world. Your father and I studied your 3D scans, trying to guess what you look like; not long to wait now. You are due in 8 weeks from writing this letter, we can't wait to hold you in our arms. Who will you look like? Will you have my dark eyes and olive skin, your father's ice blues, his pale skin, or a mixture of both of us? I wonder what your magical powers will be like. Will you be able to time travel like your father and me, or will you have your own superpower?

So, your name – Celeste is an obvious choice; the word means heavenly in Latin, and with our magical heritage, it's the perfect ethereal name for you. Your father and I agreed he'd name a boy and his choice was Gabriel, an angelic name, and I chose Celeste for a girl – for you. Your middle names, Charlotte Anna, are after your birth grandma and birth aunt. More about them later. I want you to grow up surrounded by love, so will tell you my story below, my own magical journey, just in case I cannot tell you myself. You must understand you have other family members who will love you almost as much as I do, and my friends, Alice, Lizzie, and Sarah will be your godmothers; they already know their duties! If, sadly, you are reading this alone, I will always be keeping a heavenly eye on you, always and forever; I will always be with you in some form or other; I love you to the moon and back ..."

I finished the beautiful letter from my mother, tears dripping. I blew my nose and wiped my eyes. I never thought I'd get so emotional, maybe this outburst would help me move on in the future, get it all out. My mother talked about my superpower; I always knew I had magical genes, it was never hidden from me. I couldn't time travel and Seb had accepted this early on and didn't mess around in the past since my mother's death. But I had my own special superpower, unique to me, and he recognised it for what it was long before I did, when I was very young, but that's a different story for another time. But for now, it was time to turn the page, start a new era. My mother had given me permission, I had to let go of the grief. I wanted to get back home, see my father, read my mother's memoirs, and then move on with the rest of my life, start adulting. Where to live, the North Yorkshire Moors or Richmond? What a choice.

~ The End, or Perhaps Not? ~

LETTER TO MY READERS

I hope you have not been too traumatised by the ending of *Where Time Goes*. I thought long and hard about how to end this story, it is a gothic tale after all …

Thank you to all my readers for getting this far with me and supporting me with the *Dream Die Repeat* series. I really appreciate the amazing reviews and positive comments I have received. My ten-year-old self, who always had her nose in a book, would be very proud. I sometimes have to pinch myself to be sure I've actually done it, and I'm not immersed in a dream like Ellie.

Ellie has been a part of my life and my family and friends' life since I started writing, it's been an incredible experience. I have always been grateful to my primary school teacher Tom Wilson, so it was especially emotional when we met up recently and I presented him with a signed copy of my debut novel *Dream Die Repeat*.

I am a very visual person, and I know that this has come across in my writing. Travelling to historic places for my research has been a fantastic way to soak up the atmosphere, visit places I haven't been to before whilst visualising Ellie's experiences from the past. I particularly loved my trip to Pendle and Lancashire, my first visit to this area. There was such a magical atmosphere, and in many ways time has stood still in this area since the Witch Trials of 1612. With the backdrop of Pendle Hill on a cloudy day, it was the perfect moody vibe to take me back in time.

The Sculpture trail in Aitken Wood was also fascinating, and very spooky! I'd also highly recommend the tour of Lancaster Jail, I learned about its use as a paupers jail, and saw the tiny cells where prisoners were incarcerated.

I especially enjoyed the re-enactment day at the Southwell Workhouse and Infirmary, where volunteers play the part of residents and staff. This property is run by the National Trust, I would highly recommend a visit. Follow me on TikTok, Instagram and Facebook to find out more about my visits.

Travelling to these places has also been a wonderful way to continue my book gifting mission, it is a joy to see the smile on people's faces, and getting fantastic reviews is brilliant too!

I have also been sending books to people in the public eye, those that I admire. I've always adored Joanna Lumley, and when I start something new, I often think "what would Joanna do?" Her travel programmes are brilliant, and as for 'Ab Fab' – who doesn't love her character, Patsy. I was grateful to receive a wonderful note back.

I have also received royal replies from T.R.H Prince and Princess of Wales, and Queen Camilla! It's amazing that they have taken the time to reply.

This book was only meant as a single novel, but as you know Ellie had more story to tell. Who knows what will happen next, but for now it reaches a conclusion and the final chapter of Ellie's journey. But as we all know The End is not always THE END. I have a sneaky feeling that it's not the last time you will hear from Ellie … but for now I wish to savour the moment of having three books published.

JULES LANGTON

KENSINGTON PALACE

From: The Office of T.R.H. The Prince and Princess of Wales

Private and Confidential

3rd October, 2023

Dear Jules,

Thank you for your lovely letter and copy of your book, *Dream, Die, Repeat*, which you sent to The Prince and Princess of Wales on the occasion of Their Majesties' Coronation.

Their Royal Highnesses were touched by your generous words of support for their family, and were delighted to learn that you enjoyed the Coronation festivities.

It really was kind of you to send such a thoughtful gift, and The Prince and Princess of Wales would have me pass on their warmest thanks and very best wishes.

Yours sincerely,

Mary Henry

Jules Langton

CLARENCE HOUSE

15th March, 2023

Dear Jules,

So many thanks for your very kind letter. I am delighted that you have been enjoying the recommendations on my Reading Room and was touched that you thought to send me a copy of your book, which I much look forward to reading!

With best wishes

Camilla R

JOANNA LUMLEY June 22nd 2023

Dear Jules, I am thrilled to receive Dream Die Repeat and can't wait to start reading. Thank you so much for sending it, and for the copy of Queen Camilla's letter. Hurrah for you! Such treats in store for me! Warmest good wishes, Joanna Lumley

ACKNOWLEDGMENTS

My family has been amazing, my husband Tom came up with the title for *Where Time Goes*, and also helped with the cover design for all three books. I regularly test my story lines out on Tom and he often comes up with some deep and dark ideas too. My 7 year old grandson asked his teacher if I could talk to his class about my writing. I had the best time, talking about magic and time travelling. They were a brilliant audience and asked some very interesting questions.

I am particularly interested in Victorian history, it's a fascinating era, and I wanted to show how this outwardly respectable "stiff upper lip" society also had its darker side. Thank you to Rick, my friend Lin's cousin, a real-life funeral director. He gave me a fantastic insight into burials in Victorian times, and the trade in body snatching which in this era was rife.

A big thank you to Tina from The Old Curiosity Bookshop in Hathern, Leicestershire, well worth a visit if you are in the area. As well as stocking my book in the shop, Tina has kindly invited me to talk to her book club members, twice. They loved *Dream Die Repeat* so much, I went back to talk about *Not Forever Dead* which they loved even more. I hope to return with *Where Time Goes* next year.

Thanks to Quinn's Books who have supported me as a new author, and hosted "A Conversation with authors

Carolyn Parker and Jules Langton," chaired by author Diana Bretherick. I look forward to launching a book signing event for *Where Time Goes* at Quinn's Bookshop, Market Harborough, in the new year.

Thanks to Alicia at Stoughton Grange Farm Shop in Oadby, Leicestershire. Alicia helped me cut my teeth with a book signing event. Alicia makes the most amazing cakes, the lemon drizzle being most popular. The farm shop also stocks my books.

Thank you to my Voracious Readers, who actively read and reviewed *Dream Die Repeat*, and have been following in the journey with *Not Forever Dead*, I hope you enjoy *Where Time Goes*, the final book in the trilogy.

Thank you to my team, Sarah Houldcroft – my publisher, Marilyn Messik – my editor, my graphic designer – Gail Bradley and printer – Jacqui Womersley, who has helped with advertising material.

ALSO BY JULES LANGTON

**Do you believe in a previous life lived?
Book 1 in the DREAM DIE REPEAT series.**

Ellie is living the dream – a high flying career in London and a luxurious apartment overlooking the Thames as part of a hedonistic lifestyle. So why does a tumbledown, haunted-looking cottage in the bleak wilderness of the North Yorkshire Moors bewitch her? Why does she feel compelled to buy it?

Her life is about to change: a new lifestyle, new friends, the secrets they keep, and the nightmares that haunt her. What can it all mean?

Gradually, Ellie is drawn into a magical world like nothing she had experienced before - with mysterious, spellbinding and dangerous results.

Not Forever Dead continues the story of Ellie and her magical world.

Having narrowly escaped Seb and the other witch hunters, Ellie keeps moving, but has she travelled far enough to be beyond their reach?

Will she find her birth mother, Anna, her half-sister, Lottie, and her best friends Alice, Lizzie and Sarah? Are they all safe? Will she ever be able to return to Lavender Cottage? Or is her life destined to end the same dreadful way for all of eternity without her being able to change it or even to distinguish between the good guys and the bad?

Both books available from Amazon or through my website at www.juleslangton.com.